The Other Side of the Mountain

Erendiz Atasü

Translated by Erendiz Atasü
and Elizabeth Maslen

Milet

0843553 16

Milet Publishing Limited
PO Box 9916
London W14 OGS
England
Email: orders@milet.com
Website: www.milet.com

First English edition published by Milet Publishing Limited in 2000

First Turkish edition published in 1996 by Remzi Kitabevi, Turkey

Copyright © Milet Publishing Limited, 2000

ISBN 1 84059 113 7

Printed and bound in Great Britain by
Mackays of Chatham PLC

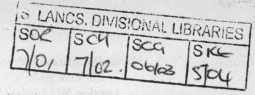
Erendiz Atasü

Erendiz Atasü is one of Turkey's most prominent writers. During her career as Professor of Pharmacognosy at Ankara University, she wrote essays on feminism and collections of short stories. Her short stories have been translated into English, French, Dutch and German. *Dağın Öteki Yüzü* (*The Other Side of the Mountain*), her first novel, was awarded the top literary prize in Turkey in 1996. Widely acclaimed, this novel established her reputation as a writer of international stature. She lives in Ankara, where she continues to write prolifically.

Elizabeth Maslen

Elizabeth Maslen is a Senior Lecturer in the School of English and Drama, Queen Mary and Westfield College, University of London. She has translated the Polish novel *Rudolf* by Marion Pankowski, and written on Doris Lessing for the British Council series, *Writers and their Work*. She has recently completed a book on political and social issues in British women's fiction, 1928-1968.

Guide to Turkish Pronunciation

Turkish letters which appear in the text and which may be unfamiliar are shown below, with a guide to their correct pronunciation:

c   as *j* in 'just'
ç   as *ch* in child
ğ   silent, but lengthens preceding vowels
ı   as *a* in 'along'
ö   as German *ö* in Köln, or French *oe* in 'oeuf'
ş   as *sh* in 'ship'
ü   as German *ü* in 'fünf', or French *u* in 'tu'

For my dear daughter Reyhan

The Other Side
of the Mountain

TOWARDS FREEDOM

THE LAST DECADE OF INNOCENCE

I was born in the middle of the century. I can remember the fifties, the years after the war, the world being rebuilt under the piercing glare of the atom bomb, to the rhythms of rumba, samba and cha-cha, backed by stifled voices echoing from instruments of death.

I remember black heaps of coal on white snow. I remember delivery boys bent under the heavy burden of their baskets of coal. I remember their dilapidated shoes exposing bare feet. I remember the cold classrooms, and living rooms where only the area round the coal-fire stove was warm enough. I remember voyages, boats that sailed to Istanbul from the Black Sea town where my father was born. I remember the miserable crowds crammed on the third-class decks, huddled together with their sheep and goats.

I remember my dreams . . . about women in Christian Dior evening gowns with low-cut necklines and bare shoulders, dancing on golden, gleaming parquet floors of halls that I had never seen but heard of, bathed in light flooding from crystal chandeliers . . . the game of 'sex appeal' . . .

My parents used to dance the tango and the waltz at the balls to mark the anniversaries of the Republic. Look at them . . . can you pick them out among the images of the past? Can you spot the men, with their feet encased in patent-leather shoes, sweating in their tails, dancing with the utmost earnestness, those provincial Kemalists? They used to look absurd seen through the eyes of the Seventies, but now seem so tragic . . .

(Is it not touching that they even took enjoyment so seriously, just like your generation?)

While the grey, chilly passageway of the fifties was opening out into the youthful spring of the sixties, I discovered my parents' library. Feride, *The Wren,* so sensitive, so merry, so sad with her broken heart, teaching deprived children in the devastated villages of Anatolia; Rabia from *Sineklibakkal,* with her heavenly honey-coloured eyes, so intense, so pious; the graceful Handan, so independent, her young life trapped and wrecked by the passion of two loves; the modern Züleyha from *The Ancient Disease*, her marriage shattered; all these heroines of Turkish fiction were the sisters of my lonely childhood . . .

Then there were all those solemn-looking books in their white paper covers, published by the Ministry of Culture during the forties, translations of world classics . . . those wonderful publications that disappeared completely during the fifties, abandoned by the Ministry. The friends of my adolescence and early adulthood: young Juliet yearning for her Romeo on her balcony in Verona; Mary Stuart wrapped in her flame-red robe walking recklessly towards the axe, rebellious and unbowed to the end. Lady Macbeth is racked by a guilty conscience; Eugénie Grandet, meek, timid, and withdrawn, waits in vain for her lost love. Natasha's impetuous heart veers between Pierre and Prince Andrei; Madame Bovary poisons herself in her dull provincial France. Sonia commits crimes to satisfy her passion for punishment. Nora slams the door behind her and walks away to freedom, my lonely girlhood staring sadly and wistfully after her, full of awed admiration. Nora, she was my heroine . . . Nora, unyielding, determined, and strong . . .

(You are getting it wrong, confused about the decades. Your sense of yourself as a woman was not awake as yet, it was only your sexual instinct beginning to resonate, timidly. What impressed you when you first read *The Doll's House* was only the pain of the broken marriage tie. You were only curious about sexuality, yearned only for that.)

I had other heroes, socialist heroes. Life was so beautiful during the sixties and into the mid-seventies, full of youth, enthusiasm, sharing, and mutual aims.

(Friendship, the spirit of cooperation, folk songs . . . they were like a great shawl spread over the incoherence and incongruities hidden in the depths . . . why don't you accept that you have never loved either the time or place you inhabited, ever since your childhood ended?)

When was life reduced to a tedious trail through the unending steppe? I did not feel well . . . though my body's loneliness was at an end.

(Like parched petals, your body wilted. Caresses that ignored all of your being, except for the flesh, injured it, burned it up, wiped it out.)

My needs and wants warred against each other. How I wish I had lived in Vienna during the Belle Époque, been one of Freud's patients, danced at the Opera Ball with a lieutenant of the Imperial Army and fallen in love with him. He would have been shot in battle, and I would have wept, wept, wept . . .

(You refused to admit that you were buried up to your neck in the common fate of woman. You closed your eyes tight, saw neither mud nor marsh. You had to marry, had to become a faithful wife and mother, that is what you thought. You were scared to death of losing your innocence.)

My marriage had its moments of bliss. Probably it was the hurricane of the eighties that wore it out. 'We thought you were a happy couple.' The forbearance you saw was only compensation for wounds we had inflicted on each other. Don't you realise murders are being committed? I am weary of hearing reports of friends being attacked or murdered, I am tired of attending funerals, losing people, shedding tears, feeling angry, tired of a life dogged by the fear of being killed . . . I am tired of washing baby clothes, of marking exam scripts, and still acting the perfect hostess to my husband's circle of friends. I am sick of playing a part in the bloodstained comedy that is being staged in this country.

I should have been in Paris in the twenties, painting pictures in a garret. Hemingway would have fought with his wife in the café below. Picasso, dressed in a picturesque sailor's outfit, would have sworn vividly as he passed along the street smelling of cheese, wine, and crêpes, where I lived. I should have been as delicate and free as my fellow countrywoman, the painter, Hale Asaf . . . I should have hidden my bleeding heart, like her . . .

And here I am, while the splintering bones of my grandmothers ache in the deep soil of the steppe - those of my grandfathers abandoned in Macedonia – an Anatolian ballad mourning within me even as a gallant tune from Thrace strikes up jauntily.

(Sheer anachronism . . . any player who is aware that he or she is acting, while on stage, cannot go on. Of course they are aware of the play, but by a kind of simultaneous amnesia, they forget what they are aware of. Later they say, 'I had a part in a farce.' Acting operates with dual awareness – one part of which is paramount. When both intensify and intersect, at that very moment either you experience a surge of creativity – like a thunderbolt – or the mind grows utterly dark. You experienced nothing. You are recalling the emotions of a later time and confusing them with earlier ones. In the years of armed political anarchy, you were an ordinary housewife. And what was your pastime? Teaching at the University!)

You did not dream of Paris and Vienna in the late seventies, your only dream in the midst of the bloody comedy you were living through, was a cup of coffee on a seashore where death was not on parade.

Then the coup of 1980 struck! The world we had known till then disintegrated. Another bloody comedy began to be performed in place of the old one.

(All the shawls that had covered the incongruities, the incoherence, were torn to shreds. Everyone stood naked. And as for me, I saw myself for the first time clearly, and I saw all the others.)

I slammed the door and walked straight ahead, like Nora; fell in love like Anna Karenina – reunited with my missing body – but did not sacrifice my life like her. I got up – like Anne Dubreuilh – from where I had collapsed. I survived. I made journeys, and lost my innocence completely. And only then could I comprehend a world which had lost all innocence. No one now can offer the excuse that their capacity for seeing clearly was damaged by the blinding light of the atom bomb. All the genies ever created have vanished into thin air! The 'iron curtain' has been torn down! You cannot hide any more on either side of it, in a state of mock innocence. And what is there left to fill the gaze? Exploitation, cruelty, and pain.

I listened once more to the ballad within me, and returned home to the steppe where the starved creatures dwell. I learnt once more how to respect my parents' and my own generations, and sometimes how to treat their passionate earnestness as a joke.

Now, I am free, for the first time.

TOWARDS THE OPEN SEA . . .
MEMORIES AND ILLUSIONS

THE WAVE

The joy of living will never be as tangible as the thick blue satin I used to handle as a child. From now on, it will be like the surviving remnants of a cloth which has been torn apart . . . will be split and will disintegrate into an amorphous grey . . .

Who dares to call this place 'Mediterranean' . . . this seaside town where sea and sky dissolve into each other? A damp, grey breath . . . I love it . . . It brings back memories of the unending seas of the North, grey and rough with no skyline at all . . . grieving but free . . . So be it, who needs joy anyhow?

I was in a north European city, when I thought of committing suicide. The winds of freedom of the late sixties were blowing round me without touching me. Twenty years have passed . . . I said, 'Let me jump into the cold grey water and let everything be over.' The river attracted me like a magnet. I changed my mind, and walked away, the instinct for life had prevailed. Now, once again, I am on the same shore.

No, she was not satisfied with her work, she could not concentrate. Her mind was taken up with the coming ceremony. She could not even remember her purpose in starting on such a text. What was it that she wanted to express? Was it the longing of a lonely heart in a cold place, to be silent? Or the desire of an exhausted body that had drawn near the selfsame shore after a lapse of twenty years, to rest? Did you, in the long run, return to the exact point you had started from in life? Certainly on that very spot on that very riverbank she had started to live the rest of her life. Did opposites end with the same results? Did frustrated youth, hungry for life, and satisfied, weary middle-age meet and merge?

Virginia Woolf had written something like, 'A drop, when complete, should fall to the ground'. Well, she wasn't a writer and could not transform her emotions into images. What made a drop a 'drop' was the spontaneous act of falling. But she had an awareness that was conscious of her lack of choice. Recording her awareness in this way helped neither in the expression of emotion nor in the creation of poetic prose. Her distress grew. She put the written page in a file she was lately in the habit of taking with her wherever she went. She would read it later, after the ceremony. There were other things she carried with her, such as a diamond ring, an evening-dress. She liked the idea of believing her mother's ring would bring her luck. The dress, in the fashion of the fifties, fitted her perfectly, showing that her mother at her age had a body with her own present-day proportions. She remembered . . . whenever her mother crossed a threshold, the place would be filled with the light of a rising sun.

Probably this had only been experienced once, but the memory grew to embrace her whole childhood. Her parents were about to go out. Her mother, beautiful and graceful, was almost ethereal. She felt she could not touch this mother, she did not want creases to appear on the elegant gown, so only a child's inquisitive fingertips brushed the blue cloth. Her mother was the embodiment of all the promise life had to offer: a beautiful and happy woman going out with the husband she loved, leaving her beloved only child at home in trustworthy company. The mother bent down and dropped a loving kiss on the child's cheek.

—Your mother was one of those eminent people who worked so hard to found this institution.

(Before she settled in the steppe town.)

—We sincerely regret she is not here with us on our fiftieth anniversary.

My mother was ill when we received the invitation.

—Did she open her bowels today?

—No, madam. She wouldn't eat either.

—Oh, you naughty girl! You didn't feed her, so her bowels wouldn't open.

—Oh, madam, how can you say such things?

—Don't I know you! You don't want to touch anything dirty. Come along, warm the soup, bring some yoghourt. Let me feed her. After an hour we will give her a suppository. Mother, mother darling, please open your mouth. Mother, do you hear me? There . . . Well done, my sweetest little mother . . . Swallow it, please, mother. Swallow, I tell you! Mother, why are you spitting it out? Mother, you're soiling my dress! Don't . . . Don't, I say! . . . God damn it! Look at her! . . . She has ruined her nightgown . . .

When I turn to the past, I remember her in her simple but elegant suits. Wherever she walked, she would leave behind the wonderful scent of lavender.

—Quick, open the window, let in some fresh air. Mother, mother! . . .
—Relax, madam, you're exhausting yourself. The old lady can't hear anything today.
—How can I relax? I hope she has another clean nightgown. Mother, see, there is an invitation for you from ——— institution. It's a great honour. What do you mean, 'Where is it?' It's an important training-college and you, when you were a young academic, were one of its founders. Please remember. Oh, look at her, she's spitting again! I'm going to get cross with you! It's rather touching that they haven't forgotten you in this ungrateful world. Aren't you at all pleased?
—It's no use talking, madam. The old lady can't hear anything. Well, she isn't always like this. But for the moment, she can't hear, can't understand.
—That's what you think. Look at that faint smile round her lips.

—She was always smiling.
(She was always morose in recent years)
—But I never heard her laugh heartily.
(Neither did I. Did she think it unseemly?)
—She was always considerate, courteous, and inspired respect.
(She was too considerate, you might say. She could be overbearing in the name of respectability. She did not enjoy life in any holiday spirit.)
—We honour her memory and, as a token of our affection and esteem, would like to present this salver to her daughter

who is with us today.

(She was like a fallen, dead seagull when I found her in her bed. I saw her profile, her beaklike nose . . . the loose sleeves of her white nightgown spreading like wings . . . her ankles, thin . . . How much smaller you grow as you draw near to death . . .)

—You are tall, like your mother. How lovely to have you here with us. She was about your age when I met her. She wasn't working here by that time. You look so like her. Children never really know their parents. You probably don't know some aspects of your mother that we are familiar with.

(Cries of seagulls fill the air, shriek upon shriek . . . Has one of them fallen . . . and died before I could see her properly? . . .)

—She was so smooth-tempered. Her temper was as smooth as her silky brown hair. She had a childlike joy about her which she always – I've no idea why – tried to stifle but never really managed to suppress.

(Wasn't she usually exaggeratedly solemn?)

—She had strong principles and never compromised.

(I am sure she had.)

—What a great effort she made, during the founding of this institution! She was so dynamic.

(Wasn't she rather reserved?)

—She worked here with real *joie de vivre*. She was engaged to your father. They were very much in love.

(Then she settled down in the steppe town where my father worked.)

—They were a happy couple, happy and in harmony.

(My mother was the survivor. Hers was a long mourning for my father. Her illness and death seemed part of that mourning.)

She was the daughter of a well-to-do family which was impoverished during the Balkan and First World Wars. Her life began in Salonika. The early stages were spent in schools for orphans and in foreign lands. She was one of the first university students the young Turkish Republic sent to Europe on scholarships. She studied Western literature, returned home, helped to found the ——— institution, and then moved to Ankara where her husband lived. She taught English for years. She had a daughter. She lost her husband . . . and died.

(Death is no longer dreadful. Neither is it remote . . . The losing of its horror and distance has turned it into an acquaintance. Nor is it incredible . . . the way my father's sudden disappearance was, years and years ago. She died a long, burdensome death, every minute of which made you feel the reality of dying. From now on, death is almost desirable . . . a greater freedom, more substantial . . . like the vast, grey, empty space that appeared in my life as a serious illness receded. The former limits of our lives disappear when we throw away or let life snatch from our grasp the good and the bad that we possess, or when we endure enforced separations. The last property we own is our bodies. Throw that away . . . and freedom!)

She stepped out on to the balcony of the hotel room, felt the salty, cool breath of the sea, smelling of seaweed, felt the coolness on her skin. The ceremony was over, now was the moment to go through the file . . .

She was gentle . . .	She was tough . . .
She was merry . . .	She was morose . . .
She was full of the joy of living . . .	She was sad . . .

Oh mother, why do you hide yourself from me? Why? Isn't it unfair to me? I want to get to know you, the mother whom I have never known . . . Where are you, mother?

I was like a drop ready to fall before I attended the ceremony; now a curiosity that almost hurts is puncturing the perfect surface of that drop . . .

Why did you change so much, mother? Did you? Was it because of my father, whose remembered image has been kept incorruptible by the uncritical memories associated with early deaths? . . . Or was it the steppe that withered you? Why was your strong, healthy, beautiful body left quivering for the lost joy of living? Why did you destroy yourself? What wrecked you, was it me? Did I frustrate you? Am I the one who is guilty?

Tell me . . .

. . . 1941

My dearest,

I have received your letter. Thank you so much. I am delighted that you are in good health. May God always keep you in good health. I miss you so much . . . I long for you . . .

Your reproach breaks my heart when you say, 'You have never loved me enough'. My darling, I know sometimes I have disappointed you, but you are the only man to whose gentleness I can completely trust myself. Please don't lose sight of the miracle we share. I have never been drawn to anyone but you, and never shall be. No other man's hand has touched me, and none shall. I am worn out with longing too, and tormented by the thought that this war will destroy the whole of our youth.

Our bed is cold without you . . . the winter is unrelenting . . . please try not to catch cold. I am sending you woollen underpants. My uncle the General (my aunt's husband) laughs at me, and says, 'Your husband is enjoying life on the sea coast, his is not real military service but a pleasure trip, you should worry about your own situation my girl, the icy weather is freezing us all here.' My heart does not understand what he means! Sleep is out of the question for me until you return. Every night I go to bed with the anguish of, 'What if we enter the war tomorrow?' Sometimes I wish I were in Istanbul, or on any seashore. The seaside climate is good for morale, you know, perhaps I would worry less there. The loneliness is terrible. But I do not think I could cope with my mother's neurosis. You know how she still thinks of herself as a nobleman's daughter, and has never got used to poverty. During the day I keep busy at school, what with lessons and students, and have no time to dwell on unpleasant possibilities, but the nights are endless. I am terribly distressed at not being able to have a child because of the War. The presence of some dear little soul would have made me feel your absence less, and would have given you cause for hope and joy. But what if . . . Those years of the First World War, full of pain and grief, still prey on my mind. My father's death, poverty, misery, the homes of relatives . . . No, a thousand times no! Our child must not and shall not suffer such fearful experiences, must not and shall not learn such dire lessons from life.

I wish to God the War would end soon, that you and I were together again, that our home rejoiced in a child.

It is a small world, my love, what a delightful surprise! Guess who my uncle the General came across while queueing for rations? My nanny Faika! We lost touch years and years ago. Poor thing, she was in a very bad way, barely surviving, on the verge of starvation. She would like to come and stay with me, as you are away in Gallipoli, doing military service for the second time, and as I am alone. I have agreed, my love. My uncle the General thought it would be proper for me to consult you before agreeing. He made a kind of teasing objection: 'My girl, how can you agree to bring a stranger into your home without asking permission of the head of the house? You are going to annoy your gallant Laz (you know every Black Sea Laz has a terrible temper).' I replied: 'She isn't a stranger, but my beloved nanny. And you can't begin to imagine what a gentleman my gallant Laz is!' It was the right kind of answer, wasn't it?

My uncle the General wants me to move from this flat we have rented into the house they have taken in the suburbs, as a precaution against a probable German air attack. I also think the city centre is too expensive nowadays for a retired general's pension. Prices have been going up astronomically, my uncle the General says that if I go and live with them, I will be free of heating and housing expenses, and be able to save a little. The city centre has been almost entirely evacuated, people are fleeing to houses in the country. But although I am dreadfully afraid of an air-raid, I mean to remain where I am, and prefer living in town to moving out into a relative's house. That is why I should like nanny Faika to stay with me, I will not be lonely then, will not be *afraid; and my uncle the General will stop worrying about me.*

Can you imagine, this aged veteran is surprised that we write to each other in the new Roman alphabet. I told him, 'But Uncle, we are the civilian soldiers of the Republic!' Was it a good answer?

Darling, there is another sad thing that has happened and has grieved me for days. Whom can I discuss it with, if not with you? If I had mentioned it to my uncle the General, he would have thought I had lost my mind and would say for sure, 'The things you brood on, as if you did not have enough worries of your own!' How could he know that you and I write poems just for each other? The poor old soldier! What has happened is this: the great English authoress, Virginia Woolf, has committed suicide. She filled her pockets with stones and jumped in the river, and was drowned. I heard her in 1929 when she gave a paper in Cambridge. She was a great lover of peace. Do you remember the passages I translated just for you, only for you, from her novel, 'The Waves'? They say she may have killed herself because of all the suffering caused by the War. Maybe . . . she was a very vulnerable, very intelligent woman. Her melancholy face was beautiful, slender, pale and dreamy, almost ethereal. You know I have read all her books. The newspapers reported that she had been very optimistic and cheerful while working on her last book. Then war broke out in all its violent intensity. I feel some change must have taken place in this highly sensitive woman's state of mind, and then she was unable to cope with the agonies of war.

I sometimes have such violent mood swings. Waves of misery give way to waves of joy. Isn't life itself made up of these essential ingredients? What is worrying is that these extremes of mood come without warning and the conflict between them is considerable. Like a cross-current, a wave! One minute you are on the crest of a wave, feeling perfectly happy , and the next you find yourself in deep water! Very well then, the question arises: how can an intelligent and sensitive soul, after going through such a crisis, go on trusting the happiness experienced on the crest, when aware that it will soon be over? And cannot he or she find consolation while in the deep water of a wave's trough, knowing that the curve of the wave will rise again soon? I wonder if the slide towards the trough fills one with the anxiety that the next wave will break so violently it will be impossible to survive?

What causes these feelings of sadness? Is it our childhood, as the great analyst Freud would have us believe? Virginia Woolf's parents died when she was very young . . . Oh, those fearful experiences a girl endures in the homes of relatives! How can she possibly ever be merry again? . . .

When she finished reading the letter, tears were streaming down her face. She had reached a perfect wholeness, or thought she had. A fierce pain seized her as a great sense of joy came to birth. Blissfully, she sensed a soft breeze caressing her skin. Her body was yielding and docile; the selfsame body that had withdrawn itself, angry and frustrated, when years ago she had thought of jumping in the river. Now it was satisfied. A longing for death loomed suddenly alongside this feeling of fulfilment. She shivered. She drew a shawl round her shoulders, retreated into the balcony, sat down, her back against the wall, and closed her eyes, enjoying the warmth of the shawl.

The Mediterranean evening flowed into her being in all its spectacular beauty. The warm air smelt of jasmine. There was a fine tension beneath nature's dreamlike, humid harmony. She touched her bared flesh, her palm found her warm breast, the skin was like the pink petals of the roses climbing up her balcony. Drops of dew shimmered on them. She pressed them against her skin, felt the texture and moisture of the petals. Her body that had been hungry for touch when young, had ached with yearning as if it were tearing apart – hard to describe – that same body was now satisfied, no longer wanting simply to accept but longing to overflow. She enjoyed sensing the flesh that was stirred and roused by the touch of rose petals. The swell of the tide rose and rose and ebbed softly, she felt its wetness.

When she opened her eyes, she saw the unending grey of sea and sky. Islands far away had begun to emerge through the mist. It was chilly. The crying of gulls went on and on. Her neck had gone stiff as she had fallen asleep. She left the balcony and entered the room, began to read once more the file that contained her mother's letters, journals, reflections, and poems. When she had finished, she began work on her manuscript.

'Now I am on another shore. Am I a water-drop in this universe, that ends up on the spot where it started to form? Do I have to fall and mingle with the earth? Maybe I shall be a seagull next time, and fly up high . . . My human existence will remain as a remote dream in a different awareness that shrouds and arcs over my consciousness.

Am I a spiral moving unceasingly away from its starting point? If so, completion means . . . what? Or am I perhaps the interplay of countless spirals, moving unceasingly away from their starting points? But then circle, sphere, water-drop . . . they are all nothing more than illusions . . . 'Perfection' does not exist . . . If that is so, the fourth dimension which is curiosity is always there to turn the water-drop we imagine is ready to fall, into a wave . . .

This evening, right now, I am leaving the shore I am on. My destination? I do not know, but I am curious to learn.'

She put her mother's name on the manuscript, and underneath her own, together with a dedication: 'To all women who have committed suicide and to those who have returned from the brink.'

She took from her case her mother's blue satin evening gown, in the fashion of the fifties, and put it on. She arranged her hair the way it was done in the photo of her mother wearing that same gown. She looked in the mirror: my mother holding her pen and the notebook she kept secretly was looking back at me, with a sad smile on her lips and a playful gleam flickering in her eyes.

ISLANDS OF THE PAST . . .
PHOTOGRAPHS AND
LETTERS OF BYGONE DAYS . . .

THE KEMALISTS

Vicdan and Nefise
(The Kemalist Girls of Cambridge)

At the Summit
(Vicdan . . . Burhan and Reha . . . Mustafa Kemal)

An Honourable Officer
(Reha)

Misunderstanding
(Reha . . . Burhan and Vicdan)

The Veteran
(Cumhur . . . Raik and Vicdan)

You Have Forgotten Salonika
(Burhan . . . and Vicdan)

A Happy Marriage
(Vicdan and Raik . . . and Burhan)

Time in Bursa
(Raik . . .)

The Other Side of the Mountain
(Fitnat Hanım . . . Mustafa Kemal)

VİCDAN AND NEFİSE: THE KEMALIST GIRLS OF CAMBRIDGE

Satellites whirling through space did not exist as yet nor were there voyages to the moon. Ships sailed to distant ports, letters were sent to loved ones, families gathered round wireless radios in the evenings.

Everyone was talking about the immense changes undergone, but our world still resembled the nineteenth rather than the twentieth century. The first bloody stock exchange called the First World War was over; wounds had been tended; as yet no one could imagine the second one, or what the world would be like afterwards. Empires still controlled our planet. Land, forest and ocean were not yet estranged from the human race.

In the year 1929, on a spring day, in the mother country of the British Empire, near the town of Cambridge, two Turkish girls stand under a willow tree on the bank of a river, Vicdan Hayreddin, born in Salonika in 1910, and Nefise Celal, born in Konya-Karaman, a small town in central Anatolia, in 1909. Vicdan is wearing a pink muslin dress – milky-brown in the snapshot – and her mother's pearl necklace. Her fragile figure is leaning against the willow tree. Her hair falls to the nape of her neck in prim waves. Nefise wears a jumper over her kilt. She sits down squarely on the bank, her bare feet in the river; her gym shoes stand beside her. The wind ruffles her dark cropped hair, giving her the air of a naughty boy. There are sweat stains on her jumper under the armpits, whereas Vicdan looks cool and composed, all ready for tea at five o'clock. Their smiles are so genuine . . . they are in mysterious harmony with the place and the year 1929.

Vicdan lacks the spontaneity of her friend. At times she secretly admires Nefise's behaviour, and at other times finds it improper.

They boarded the Italian liner *Théophile Gautier* at Istanbul. When they stepped ashore at the port of Marseilles, Vicdan felt like kneeling down and kissing the ground like Nefise and the other passengers, but she could not – Vicdan cannot touch soil, handle plants, pet animals; she has a secret aversion to such things. In the snapshot, she looks as if she is sensing the harmony growing within her, as the spring breeze penetrates the pores of her skin like a remote humming, without her acknowledgement.

During the severe storm they encountered between Naples and Marseilles, Nefise was very seasick. 'Mauvais temps, Signorina, mauvais temps, not to step out of your cabin, s'il vous plaît.' Vicdan will remember to her dying day the steward with his rolling gait as he tried to soothe the passengers. Well, at least she had proved stronger than Nefise when faced with the sea.

Nefise would make fun of Vicdan's fastidiousness. She would proclaim with pride: 'I am a child of long-suffering Anatolia, I can live on air.' She certainly had the ability to survive in any time or place, ever since she sold lemons in the Karaman marketplace, shouting at the top of her voice until her young larynx had all but been torn to shreds, during the days when she had known the extremes of poverty along with her mother and brother after the death of her father. She did not lament her losses. Her existence seemed to be an extension of the soil on which she used to run and play as a barefooted child.

Vicdan has walked away from the willow's branches towards the grass on which Nefise has spread a rug for her, and has sat down. She smiles at her friend. There must be three years and a trip to Berlin between this snapshot and the earlier one. In the summer vacations, Vicdan would board the *Théophile Gautier* and sail to Istanbul, as she could not bear the homesickness for her mother and brothers.

Nefise undoubtedly preferred trips to the Continent as opposed to voyages through the Mediterranean. It was the most prosperous period of their lives. The scholarship funding they received from home was more than sufficient. The currency of the young Republic was still among the most buoyant in Europe. But Nefise had a real struggle persuading Vicdan to travel to Berlin with her during that summer vacation instead of sailing back to Istanbul. – Did the distancing between them show itself on that trip? – I shouldn't think so.

Another snapshot . . . Two young women, Vicdan and Nefise . . . Nefise's head rests on Vicdan's lap, Vicdan's hand on Nefise's brow. The love they feel for each other is clearly visible. Whom do they have except each other? A pair of young women, two fatherless girls in a foreign land. They must achieve graduation; it is a duty they owe to their country, a responsibility weighing heavily on their shoulders. What happened to their other friend is a terrible memory always haunting their hearts, the image of a young girl who had longed for England when at home, and who had flung her graceful body off the cliffs at Dover into the icy waters of the Channel, as soon as she disembarked . . . Her body torn apart by the rocks . . . an ever-present memory . . . a tireless custodian of their hearts which might otherwise fly off on the wings of youthful ycarnings.

5 October 1934

Vicdan Hayreddin,
Sakızağacı Road, No.8,
Bakırköy, Istanbul

My dearest Vicdan,

I was not destined to finish the letter I had started to write to you on the typewriter. My eldest brother took it with him when he left for Diyar-ı Bekir where he has been posted. I enjoyed using it so much! Well, never mind.

Dearest Vicdan, I do look forward to receiving a letter from you. In the postcard you deigned (!) to send, you wrote that you were not feeling well, that it was just a cold, and since then I have not heard from you. I am really worried. God forbid, but could it be some lung infection, like pneumonia or pleurisy? Why are you tormenting me by keeping silent? You naughty thing, what's the reason for this neglect of yours? Or should I say laziness? Please let me know how you are.

How is everyone at home, your mother and your brothers? Please give my regards to aunt Fitnat Hanım. Has Burhan joined the Law Faculty? Does Reha mean to enrol at the Military

Academy? Is little Cumhur old enough for primary school?

Though it is more than four months since we came back from England, I still haven't been assigned a post. How about you? You remember of course that we mailed our papers, giving the exact date when our studies began in England, to the official responsible for students on scholarships. The man who holds the post now insists that these papers were not passed on to him by his predecessor. I wrote to Cambridge and had a reply by return, and a copy of the original papers. With these new documents, I travelled to Ankara and appealed to the Ministry of Education – in vain! I cannot find words to convey the chaotic state the Ministry is in!

I exchange letters with friends back in England regularly. Everyone asks about you. How they love you! They never liked me half so much! Is it because you have a fair complexion? I am only joking, so please, dear sister, don't take it to heart!

Our landlady Miss Meadow has gone back to Spain by boat. You'd think she had fallen in love with the country and the people. She writes that Spanish men have a certain magical chivalry. Dear Vicdan, the Spanish Republic is leftist, I presume, I am right, aren't I? If we are to believe Miss Meadow, those in sympathy with Germany are gaining ground in Spain. She is anxious for her beloved Spain, and frightened at the possibility of civil war! I can't imagine that gracious Europe, the birthplace of rationalism, science and art, will submerge herself in a bloodbath yet again. I am certain that Britain, with all her stable foundations and institutions will never permit this German craze.

Vicdan, I miss you, miss England and Cambridge so profoundly, you cannot imagine . . . Dear Cambridge . . . I am so far away from her . . . As the distancing mists of time and place gather between us and the peaceful city of our youth, the romantic love I cherish for Cambridge deepens.
Your loving sister,
Nefise Celal
c/o the Proprietor of 'The Republican Pharmacy', Karaman/Konya

20 November 1934
Ankara

Dearest Vicdan,

I cannot believe it has been almost six months since we last saw each other. I started work in the Gazi Teacher-Training College a fortnight ago. I imagined you would be teaching in one of the schools in our capital. No trace of you . . . I am so disappointed. Your insight has proved right as always. Remember, you used to say back in Cambridge that I would miss you and the town. Yes I do, terribly . . .

I wandered round our Ankara, wishing you were beside me. I was happy to see that our new capital looked like European cities with wide, clean avenues, but more like a German town (not surprisingly, with all the new government buildings designed by German architects), than an Anglo-Saxon one. Some buildings reminded me of Berlin.

The Teacher-Training College is four kilometres out of town. No houses nearby. The barren hills of central Anatolia, black and grey, roll on endlessly like the Sussex Downs. How the meadows of England spread out without end, green all the year round!

There is a rock half-an-hour away from the College. Some evenings I go there by myself, and gaze at the mysterious castle of Ankara, perched up high. As the shadows of evening fall, the towers seem to me like guards muffled in their dark-blue coats, on night watch. 'They are the gendarmes of our city,' I tell myself.

How beautiful the steppe, the hills and the castle are in the moonlight. Unfortunately I cannot go for walks at night, in case people think I've lost my mind.

Remember how we used to walk in the moonlight in Cambridge? We felt safe. We never worried that we were women . . .

I am the only woman teacher here. You can imagine how lonely I am. I cannot make friends with my male colleagues, gossip about love-affairs begins at once. Maybe, as I was always at girls' boarding-schools, I can't find much in common with men now, anyway.

I hear bad news about my mother. My brother says in his letter that she is too frail to leave her bed. My brother would never have written like this to me, would never have caused me anxiety if the situation weren't serious. Vicdan, how could I go on living, if I weren't to set eyes on my mother again? I can't leave the college, we have a sacred duty here. I have to wait helplessly.

I pray to God that you and your family are in good health, and kiss your sea-green eyes lovingly.
Your sister Nefise.

P.S. Vicdan, nowadays, I don't know why, I often think about our trip to Berlin. Vicdan, for God's sake, please tell me what I have done.
Nefise

On the thirtieth of November, Vicdan Hayreddin is at number 8, Sakızağacı Road, in the sitting-room of the wooden house, looking out over a Sea of Marmara once alive with fish, their scales of mother-of-pearl. She is holding Nefise's letter. The blue light of an Indian summer comes in through the open window, along with the smells and voices of an Istanbul that still enjoys spring all year round. The smell of the sea and of grass, the shrieks of seagulls, sirens of ships, children's voices . . . Soon he will come – Raik, the maths teacher, born in 1903 in Trabzon, another war orphan – and give Vicdan the first kiss of her young womanhood, behind Fitnat Hanım's seaweed -coloured, silk tasselled, shantung curtains, that survived the Balkan War, World War I, and the War of Independence, whose worn-out parts have been skilfully concealed between the folds. If Fitnat Hanım gives her consent, the future betrothed will enjoy a boat trip in the moonlight. Raik rows well, as he should, coming from the Black Sea coast! He will not touch Vicdan for a second time today, although perhaps he may plant a tender kiss on her hand after helping her step ashore from the boat.

Vicdan is in love with Raik. She has been hurt by Nefise. Because she doesn't discuss the reason with Nefise, the rift between them has deepened. Revealing even the outer layer of her heart's hurt would wound Vicdan's self-respect. And what of the deeper layers? Impossible! Nefise, after she had got over her initial embarrassment would laugh at her! 'Sister, see how things worked out! What if I did apply to the Ministry before you did, and didn't tell you? Wasn't my documentation completely lost in the chaos of the Ministry, our brand-new Republic inherited from our absurd Empire? Isn't your assignment about to be finalised too? Why these arrogant airs?' Could Nefise be brazen enough to react like this? Well yes, she could.

The real reason for the hurt has nothing to do with assignment to a post, or documents, and so forth. Who cares about not receiving a salary for a few months? Vicdan is as experienced as Nefise in going to sleep on an empty stomach. She, along with her mother, stepfather and brothers, is suffering severely from lack of funds.

The world crisis of 1929 has at last reached Turkey. Vicdan manages not to be indignant with the Ministry, and waits patiently for the State, which she steadfastly refuses to criticise, to remember her. Vicdan is astonished that Nefise, with her ability to adapt, has fallen prey to loneliness and disenchantment with Karaman, the small town where she was born and brought up. Vicdan does not long for England, she has been completely re-absorbed by the loud-slamming doors and fainting, weeping household of her mother, and has taken refuge in the exasperating but secure atmosphere of her surroundings . . . and of course in newborn love . . .

She has locked up her longing for England and her hurt about Nefise in hidden compartments of her soul, along with many other distresses; but Nefise keeps forcing the locks with her continual letters.

Nefise, my confidante, who alone knows my childhood hurts, how slyly you staked out your separateness from me! . . . If a strange coincidence hadn't betrayed you, I would never, ever, have dreamed that you applied to the Ministry long before I did, declaring that I had not as yet come back from England. No power on earth would have made me behave in such a fashion. When your little trick did not work, you tried to share your anger at the Ministry with me! You were almost going to suggest that we should offer a united front! You have wounded me! . . . But . . . your mother is ill . . . may die . . .

Ever since her father's death in 1920, Vicdan fears that she will lose her mother too; and once again identifies with Nefise as she reads about her friend's anxiety; the warm tide of love, longing, and memories they share rises in her heart. But just as Vicdan is about to surrender to the waves, the tide ebbs . . . Her heart is left high and dry. Vexation pierces it like a red-hot needle!

It is not easy to forgive someone so much loved, with whom you were once so completely at one.

After the moonlight boat trip, her heart washed by other seas, Raik's warmth flickering on her lips and in her palm, Vicdan will read her friend's letter once more and discover some quality which she can respond to, Nefise's vulnerability and frailty hidden beneath her impetuosity and aggression. (Vicdan, you knew it already!)

Yes, but I had forgotten, and chose not to notice it after Nefise hurt me . . . but Raik has kissed me . . . and now again I remember . . .

And yet again Vicdan will discover her friend's sensitivity, hidden beneath the calloused tissue of Nefise's soul, in the superb prose Nefise will produce when translating works of English literature into Turkish. Vicdan will read them once more ten years later, and identify once more with her friend's tenderness, after her death. What reunites Vicdan and Nefise, on the evening of the thirtieth of November, 1934, arc the seeds of creativity in both their hearts, ready to burst and just waiting for the right moment to germinate, rather than their shared anxiety for Nefise's mother! That same mother who will go on living year after year with the silent stoicism peculiar to the pious, after burying her daughter.

The night passes, the thirtieth of November flows into December the first, as Vicdan writes a letter of reconciliation to Nefise. She doesn't yet know that their friendship will never be as it once was; Vicdan has not yet learnt that her young woman's heart, bursting with new love, will not always be so strong, that love diminishes, wounds reopen, forgiveness may grow stale. She is still too young to know . . . and too happy.

Raik proposed to her during their boat trip, only the phosphorescent sea and the silver-scaled fish hearing Vicdan's shy voice, full of love, saying, 'yes'. Now Vicdan is strong enough to confront Nefise and herself. Why does Nefise keep on remembering Berlin?

Was it there that she hurt me with her blundering? A little . . .

Vicdan is accustomed to enjoying open-hearted communion with Nefise, always followed by a certain brusqueness on Nefise's part . . . She has accepted Nefise as she is, still like an impudent adolescent. Or was it after their return from Berlin? (Vicdan, you are not open and honest with your own self! The real problem was the question of Hugh Eliot, wasn't it? Nefise's attempted duplicity at the Ministry is only the label you have, to your secret relief, hurriedly pasted over the compartment where you crammed the pain that question caused you.)

Hugh . . .

The Hugh Eliot problem that surfaced after their return from Berlin . . .

They went to Berlin in 1932 . . . saw the wide avenues, the smart cafés, the magnificent Brandenburg Gate, the Palace of Charlottenburg, the Pergamon Museum. They shook their heads knowledgeably before the Altar of Zeus, the gift of Sultan Abdülhamid the Second to the Germans; they were completely agreed that such an insensitively conceived gesture would never have occurred under the Republic. They strolled arm-in-arm along the boulevard Unter der Linden, looked in dazzling shop windows, saw sophisticated women, brilliant with diamonds, in the same streets where crippled war veterans stood begging and the unemployed loitered. They heard suggestive songs overflowing from cafés, and the constant rhythm – rap, rap, rap – the sound of jackbooted feet pacing.

They were staying with the Trotts. It was an address recommended by the University; there were Cambridge dons among the Trott family. Sky-high prices, never falling since the war, had compelled the Trotts to turn their home into a boarding-house. They had lost their elder son in the First World War, their younger one, Hans, had enlisted in one of the youth movements of the National Socialist Party. He wore an emblem on his arm that Vicdan and Nefise thought intriguing and original. When they wondered what it was, Hans shouted, 'The Swastika!' He was a charming boy with a fair complexion, and spoke English fluently. He was a pleasant companion in those moments when he forgot he was a Nazi. But without warning he would be gripped by some mysterious power, like a dervish in a trance, or an epileptic, and in a hysterical voice that would rise and rise to the point where sound ceased, he would scream out phrases like 'the trampled honour of Germany', 'the revenge of our noble race', 'the Third Reich'. His ecstasy of rage always went with fevered, wild gesturing. And his Nazi salute! That was unbelievably amusing! Vicdan and Nefise would giggle and whisper to each other that Hans was having yet another political fit!

A large portrait of Hitler hung on the wall of the Trotts' front room, right opposite that of their elder son who was killed at Verdun.

Frankly, Nefise and Vicdan were not interested in politics or in political leaders. They had faith in their own country and their own leader, and were light-hearted. Could this little man called Hitler, so small and ugly, offer the conquered German nation what Mustafa Kemal Pasha, the war veteran, their 'Gazi', had achieved for the Turks? Well, the Germans should be thankful then. All these roaring voices, the continual shouting, must be characteristic of the German nation. Well, you could not expect every society to be as impassive as the British.

One evening the Trotts took the girls to a cabaret. 'It is not very suitable for *"die fraülein"*, but a trip to Berlin would not be complete without a visit to a cabaret!' Vicdan and Nefise watched the show with its bedroom aura, wide-eyed and astounded, as they witnessed the licence of the show-business Berlin of the thirties, without fully grasping what it was all about. Strangely, their innocence emerged unscathed. They were students of Western literature: Germany was, for them, equivalent to Goethe, Schiller, Heine: misty forests, tranquil lakes, remote and solitary castles, water-nymphs, platonic love. The physical Berlin, in which they found themselves, was completely different. However, their young and inexperienced minds, while incapable of analysing the situation politically, could sense the existence of a subtle relationship between defeat in war, hunger, unemployment, vulgar riches, lewd entertainment, and National Socialism.

Berlin was turning from an enjoyable adventure into a chilling nightmare. Every day they confronted new forms and faces of the madness they had thought was confined to Hans alone. Berlin was a clown with an angst-ridden heart, walking a tightrope, which was destined to break. They began to miss their sober, sedate and moderate England.

An incident Vicdan and Nefise were forced to witness a few days before their return from Berlin shattered their equilibrium more than they realised at the time.

They were going back to the Trotts' after a shopping expedition. They heard rapid footsteps, shouts, sounds of smashing and trampling. In a way they had grown accustomed to the hubbub of Berlin, so they paid no heed at first. Then suddenly there were uniformed men wearing the swastika. The girls were alarmed and started to run – it was too late – they were surrounded. The men seemed not to notice them, but soon Vicdan and Nefise were terrified. One moment the street was deserted, the next teeming with Nazis who worked steadily, with machine-like precision, breaking the shop windows one by one. Splintering glass and the crunch of boots echoed on the pavements. A man was dragged out of one of the stores, and collapsed under the blows to his back, head, and belly. Vicdan and Nefise had quite a close-up view of the man directing the operation. He was young, in control, organising everything carefully and cold-bloodedly, certainly not shrieking the way Hans did. He was completely sober. The girls' blood froze in the terror of the moment. At a single stroke, like a thunder-clap, all the different impressions of Berlin stored piecemeal in their brains fitted into each other and into the body of the baton held in the SS leader's resolute hand as it rose and struck.

In their attempt to run away, Vicdan's hat fell off and one of Nefise's shoes was discarded.

All at once, the Nazis vanished. The street was deserted. No sound, no one breathing. The beaten man in a pool of blood. His bones were broken, his body like an empty sack.

For a moment Vicdan and Nefise could not move, then instinctively they turned towards the wounded man. Nefise was the first to understand the situation, she nudged Vicdan and whispered 'Let's run!' . . . 'That man needs help,' Vicdan protested. Nefise's face was white with fear. 'Are you out of your mind? He must be a Jew,' she said, grabbing Vicdan's arm and pulling her away.

As soon as they had reached the boarding house they each said to the other, 'Don't let's mention anything to the Trotts.'

At supper they told the Trotts they were tired and had decided to return to England earlier than they had planned, and they asked Hans to book seats for them on the train to Calais.

That night in their room, they undressed and went to bed in silence. They whispered 'good night' to each other and put out the bedside lamps. Each was alone in the dark with icy fear and the guilt of not daring to help a wounded fellow-human being.

The children of peoples who have suffered for a long time, have bitter memories they would rather not confess even to themselves. What the girls had witnessed released the hidden poison. Like wounded animals, their inner selves which were conditioned to pain and anguish sensed the coming of a great catastrophe. What they understood they would have liked to forget at once, but it was not possible. They could not bear to face what they had sensed, not under the heavy burden of their own past . . . They were as desperate as lost children in the household of these people called Trott, whom they could not analyse, classify and identify.

Nefise slipped into Vicdan's bed. They hugged each other and wept silently.

The first time Vicdan saw a dead body – a hanged man with his swollen, purplish feet, his protruding tongue – she was just a child in a West Anatolian town. He was a deserter, a soldier executed by the nationalists. Later, others were hanged on the gallows. Children played truant from school to see them. Men on the end of ropes . . . Vicdan remembers one particular deserter who suddenly appeared in the yard where she was playing with other children. A tall man, a worn-down peasant, driven from one front to another, year after year. How he begged the children – his eyes wild with fear – not to tell anyone that they had seen him. All he asked was simply to survive; did he not deserve it? Vicdan's heart aches with compassion and grief.

Vicdan's family supported the nationalists. Little Vicdan felt she would give up her life for her country's freedom, for her nation, for Mustafa Kemal Pasha; true, but the ailing peasant and the men on the rope-ends brought an inexplicable dread and pity into her heart. In her sleep, fearful images of hanged men haunted her, yet she mentioned her horror to no one.

Her mother, Fitnat Hanım, realised what Vicdan had seen. The night she screamed, terrified, in her sleep, Fitnat Hanım took the distraught child into her own bed, hugging her and talking to her. Fitnat Hanım was a stern woman who treated her children with severity, but that particular night she was lovingly tender. She told Vicdan that as long as their homeland was trodden down by the enemy, it was a sin and a shame to let yourself be seized by fear. Fear of death lay in wait in every heart, she said, but you had to learn how to live with your fear and how to overcome it. She told Vicdan about Salonika, the charming city by the sea far away in Macedonia, the bustling harbour, the lost country, the lost home gone for ever. She described their beautiful house there, built of stone, decorated with reliefs, and the garden which they had to abandon, along with all their belongings and flee when Salonika was taken by the Greek army. She told her how they had suffered. The Greeks drove the Turk out of Macedonia and Thrace. And were they now going to drive the Turk out of Anatolia too? Where to?

'Our duty,' she said, 'is to pray to God for the liberation of our country and to support Mustafa Kemal Pasha! The victory will be ours!'

Vicdan's father had just died. He died without seeing the nationalists gain power in the town of Alaşehir. Months before her father's death, young Greek soldiers, palicaries in blue uniforms, had taken control of the Alaşehir streets. A brooding, silent air of mourning hung over the Muslim houses. Hatred and fear began to circulate in whispers . . . Houses closed their doors and turned inwards . . . No, not all Muslim houses . . . Children were warned not to go near enemy soldiers, when walking to and from school. Reality mingled with fanciful exaggeration . . . Did these men really assault women and children? Vicdan remembers one, a smiling youth . . . He offers a candy to Vicdan . . . Vicdan runs away at once . . . Maybe he is sincere, maybe the candy is not a trap. Still Vicdan moves quickly away, her heart beating in panic.

One evening palicaries came to their door. They were rounding up Ottoman officers. Some informer must have told the Greek patrol that Hayreddin Bey was a retired colonel. Hayreddin Bey was old and tired, tired of warfare. Fitnat Hanım was only a very young woman but tired, tired of migrations. Husband and wife were both from Macedonia. Vicdan's mother had not worn a headscarf at home, but on hearing the news of the

Greek invasion of İzmir, she covered her hair with a black scarf and would wear it until the day the occupation was over.

From time to time Fitnat Hanım would put on coquettish airs with her husband, who was quite a lot older than herself. She was always treated gently both in her father's and later in her husband's homes. The Balkan War plunged her from her throne in her husband's heart into a state of mere survival among the hungry, sickly crowds of Balkan refugees gathering with their children in the cold inner spaces of the mosques. Her husband was at the front.

After the Balkan collapse, Colonel Hayreddin Bey retired from military service. The family settled with their three children in Alaşehir, a small town in Western Anatolia. Now, before the heartache for their lost homeland had lost its feverish intensity, the new homeland was about to be taken away.

Before the Balkan War, Fitnat Hanım did not, could not, cope with things going wrong, would faint if the slightest misunderstanding occurred in her married life. But after the Balkan War, her habit of swooning vanished. When the palicaries were at their door, Vicdan and her brothers thought their mother would faint again. But on the contrary, she was resolute and erect as she opened the door. She said to them in Turkish, 'You should be ashamed of yourselves, my husband is an old man,' and she turned to the informer Yorgo, who was trying to hide behind the soldiers, and said, 'Shame on you, Yorgo, you are a child of Anatolia! Remember the times Hayreddin Bey has helped you with your problems, you ungrateful man!' Yorgo could not look her in the eye. Fitnat Hanım repeated what she had said in Greek. The palicaries pushed her aside and entered. Vicdan and her brothers – squatting in a corner – were weeping. Fitnat Hanım confronted the soldiers again and said, 'You cannot take the man of the house away. God's curse on you!' Meanwhile Hayreddin Bey had put on his uniform and military medals and come into the front room. He tried to force his aching back to stand erect. 'Don't exhaust yourself, my lady,' he said, and stared at the Greek soldiers – arguably young enough to be his grandchildren

– with eyes full of pity and contempt. 'Let us go,' he said, kissed his wife and children and left with the palicaries.

Fitnat Hanım and her children Vicdan, Reha and Burhan hugged one another and waited . . . for days . . . Not consciously, but with their physical bodies the children remembered another time when they hugged their mother's body and wept . . . the migration from the Balkans.

Fitnat Hanım could only hope for her husband's corpse. But one evening he appeared, walking with difficulty. Fitnat Hanım and the children covered the old veteran's skeletal body with theirs. 'What have they done to you?' shrieked Fitnat Hanım. 'No time for weeping, my lady, pull yourself together,' said Colonel Hayreddin Bey. He would not talk about what they had done to him. After the children were asleep, he told his wife, 'I don't have much time. After I am gone, don't linger in this town. Take the children, and go to Istanbul, to your brother's. This business looks as if it will last a long time. The poor palicaries . . . They have become puppets in the hands of the British.'

Whether he died of the humiliation he suffered in Greek hands or from some mortal blow, nobody knew: the old veteran certainly died with deep emotional scars. What he found unbearably painful were the Greek flags that some Muslim homes were flying. He could make no sense of it. He also learned that it was not the informer Yorgo who had betrayed him: poor Yorgo was simply too frightened to refuse to lead the palicaries to the Colonel's house. But Haci Muhiddin Efendi, a native of Alaşehir who loathed the Balkan immigrants, – he was the one who betrayed Colonel Hayreddin Bey!

Haci Muhiddin Efendi, who had a Greek flag draped on his house. Hayreddin Bey could not understand it, and so could not bear it, and broke down. Muhiddin Efendi – who had made the pilgrimage to Mecca. Nobody knew that Colonel Hayreddin Bey, once a devout Muslim who prayed five times a day, whose youth had wasted away on the frontiers of a collapsing empire, fighting so that those like Haci Muhiddin could go on living safely at home, had died a complete atheist at heart.

Vicdan wept and wept the day her father died; it was hard to stop the blood flowing from her nose. Then she started having trouble with her eyes. The doctor to whom her mother took her diagnosed that her eyes had been weakened by excessive loss of blood. Ever since that day, Vicdan has worn spectacles with thick lenses. Ever since that day, she feels nausea when she passes houses from whose gloomy depths can be heard the sounds of rosaries clicking and the tapping clogs of the faithful, going to wash their feet in ritual ablution before praying.

Soon after her father's death, Vicdan, together with her mother and brothers and her nanny Faika, moved to Istanbul and took refuge at her uncle's. Istanbul was under allied occupation. Vicdan's unhappy mother could hardly bear having to seek shelter under her brother's roof, as he was a wealthy merchant who was profiting from the current political situation. The debauched life her brother enjoyed with the army officers from the allied forces, together with the opulence of his prosperous mansion, were heavy insults to the memory of Fitnat Hanım's dead husband and of Salonika, their lost home . . . Vicdan and her brothers survived, and little else, in their uncle's house, leading timid, hesitant, inconspicuous lives; uncertainty and insecurity became inseparable, if subconscious, parts of their inner selves. They could be exiled at any moment into the unknown . . . They neared adolescence carrying the scars, in their young souls, of the constant threat of destruction.

One evening, Vicdan heard her mother whispering to a visiting woman relative, a Macedonian, 'I cannot approve of my brother's morals. We must move before my children are ruined in this corrupt household.' So, 'Time to migrate,' thought Vicdan.

Vicdan's memories of her uncle's household are vague. She cannot work out why those elegant halls, airy and full of light with their lofty ceilings, linger in her memory like dark, stinking ghosts. Why does this graceful house make her think of gasping for breath in foul nooks and crannies, and of fumbled gropings in the dark? Was it reality or illusion? Hard to tell . . . dreadful, ill-omened and masked . . .

Vicdan was soon free of her uncle's house. Her mother, Fitnat Hanım, married the first man who asked for her hand. So Vicdan and her brothers found themselves in the dormitories of schools set up for orphans. Their stepfather was originally an Azeri from Azerbaijan who supported the Kemalist nationalist movement. Even during the wedding ceremony, Fitnat Hanım did not take off her black headscarf.

Until the moment of Independence, life for Vicdan was as monotonous, grey, and claustrophobic as a corridor in the school for orphans. No air, no light . . . She made friends with Nefise, among the orphan crowds, youngsters whose fathers had either been killed in one of the recent wars or had died of ill-treatment during the years of the occupation. Children who seemed to have lost happiness for ever . . . She felt a stranger in her mother's house at weekends. Not that she disliked her stepfather, but she kept remembering her father, missing him, missing his voice, missing his smell, and weeping in secret.

Then came the victory . . . Refet Pasha entered Istanbul with the triumphant army. All the orphans in the boarding-schools, hordes of them, went to meet the General with flowers in their hands; young war widows also, crowds of them, with tears in their eyes.

Once again, the sun shone on the seven hills of Istanbul; once again fair winds blew from the Bosphorus. The corridors of the teacher-training school for girls turned into sunny tracks leading the orphans to the expectant, wide-open, loving arms of a radiant life, into joyful roads, merry with laughter, accompanied by piano music and foxtrot or charleston rhythms.

Vicdan's mother pulled off the black scarf she had worn over her fine head of hair ever since the occupation started, threw it away, and never again covered the rich brown curls tumbling to her shoulders. Then she hurried to take a literacy course, so as to learn the new Roman alphabet, and felt proud of her daughter who would soon become a teacher. Her sons in their military boarding-school began wearing the uniform of the young Republic with pride. Vicdan grew accustomed to her stepfather.

Once again, life smiled. In 1927, Vicdan's mother gave birth to another son who was called Cumhur after 'the Republic'. In 1928, the Ministry of Education directed a decree of President Gazi Mustafa Kemal to the teacher-training schools: 'In order to build up our "army of enlightenment" as soon as possible, our Republic will institute scholarships for students to be educated in the cultural centres of Europe. Please determine which of your students is qualified to enter for the examination.'

On the day Vicdan learnt the result, she did not walk, but flew like a seagull winging swiftly through the enamelled blue of Istanbul. Her mother greeted her daughter's success with joyful enthusiasm, and presented Vicdan with her pearl necklace, her only remaining piece of jewelry.

The anguished obsession with death that had been consuming the heart of Vicdan's mother ever since the Balkan defeat, turned into an anxiety that she would die before being reunited with the daughter she was sending to faraway lands.

There she is, Vicdan's mother, standing at the Istanbul harbour, on the verge of collapse, sniffing at lemon cologne and essence of mint, but managing somehow to stand erect and wave to her daughter on the third-class deck. Here they are, Vicdan and Nefise's mothers, Fitnat Hanım and Hatice Hanım standing side by side, the former holding her head up, with its brown curls burnished and shining in the autumn sun, the latter muffled up in her black charshaf, both hiding their tears and nursing hope and pride in their hearts for the daughters they are seeing off on their way to the bright future of their Republic.

England welcomed them warmly and with a friendly curiosity merging with respect for the new Turkish Republic that had avoided all the traps laid by the British Empire, for Mustafa Kemal Pasha who had outfaced the great world powers, and for İsmet Pasha who had managed, at the Lausanne Peace Conference, to evade all the skilled manoeuvres of Lord Curzon, the bright star of the Liberal Party. The British Empire had rearranged her skirts a little to make room for the young Republic of Turkey.

16 March 1920
The infidel struck three of us dead as we slumbered
Did all the English partake
In the taking of lives before dawn
No, just two villains
16 March 1920
When confronting the garrison
I did not abandon my rifle
But shot dead two Englishmen
To save your honour, my fair Istanbul
For you my blue-eyed beauty, I sacrificed my life

They struck three of us dead
The infidel finished two of us with bullets

Only nine years had passed since 1920 . . . 'It is all British trickery,' Vicdan's father used to say. 'Don't ever bear a grudge against any nation, my child,' said Mustafa Kemal Pasha, 'our foes are not people but politics.' 'Do not fear for your sons,' he had called to the mothers, referring to the Anzac soldiers who died in the Dardanelles, 'they sleep peacefully in our bosom.' 'Don't ever bear a grudge against any nation, my child.'

Besaboro,
Cornwall
11 August 1934

Dear Vicdan,

I think it is high time that I should write to you, before you forget your English. I certainly haven't forgotten my Turkish yet. I can still say in Turkish, 'Do you think, madam, that it will rain all day, or is it going to stop?' Or, 'What a beautiful winter day . . .' At regular intervals, I recite the Turkish poems I've learnt by heart, but it isn't very rewarding as my only audience consists of Ethel and Mildred.

My dear Vicdan, I do find it hard to believe that you are so far away, on the other side of Europe. We shall all miss you very much.

I haven't been able to get a job yet. I don't mind much, in fact, but unemployment tends to be a grave problem for the poorer sections of society. Well, we girls, Ethel, Mildred, Joan, Heather, and I, shall all be in Cambridge next autumn, starting as postgraduates, as we are all unemployed. Only you two, Vicdan and Nefise, will be missing. It will be pleasant to roam around those ancient streets and beautiful Backs again – how I wish you could be with us!

What did your family think of our graduation gowns? Did you parade in yours through the streets of Istanbul?

I do wonder what you are doing and when you will be starting to teach at the University. I am all impatience to receive your letter with the answers and with one of those splendid Turkish stamps like the ones you used to get when we were all together in 15 Park Road.

Does that address seem very far away to you now? Well, it does seem a little remote to me at the moment; probably it is ages away for you.

I am enjoying my holiday, being lazy, sunbathing, and spoiling myself. I've completely forgotten the existence of such things as essays on literature.

My fiancé Poffle is in Cornwall with his parents, only thirty miles from here.

Well, I don't think I have any other news to give; I don't know how often you see Nefise, but please give her my love when you do.

Before I forget, do you ever read English newspapers? Would you like me to send you the Times Literary Supplement, for instance? You shouldn't forget England . . .

Now I really have to finish and write your intriguing address on the envelope.

Love from Eileen

P.S. Please write down the Turkish poem I know by heart, and send it to me. I have no idea what it looks like in pen and ink, and am keen to find out.

Address: Miss Vicdan Hayreddin
Sakizagaci Sok., No 8
Bakirkoy, Istanbul, Turkey.

2 October 1932

Miss V. Hayreddin
15 Park Rd, Cambridge

Dear Vicdan,

I do hope you haven't got the wrong idea about my taking Nefise to the Ball , and you aren't hurt.

To tell you the truth, I haven't got the faintest idea at the minute as to why I asked her and why she accepted.

I don't think I did it to hurt you. Although you did turn down my proposal, I wouldn't for the world do anything to hurt you.

To cut a long story short, my lovely, adorable Turkish tulip, I am still in love with you. If you change your mind, I shall be waiting . . .

Yours as always
Hugh Eliot

—Miss Vicdan Hayreddin, you have lived in England for six years. Did you ever fall in love or consider marrying an Englishman?
—No, never.
—Was it because you didn't like them?
—No, they are true gentlemen.
—So . . .
—I was in love with my country.
—What will-power!
—You think so?

(What do you think, Vicdan? Was it will-power, caution, or discretion?)

1 January 1932

Miss V. Hayreddin,
15 Park Rd., Cambridge

Dear Vicdan,

Thank you very much indeed for the woollen scarf you gave me for Christmas. I hope you liked your present. Unluckily, you missed the Christmas party – how disappointing that both you and Nefise should miss the New Year party too. Ah, you Turkish girls . . . How on earth are we going to make you like parties? Do you know that Hugh Eliot is head over heels in love with you? Your Indian suitor Abdulrahman Khan and Nefise's Egyptian Ali Cenab were there. They sat around throughout the evening, looking sulky because you weren't there.

Yours sincerely,
Mildred

P.S. I will come straight to 15 Park Road as soon as the Christmas and New Year festivities are over. Miss you all.

England had received them warmly, offered them congenial lodgings and friends they could depend on. Had England always sustained them with memories of security and happiness, and cherished their optimism? Had England always been that misty green vision, adorned with pearly morning dew?

They landed at Dover on a wet, grey day, and felt in their bones the loneliness borne in by the humid smell of ocean.

No one ever touches anyone in this country . . . Don't you ever feel the cold? No one laughs heartily in this country . . . Don't you ever feel pleasure? Look, there's a funeral in that small churchyard. No one is weeping! What formidable self-control these people have! Has the cool damp air congealed their senses, confined their feelings to the strait path of respectability? How are we going to survive in this country for six years, how am I going to bear the weariness weighing down my limbs, silencing my tongue? The heavy grey sky lours over my body, pressing me down to the earth . . . I must keep away from open windows on upper floors, from seashores when the tide rises, from cliff tops, from the wish within me to merge with the earth and to be free once for all of this agony. Nefise, my sister, where are you? I'm reaching out for your hand . . .

Why doesn't it ever thunder, why doesn't rage ever erupt? No one stirs . . . Everyone keeps to his allotted station, abiding by the rules of a game called consensus. How quietly they hate one another! The upper classes politely scorn the middle classes who politely scorn the lower classes who politely scorn people coming from the dominions and empire. The tranquillity will kill me! Vicdan, my sister, give me your hand . . .

Where do we stand in this country? So far no one has shown us contempt. They haven't worked out yet where to place us according to their consensus. The rising of our country from the dead must have shocked them.

Listen, you England! We shall not stay long. We belong to the Republic of Turkey, the only country that could say 'No!' to your Empire. We shall only have to endure you for six years, that is all. Stretch out your green branches to me, England, welcome me with your soft verdure, or else how am I going to bear you?

Stop a minute! Isn't the quiet here like the silence in our own country? Yes, but in quite a different guise. Never mind, it is still similar. A variety of people are living here, just as in our country, speaking different languages, cherishing a variety of beliefs. Yes, but in quite a different guise. Never mind, it is still similar. Kindly women live here, caring for the young, just as in our country, though they do not clasp us to their bosoms heaving heavy sighs. Never mind, they do offer cups of tea, their mild smiling eyes full of affection . . . Young girls live here too, warmly sincere, who could become sisters to us.

Disasters do not often happen here. Very different from our country in this respect . . . but isn't it lovely? Life flows steadily on here. Very different from our country in this respect . . . but isn't that consoling? There are so many things to be learnt here . . .

Hey, England, do you know what, I have started to love you! I am young and full of optimism, my country has been rescued from destruction, she has risen from the dead. See how she stands erect, so far away, and so impatient for my return. But you are so very close, England. Hey, I do love you. I have identified my youth with you. I shall always love you.

'We used to roam the meadows, on moonlit nights. We never worried that we were women and never felt afraid.'

In 1932, in Berlin, in the apartment of a petit bourgeois family voting National Socialist, two Turkish girls are weeping silently, for the birth of the Third Reich, for the approaching calamity; they are like lost children, helpless and longing for home; but where is home?

Isn't 'home' the place you know best? Vicdan and Nefise have wandered all over Britain, have seen every inch from Land's End to the Lake District, from Sussex to the glens of Scotland, from the chalk cliffs to the shores of the North Sea.

'Where is home?' wondered Vicdan. Alaşehir, the small Anatolian town that betrayed her father? Or is home the interminable dormitories of the boarding-schools? Or her mother's household, number 8, Sakızağacı Road? Or the beloved seaside town she lost when she was only two years old? (You must forget Salonika, Vicdan. The town no longer belongs to your country. If Mustafa Kemal Pasha has forgotten Salonika, where he was born and lived the happiest days of his life, so can you, Vicdan. You must. Forget, Vicdan, forget, erase from your subconscious if you can, the tremors of terror and anguish your infant body picked up from your mother's flesh, on the migration routes. You too, little Reha, little Burhan, you forget too, if you can. Forget, little Vicdan, forget hatred for the Greeks, revenge, fear, and anger. 'Peoples are not our foes.' Forget, little Vicdan, forget your uncle's mansion, what you went through there, forget if you can . . . Forget your father's death, forget your fellow Muslims' betrayals if you can . . .) I have forgotten everything, I have passed through fire, I am purified . . . but still the question remains, Where is home?

'Where is home?' wondered Nefise. The shabby market of the small town in Central Anatolia where she used to sell lemons as a child, after her father's death? The dilapidated wooden house with a leaking roof, and the smell of fried onions and damp? Her aunt who died after a miscarriage, losing torrents of blood? Her mother who still carried the scars from her husband's boots, the memory of a brutal kick, on the belly and in the heart? Hunger? The fear of invasion as the Greek army closed in? Where is home, South-Eastern Anatolia, remote and lonely? Eastern Anatolia, beyond the snow-capped mountains? İzmir under Greek rule? The Black Sea coast, further away and less familiar than the shores of Scotland? Haughty Istanbul? Unknown Ankara? The question remains, Where is home?

In 1932, in the home of a family voting National Socialist, two Turkish girls are weeping, one for the home she has lost, the other for the one she has not yet discovered.

We are Turkish, that is certain. But still the question remains . . . Where is home?

Nefise, in her grey-blue nightgown and brushed-satin slippers, lies on a divan in the hall of 15 Park Road, Cambridge. She has a wine glass in her hand, and is trying to beat the hangover from the ball of the previous evening by drinking more champagne out of the bottle which was a gift from Ted Campbell.

Vicdan stands in the doorway, staring at her in amazement. Nefise's gown and pose call Jean Harlow to mind – the only items lacking are ostrich feathers for the skirts of her nightgown – while her lips beneath her crimson lipstick, her dark complexion, round face, and fine black eyebrows resemble Pola Negri's.

Vicdan has not yet heard that Nefise went to the ball with Hugh, but she suspects she did. She is hurt, because Nefise has kept the name of her partner secret. Vicdan was away on the night of the ball, on a visit with Miss Meadow – their landlady – to Miss Meadow's sister who lives in the country. Now she is back and completely lost for words, doesn't know where or how to begin, how to address this Nefise who has undergone such a rapid metamorphosis, and looks like a film star.

Vicdan: Did you enjoy yourself?

Nefise: Yes, very much. How about you?

Vicdan: Oh, I had a lovely day in the country.

Nefise *(in a sudden burst of anger)*: I am sick and tired of meadows, fresh air, and all that . . . I adore music, dancing. I long to feel alive . . .

Vicdan *(surprised and hurt)*: Nefise, you aren't yourself.

Nefise *(still aggressive)*: You are so reactionary. That's what you are! You are in tune with this reactionary country. I mean Britain.

(Reactionary? Vicdan feels hurt again. How can a Kemalist be reactionary? No . . . Vicdan is no reactionary. She is reserved. That's all. But she has a revolutionary's soul. Throughout her long life, Vicdan will suffer from the torment of being torn between her eager, energetic spirit and her patina of reserve.)

Nefise *(calms down)*: I met someone at the ball, I danced with him.

Vicdan *(gently, trying not to sound curious)*: Someone other than your partner?

Nefise: He was wandering around looking sulky. He's a lieutenant.

Vicdan *(thoughtfully)*: Who?

Nefise: The young man I met at the ball. Ted Campbell. He comes from an aristocratic family.

Vicdan *(loudly)*: An English lieutenant!

Nefise *(defiantly)*: Yes. He's going to India soon, and wants to take me with him . . .

Vicdan: To India?

Nefise *(lifts up her hands and looks at them closely, then dreamily)*: He asked me to marry him. This must be what they call 'love at first sight'.

Vicdan *(she is breathing with difficulty and shouting with rage. She will only realise later what a heavy blow her words deliver)*: What are you talking about? Have you taken leave of your senses? How on earth can you, a citizen of the Turkish Republic, think of marrying an officer of the British Empire?

(Nefise is genuinely surprised; she obviously hasn't considered the matter from this particular angle. She is intoxicated by her own femininity which she glimpsed for the first time the previous evening.)

Nefise *(whispering)*: We kissed.
Vicdan *(still indignant)*: How can you believe promises made under the spell of wine on a romantic evening? India . . . What the hell are you going to do in any part of the British Empire . . . Ohhhh, those bloody British, and their damnable Empire! . . . How long, do you think, can they go on dominating the earth? *(Nefise looks at Vicdan, like a wounded gazelle.)*

(Is this you, Vicdan, calm, considerate, always courteous? You can't recognise yourself, can you? How did you manage to conceal your rage until now? Who is the real target for your indignation – the British army, or Hugh? Who is it?)

Vicdan *(calming down)*: Nefise, we have to go back to our country and teach young people. This is what's required of us and it's our bounden duty. We have got to work for the state for twice the length of time we spend here. Six years . . . That makes twelve. If you marry a Britisher and stay here, who is going to pay the scholarship money back to the state? Your family? We aren't rich, remember . . . Neither you nor I . . . *(Nefise listens to Vicdan but understands nothing. She is still living the ball, how she flew from Hugh's arms to Ted Campbell, from waltz to tango, from the sweet scent of roses to the salty smell of a man's body.)*

(Nefise has always known that Vicdan inhabits an emotional, nostalgic sphere of existence and is rather maladroit when tackling the practical matters of everyday. Now she is amazed to discover a new Vicdan who can sum up their lives so precisely, so simply and so ruthlessly.)

Nefise: I had forgotten. You are right.
Vicdan *(tenderly, now)*: Nefise . . . this isn't our home. Our country is waiting for us.
Nefise *(with a deep sigh)*: Of course . . . I went to the ball with Hugh.
Vicdan *(trying to hide that she is hurt)*: So I guessed.
Nefise: How?
Vicdan: By the odd way you've been behaving.
Nefise: Are you hurt?
Vicdan: Certainly not. I was only hurt because you kept it a secret.

Nefise: He's in love with you.

Vicdan: I'm not in love with him.

Nefise: Are you sure?

Vicdan *(in a small voice)*: Of course. *(She hesitates)* Why did you go with him?

Nefise: I wanted to go to the ball. He shouldn't have invited me. He wouldn't have, if he really loved you.

Vicdan: I'm not interested. All that bothers me is you. I don't want you to be deluded.

Nefise *(with a bitter smile)*: Shall we always be living like this, hiding from men?

Vicdan: There won't be any need to for us to hide ourselves or what we feel, once we are back at home.

Nefise: Everyone will be waiting for us, eh, for the heroic Turkish girls who have conquered Europe?

(Silence . . .)

Nefise: How do you know the British Empire will collapse?

Vicdan: I don't know it . . . I sense it . . .

Nefise: I can't understand what comes over me sometimes. Something evil goads me, like the Nazi demon in Hans Trott. At such times I can't think of anyone but myself. I have an evil soul.

Vicdan *(hugging her friend)*: You aren't evil. Nefise, we're lonely. We miss our home, our families, our country.

They both remember at the same moment their friend who killed herself in that first month they were in England. Her body, torn to pieces on the Dover rocks! They do not speak, their eyes fill with tears. Peace descends on them. No, no, there can't be a problem called 'Hugh' between Nefise and Vicdan.

Nefise: I sometimes miss my mother, that's all. There's a demon inside me.

Probably 'Hugh' is another manifestation of a different and crucial problem. Hugh's letter of apology has healed Vicdan's self-esteem; the pain has eased only to reveal the existence of another hurt. Vicdan understands what constitutes Nefise's demon: the need to take her place. Hugh was only an excuse. If Nefise had actually been in love with Hugh, Vicdan would probably not have felt so unhappy and so unsettled in her relationship with Nefise.

During their coming years in England, when Nefise and Vicdan cling to one another in their agitated need to survive, Vicdan will continue to deny the division between them, although her hurt increases.

While Nefise will find that her demon returns with greater strength after each exorcism, and will be unable to do anything about it.

> Nefise: I am evil.
> Vicdan *(lifting her cheek from Nefise's)*: Everyone is, in a way.
> Nefise: You aren't. You are very, very good. *(She presses her face against Vicdan's again, although Vicdan has imperceptibly drawn away.)*

(Where are your demons, Vicdan? Where have you hidden them? A day will come when your demons will become your inquisitors. Life and history are not forgiving, and make us pay even for the concealment of our demons . . . Even virtue comes at a price.)

Miss Meadow sensed the tension between Vicdan and Nefise. Nefise had broken the rules, had refused to honour their silent agreement and had gone to the ball with the young man who was courting Vicdan. Miss Meadow knew that Nefise had accepted Hugh's invitation, since female students had to report the names of their partners to their landladies as well as to the administration, according to the regulations of the twenties and thirties. If the administration did not think the young man suitable, his name would be rejected. His credentials – he would in all probability be a student at Cambridge – and his social standing would be considered before consent was granted. Certainly, the son of a good family like Hugh's would be considered acceptable.

Miss Meadow thought it would be wiser not to leave Vicdan alone on the night of the ball, and took her as her guest to her sister's country cottage, which Vicdan loved.

Miss Meadow had been one of the young women the British

Empire brought up to be devoted wives and mothers, until the First World War sentenced her to lifelong celibacy. During the twenties and thirties, being one of those women who had lost all hope of marriage and motherhood in the Great War, she focused her maternal urges uncomplainingly on young people other women had given birth to. Like all good Anglicans, Miss Meadow believed in God, in King and Country, in commitment and virtue. She never doubted that sooner or later virtue would be rewarded in the Kingdom of Heaven, and so was always able to retain her peace of mind. When the depression of 1929 knocked at her door, she immediately turned her house into a hostel for university students; she felt happy about this, as she would be of use to young people. She was an ideal landlady, affectionate, concerned but not intrusive. Young women from all over the world, from India to China, had been her guests, but Nefise and Vicdan were the first Turkish people she had encountered. Being a citizen of Empire, she was used to different nationalities, and her affectionate nature restrained her from adopting the high and mighty attitude of some of her compatriots.

Before Vicdan and Nefise settled at Park Road, Miss Meadow had been warned by the meticulous and efficient University administration, which functioned like a well-oiled machine, that these young girls were from a severely scarred country. They had lost their fathers when they were very young. The chances were that they had serious problems within their families. And, most important of all, 'the third of the scholarship girls in the Turkish group had committed suicide, although she had voluntarily come to study in England.' Miss Meadow felt distinct contempt for the authorities as she read the final sentence. There was absolutely no need to warn her that the British Empire intended to keep on good terms with the Republic of Turkey, as a reason for offering love and sympathy to two fatherless girls.

Vicdan and Nefise were not difficult cases. They were open-hearted and courteous. They obeyed the rules and also kept their rooms and belongings clean and tidy. They soon got used to the wet English climate. Wearing their gowns and carrying their umbrellas, they cheerfully mounted their bicycles, gliding along the narrow medieval streets, crossing the elegant bridges over the river where graceful swans sailed, wandering through the endless green fields. They hurried from libraries to concert halls, from one Gothic building to another. They readily accepted everything England had to offer without any obstacle emerging from their inner worlds. Their spirits absorbed, as dry soil sucks up water, the gracious university life of Cambridge.

Miss Meadow, although a devout Christian, was aware that other religions existed in the world. In a country where class divisions of labour had begun long ago, Miss Meadow had learnt as a child to tolerate those areas of life which it was not her lot to share. She gave two Korans, translated into English, to Nefise and Vicdan.

The girls were extremely enthusiastic. For Miss Meadow, it was difficult to grasp that the girls were reading their holy book for the first time, and in English as well! And she found it quite delightful that the girls, their faces flushed with excitement, would rush to tell her about passages they had read and understood. The contrast of submissiveness and violence woven into these texts intrigued Miss Meadow. But she realised that the doctrines laid down in the Koran did not much affect either Vicdan or Nefise.

Miss Meadow was curious about Turkish tradition. Tradition? What tradition? Could tradition survive the annihilation of war and migration? Miss Meadow was puzzled to discover that the girls could not have been farther removed from the concept of tradition if they had grown up in the bosom of the wild. But the delicacy of their behaviour, their consideration for others showed they were descended from a civilisation with deep roots. Could courtesy survive when tradition crumbled? Well, it did. Eventually, Miss Meadow made contact with the families of Vicdan and Nefise. Small parcels of presents were exchanged between Cambridge and Istanbul, Cambridge and Konya-Karaman.

In a way, Miss Meadow understood why the girls only had fleeting relations with the opposite sex; and in a way she did not comprehend it at all. Miss Meadow was undoubtedly a virgin; hers was a body that had brushed against masculinity long ago, before the War, and then only tentatively, and had been disciplined by solitude ever since. From one point of view, the caution of Nefise and Vicdan did not surprise Miss Meadow at all. Differences of religion could have been a stumbling block, after all. But then, why did they run away from their Muslim suitors? Miss Meadow was convinced that the Egyptians and Indians had even less chance than the British, as far as Nefise and Vicdan were concerned. Well, she knew that the girls were committed to compulsory teaching careers when they returned home. Could this be a factor? Still . . . A knowledge rooted in nature, which long years of a lonely life remote from men could not erase from her flesh, said 'No!' and prompted a difficult question that constantly occupied Miss Meadow's mind. What will become of these girls? The other guests at her boarding house, Eileen and Mildred for instance, were either betrothed or about to be engaged. But, what would happen to Vicdan and Nefise? They met a lot of young men at the libraries, concert halls, picnics and their behaviour was frank and open so long as no question of love or marriage was raised. They were good friends with Toby, Miss Meadow's nephew, who was a little younger than them. Of course, no self-respecting young woman would contemplate flirting with or marrying a man younger than herself in the Cambridge of the twenties and thirties. Hugh Eliot was pursuing Vicdan, but Miss Meadow doubted that he would be successful. Then the unexpected happened: Hugh asked Nefise to be his partner at the opening ball of the academic year.

Always the observant landlady, Miss Meadow realised on the morning she returned home from her sister's with Vicdan that Nefise had a hangover, but she made no comment. She left the girls alone, respecting their right to settle their own accounts. They had certainly experienced something traumatic. How could Miss Meadow ease their pain?

For some time now, she had noticed subtle changes in the girls' behaviour. It started in fact after they returned from their holiday in Berlin. Had something happened there? Why did they go to Berlin, why not to Paris, for instance? Paris with its *joie de vivre*! The moroseness of the German spirit reminded Miss Meadow of those deep muddy hollows in forests where the sun could not penetrate. All kinds of insects, parasites, mould and rot lurked in those deep, musty corners. English fields kissed by the sun were different. The spirit found perfect harmony, met God in English fields, sometimes even in its own image.

Tomorrow we should go into the country. Must give my nephew a call. Let him take us all in his car to some place where we can get some fresh air.

Yes, something had certainly happened in Berlin . . . Ever since, Vicdan's patriotism and her affection for her family back in Turkey had intensified. Nefise was moody, had grown nervous, spiteful and aggressive. She seemed to be absorbed in a quest but not to know what she was looking for, as if she had just discovered a long-existent lack.

As soon as they got back from Berlin, they described their holiday to Miss Meadow, as they always did any fresh experience, but neither of them mentioned the street violence or the night they shared the same bed. Nefise chattered away until she ran out of breath. 'Oh, Miss Meadow, we felt completely at home when we reached Victoria Station.'

Miss Meadow realised that the interminable drizzle of London, the sedate businessmen filling the city streets in their sombre attire, never contemplating for a moment that their bowler hats might lose their trim form even if the world were to crumble; the morose but solid edifice of Victoria Station, giving the impression that it would stand its ground even on doomsday; in short, every item of the establishment that bored and stifled the youth of Britain was a restorative for Vicdan and Nefise, whose souls had been battered by cataclysmic upheavals.

Something must have happened in Berlin.

Miss Meadow, with the sympathy women inevitably cherish

for members of their own sex, went into the bedroom where the girls were sleeping, still trying to work out some way of helping them through the crisis, as she tucked them in tenderly and gently stroked their hair.

They were sleeping like babies, innocent, still unaware of so many aspects of life. Yet they were like the wise old women of bygone ages, experienced and mature. How else could they forgive and forget their homeland being torn apart?

Politics was an element in the division of social labour which did not fall to Miss Meadow's lot. It wasn't up to her to criticise the British Empire. All the same, sometimes she could not help feeling that some of her country's interventions did the world no favours. But no, no, Miss Meadow knew her place. She was just an ordinary woman; it wasn't her business to express political opinions.

Miss Meadow's eye caught sight of Mustafa Kemal's picture. She picked it up and examined it carefully, in the pale moonlight that filtered through the blinds.

Miss Meadow recognised the love and admiration the girls felt for the hero who had cured their country's ravaged flesh; but such devotion did not lie within Miss Meadow's field of experience, and in order to comprehend it fully, she had to compare it with emotions she had known or had witnessed. She could only compare the love Vicdan and Nefise cherished for Mustafa Kemal to the emotion felt for Jesus, that burned in the hearts of Catholic nuns, the virgins wearing Christ's ring.

The face of the man in the picture made Miss Meadow think of spring skies, the expression was both bright and clouded. The fecund expanse of spring sky, brooding, mettlesome, full of light. This face was different from all those she knew. She could only think of pictures of Christ, the features were so removed from the ordinary. Not that Christ and Mustafa Kemal resembled each other . . .

Christ looks up to heaven, to his Father, with infinite submission and the unending, desperate sorrow born of his complete understanding of life. That he can sense every detail has created a permanent transparency in his soul, which lights his face softly. Light is diffused, deep in his eyes. His is a tranquil visage, infinitely sensitive. When sorrow merges with submission, it is transformed into something tender, into 'love'. Christ, a lonely man? . . . How could it be otherwise? Could there be different kinds of love from the Christian kind, a revolutionary way of loving?

Miss Meadow stared at the uncompromising eyes of Mustafa Kemal and thought he was a creature that was not human . . .

> He looked like a blond wolf
> His blue eyes were lightning flashes
> He walked to the cliff edge, leaned over and paused.
> He would spring from the Koca Hill to the Afyon Plain
> Leaping on lean legs and gliding through darkness
>   Like a shooting star

Miss Meadow would never know this poem. There were still ten more years before it would be written and Miss Meadow would be long dead by the time the poet, Nazım Hikmet, was famous. But in the year 1932, in Cambridge, in one of the bedrooms of 15 Park Road, Miss Meadow, meditating in the pale moonlight of an Indian summer on the portrait of a hero, thought he was a phenomenon glimpsed at in an intersection of inexplicable coincidences belonging both to nature and history. The force of natural insight, which the human race had used, spent and spoiled while moulding small minds and selfish wants, was concentrated, intact as ever, in every aspect of his visage. Supremely concentrated, perpetually alert, dynamic, vigilant, like a mighty conductor radiating spark-filled waves . . . The past was incorporated in his being. His eyes, looking straight ahead, pierced through history and gazed beyond time with a look of near-desperation, the joyless smile of those who hate violence, yet have been compelled to use it, lurked in his eyes. Those eyes with their boundless perceptiveness could not, would not, glow contentedly . . . A lonely man . . . Almost desperate . . . 'A great man can perceive the future,' thought Miss Meadow, 'can see not only tomorrow but the day after that, so even his hopes are desperate.' Aware of everything, but still resolutely looking forward. Miss Meadow had read Hesse's Siddharta. It was written there that the ancient men of wisdom did not have feelings similar to those of ordinary mortals, and could not love or hate in their way. Buddha could not fall in love, since all his being was made up of love. Could Mustafa Kemal love like any other man, feel rage, or bear a grudge? What could it be, if not love, that reached from the hero to these lonely fatherless girls, far away from their homeland? Hope radiating from him, leaving him grim-faced, circulated through the veins of Vicdan and Nefise, sleeping like babies, in the pale moonlight, in the city of Cambridge, seven years before the Second World War.

Nefise was not asleep. Soothed by Miss Meadow's sympathy, she pretended to be, just to have Miss Meadow a little longer at her bedside. Emotional hurricanes raged within her.

How thoughts and feelings, passions, the whole range of individual reactions flowed from one human being to another, uniting them, protecting them, supporting them, then dividing them and maybe destroying them, against the background of history, the blood shed by nations. Whom could you trust? A young aristocratic Englishman infatuated with Nefise? Miss Meadow, so warmly compassionate to them both? British battalions executing Ottoman soldiers? Nefise, thrusting a dagger into Vicdan's back? Emotions, like a thrilling adventure, open the way for unexpected incursions and occurrences . . .

Why couldn't she stop hurting her best friend, Vicdan? Why did she answer, back in Berlin, the stupid question put to them so often, 'Which of you is more typically Turkish? One of you is dark, the other blonde', in that way? 'Of course, I am,' Nefise always replied, 'I come from the heart of central Anatolia, my friend Vicdan comes from Macedonia, north of the Aegean Sea, so she is less Turkish', while Vicdan kept quiet and only smiled. One day Vicdan asked mildly, 'Why do you say that? Mustafa Kemal

Pasha is from overseas too, so is he also less Turkish?' Nefise openly scorned her friend's gentle protest. What connection could there be between Vicdan and Mustafa Kemal?

A few days later, the violence they witnessed on the street taught Nefise an unforgettable lesson, the real meaning lurking behind such phrases as 'less or more Turkish'! How could she hurt Vicdan, especially in front of people asking such tainted questions? Why had the barrack discipline that regulated the family they stayed with in Berlin, attracted her so much at first, and then scared her? How could she, even for an instant, think of Britain as her home? Why did she accept Hugh Eliot's invitation, giving him the idea that he could flirt both with Vicdan and herself? Why did she abandon Hugh at the ball and veer towards Ted, the young aristocrat wearing the uniform that had invaded her country? Why did she feel drunk with power when Ted was flirting with her, and Hugh was sitting in a corner, sulking? Why? . . .

She had let Ted touch her . . . Ted, who called her, 'my dark tulip' . . . Hugh used to call Vicdan 'my Turkish tulip' . . . What lack of imagination! Nefise was disgusted with men with their small imaginations, as she lay awake in her bed, battling questions, searching for answers, struggling with feelings of guilt. While her body, roused by all this stimulus, needed more than ever the touch of a man, to absorb it, then to melt and overflow with it. Every atom of her flesh grew tense, on fire, ached with need.

The ancient knowledge of the female woke in her body alongside desire. The ancient knowledge whispering to her that the feelings of the noble soldier of the British Empire and of the female citizen of the Turkish Republic, could only be as one when their bodies were far apart. As soon as their bodies united, the man's emotions would fade away. Nefise would become an Oriental shawl, to be worn-out, owned by the uniformed aristocrat, who thought the world belonged to his kind. No, she would not even remain unsullied, like a silver souvenir. No, no. She would not be a Turkish carpet to be trodden on until threadbare . . .

A slender image, carved out of time and pain, shimmered in the moonlight. It was the image of the English authoress Virginia Woolf. Nefise, along with Vicdan, had listened to her paper at a conference in Cambridge a few months earlier. Woolf talked about things they had not thought about before, speaking of insights they had not sensed through spine or brain before. She talked about time and womanhood, about the crushing weight of centuries that had rolled over the female sex. The knowledge and the exquisite taste of all these centuries had filtered through the sediment of pain and guilt they bore, and imbued the writer's sensitive features. A sad woman . . . A great woman . . . A lonely woman . . . How could it be otherwise . . . They had felt it . . .

They had sensed it . . .Woolf's eminence and independence were not enough to defeat pain . . . That insight threatened Nefise and Vicdan. It was just not enough . . . Neither Woolf's nor Great Britain's eminence and independence were enough to defeat the pain of womanhood.

Nefise wiped away her tears. She had to go back to her country. She had to heed the summons of that other man who offered her a country, a homeland – the man whose picture hung beside her bed, whose love was in her heart.

Nefise's heart and mind, full of the dauntless energy of youth, strove to find a way out throughout that sleepless night, while her whole being suffered torments in the traps of passion.

Nefise did not recognise the femininity enshrined in her tense muscles, the sexuality that quivered with instinct, intuition, inspiration . . . For her womanhood was a female figure crouching, frightened and vindictive, bearing the marks of slaps and kicks on her skin and deep in her heart, bleeding secretly in lavatories. Nefise did not want to be like this . . . She had to obey the champion who held out a magic staff, carved out of wisdom and exquisite taste, for her to grasp and leap over the centuries. Could she do it? She did not know. She had to try. She had no other choice, no other ray of hope to lighten the dark and crushing doom the centuries had heaped on the womanhood of her country. She had to trust this champion and her taciturn people who sometimes frightened her. She had to hold on to the faith and trust in the beauty she had lately started to find in the folk-songs, poems, and ballads of the silent, sad, submissive people of Anatolia. The way out for Nefise was Turkish, her mother tongue.

Nefise would become one of those great writers, poets, translators who create their own tongues. She would link the nomadic freedom, the steppe-like simplicity, the Eastern tranquillity and the Muslim patience of the Turkish language with the refinement, the riches, the dynamic vitality of the West. This would be her contribution to the great Anatolian revolution that gave her, Nefise Celal, born in the small town of Karaman, in central Anatolia, her role in life; and it would also be the expression of her gratitude. Nefise had no other mission, no other independence, no other identity . . . She had not . . . and she would not have . . . She had to return to her country and to her hero . . . when the time came . . .

But tomorrow I must go to the green fields, to the heart of the England that I love. Heartache is best soothed there, in the fields kissed by the sun, among the willow trees, feeling the coolness of the breeze, where 'separation' does not exist.

I WANDERED lonely as a cloud
That floats on high o'er vales and hills,
When all at once I saw a crowd,
A host, of golden daffodils;
Beside the lake, beneath the trees,
Fluttering and dancing in the breeze.

Continuous as the stars that shine
And twinkle on the milky way,
They stretched in never-ending line
Along the margin of a bay:
Ten thousand saw I at a glance,
Tossing their heads in sprightly dance.
The waves beside them danced; but they

Out-did the sparkling waves in glee:
A poet could not but be gay,
In such a jocund company:
I gazed – and gazed – but little thought
What wealth the show to me had brought:

For oft, when on my couch I lie
In vacant or in pensive mood,
They flash upon that inward eye
Which is the bliss of solitude;
And then my heart with pleasure fills,
And dances with the daffodils.

To the open country, the open country, where larks are singing . . . To the daffodils with their golden wings . . . To the sweet haunting smell of lilac . . . To scattered daisies, with their golden eyes . . . Come to the countryside.

They are riding in Toby's Ford, the 1925 model. Nefise, Vicdan, Eileen, Mildred and Miss Meadow. Toby surrenders the wheel to Nefise for a short while. They are flying! Vicdan, too shy to admit that she loves speed, gives little shrieks of protest. Eileen and Mildred shout for joy! Miss Meadow cries 'Ooooh! Ooooh!' as her plump body bounces on the crowded back seat. They are on wings at fifteen miles per hour!

To the countryside where clover spreads over the ground, where willow branches stoop down to the stream, where trout glisten in the river. To afternoon drowsings under yew trees, soothed by the enchanting smell of honeysuckle. The dreamy veils of buttercups are crowded by lily of the valley, while twilight falls along lanes adorned with primroses . . . purple twilight comes, like the wistfulness of purple violets . . . and autumn leaves drop, swirling into heaps throughout the countryside as it bares itself, crackling, for winter.

Seasons superimpose themselves in the memory, colours, flowing into each other, paint the pastures. Each season, of itself, is a perfect part of this whole. Take it away from the others and the painting changes even though the harmony remains.

From her straw picnic basket, Miss Meadow brings out crystal glasses, neatly folded napkins, sandwiches of rye bread with marmalade and butter, cheese cut in thin slices. They fill their glasses with champagne, chin-chin! 'Bye, bye bluebird' is playing on the gramophone. Girls dance with each other, they dance with Toby, even Miss Meadow dances. Laughter and happiness. Nefise recites to a daisy:

In youth from rock to rock I went,
From hill to hill in discontent
Of pleasure high and turbulent,
*   Most pleased when most uneasy;*
But now my own delights I make,
My thirst at every rill can slake,
And gladly Nature's love partake
*   Of Thee, sweet Daisy!*

Thee Winter in the garland wears
That thinly decks his few grey hairs;
Spring parts the clouds with softest airs,
*   That she may sun thee;*
Whole Summer-fields are thine by right;
And Autumn, melancholy Wight!
Doth in thy crimson head delight
*   When rains are on thee.*

Vicdan recites 'Daffodils'.

Now it is Eileen's turn. Miss Meadow, Toby and Mildred watch her, wide-eyed with admiration. Vicdan and Nefise laugh up their sleeves. There is not the slightest change in Eileen's solemn stance. She continues right to the end of the poem with unaltered determination. Although her patience is wearing a little thin as she reaches the final words, she manages to complete her task. Applause and laughter! Miss Meadow's admiration is so great, she cannot even laugh, and keeps saying 'Gosh!', the exclamation marks resonating in her voice. Eileen laughs with childlike pride, her gray-green eyes shining with pleasure as she acknowledges the applause. She has just finished reciting in Turkish Abdülhak Hamit's elegy for his young wife, who died in Damascus:

Çık Fatma lahitten kıyam et
Gönlümdeki yadına devam et

(Arise from your tomb, Fatma,
Live with your memories in my heart)

Then Vicdan sits down on the rug Nefise has spread on the grass, and Nefise rests her head on Vicdan's lap.

A summery day in autumn . . . The year is 1932. There will be seven years before the outbreak of war, ten before Nefise's death from cancer of the pancreas, sixty before Vicdan's body is extinguished, tiny and shrunken with Parkinson's disease. Eileen will die in 1977 of cancer of the stomach. Mildred will live to the end of the century when English fields will shed acid tears. Miss Meadow will die of old age at the beginning of the sixties. Miss Meadow, Eileen, and Mildred will never again set eyes on Vicdan and Nefise after the Turkish girls leave England, but will keep corresponding until one or other passes away. Toby will go to war and will not come back, just like Hugh Eliot, and Hans Trott, who is studying 'the glorious history of the Reich' during that fine Indian summer of 1932. Hans will fall at the siege of Stalingrad, Hugh in Normandy, Toby in the Far East. Ted Campbell will come back safely, and will often remember Nefise until the atrocities of war freeze all tender feelings in his heart.

The day after the picnic in the meadow, Nefise and Ted met by the Cam. Ted had been uneasy after the intoxication of the ball had worn off. He had not the slightest idea how his parents would react to the possibility of a foreign – Turkish and Muslim – daughter-in-law, or whether such a marriage would be legally acceptable, in view of his commission in the British Army. He was still under Nefise's spell, but could only hazily remember having proposed. A man of honour must never go back on his word, apart from the fact that such behaviour would definitely not be right. If Nefise were to accept his proposal, Ted would have to go the whole way.

Nefise turned him down. They shook hands and parted. But Ted could not feel relief; he had not been prepared for that kind of refusal.

'I am a Republican,' Nefise had said, 'and you are an army officer serving an Empire. We have nothing in common.'

Ted had been shaken; he found politics unsavoury. However, while an honourable officer might not be interested in politics, he would not hesitate to die for his King and country if necessary.

'What country?' Nefise had said, 'Is India your country?'

Ted had never given that a thought!

'Dear Nefise, I respect your decision although it pains me. But please allow me to say that I find it utterly astounding that you should confuse something as humdrum and vulgar as politics with private life – we British tend to regard that as sacred.'

'Is that what you think?' Nefise had said, 'Can't you see that the way politics work sometimes leaves people with no privacy at all?'

Ted, child of a country which had never known enemy occupation, had understood nothing of this.

He would learn . . . ten years later, based in the Far East, when a telegram from London arrived, informing him of the deaths of his wife and two sons in one of the air raids which annihilated parts of London. Before the pain of loss pierced and cracked his carefully guarded heart, well-equipped and disciplined as it was by virtue of his class tradition and military training, his first reaction was to remember Nefise . . . the dark Turkish tulip . . .

Ted sincerely wished her a happy and secure life in Turkey which for the time being had managed to keep out of the war. He was never to know that she had already died.

Attention! Everybody ready! Toby adjusts his camera.

Vicdan smiles tenderly as she looks down at her friend Nefise, whose head rests submissively on her lap. As Vicdan lifts her pretty little hand and brings it down to touch Nefise's brow . . . click . . . Toby has pressed the button.

Once again Vicdan will put her hand on Nefise's feverish brow, her lips will brush Nefise's . . . ten years later.

A grey day in November, 1942. The dark blue corridor of the Numune Hospital in Ankara leads Vicdan to an ending. She hates the month of November ever since Mustafa Kemal's death, and now she has to face another conclusion. She knows a part of her life is expiring together with Nefise. Their friendship is ending at last. They have remained true to each other throughout the eight years since England, with the invincible loyalty of idealists. They, Nefise and Vicdan, children of a nation that had been executed and had risen from the dead, believe in the miraculous deeds of mankind. They, the miracle workers, the creators and the witnesses of the resurrection, have dedicated their private lives to the revival of dead relationships. It is easier for Nefise to end relationships. She has married twice in her short life. Two disappointments . . . Attachments are so precious and precarious for Vicdan, after the deprivation of her childhood years, she cannot possibly end them . . . Absolute loyalty . . . She has not now and never will have as close a woman friend as Nefise . . . Her ties with her own sex will be severed until the baby that occupies her lap during the postwar years will grow up to be a woman.

Vicdan knows Nefise is dying. To an outsider's eye, Vicdan is quite calm. A certain slowness is perceptible in her movements; she does not speak, for in this way she can keep her inner self and its suffering under control. Sorrow is a physical sensation for Vicdan, carving out a painfilled hollow from heart to belly. She does not weep, perhaps cannot. She is no longer the little girl, who wept her heart out when her father died, until her eyesight failed. She has learnt to confront misfortune steadfastly. But the sadness of her heart is not unsullied and intact. Contradictions strain and intensify the various shades of sorrow, cracking them, breaking them into tiny slivers of glass. Wounds bleed, a sense of loss tears Vicdan's inner self apart. Her friend's life that is ending at thirty-three, their relationship that is ceasing, memories pierce her heart. Her England too is perishing along with Nefise . . . England under the blitz . . . Dewy meadows are fading away, the coolness under the weeping willow, the nature poetry . . .

Nefise is burning with fever, her mouth is dry, her lips are cracked, her mind is confused from time to time, and sometimes clear.

So you have come
Could you imagine I wouldn't!

Vicdan puts her hand on Nefise's forehead. The slivers of glass piercing Vicdan's heart melt at that passionate touch, unite and are purified, pain condenses into tears. Vicdan moves her wet cheek close to Nefise's.

Don't weep . . . My life has been short . . . Why have I always hurt you?. . . You are better than I am . . . That's why

No, it isn't true. You have always been my sister.

I shall die before the war is over . . . What will become of our country?

She will survive.

I have finished my mission . . . haven't I?

Yes, you have. You have beautified our language, translated the most delightful love stories into Turkish (Where is your husband, Nefise? Why isn't he beside you?) You have trained hundreds of students (Where is your son, Nefise? Why are they keeping him away from you?)

You think they are good. . . . my translations?

They are superb.

I am dying in November . . . like Mustafa Kemal . . . Too hot . . . Wish it would snow . . . Remember the picnic in Cambridge?

When you read Wordsworth's poems, and Eileen recited 'Çık Fatma Lahitten kıyam et' (So you can smile while you are dying) and Toby took pictures.

Wish we were in England . . . in the meadows . . . endlessly green . . . and cool.

Vicdan puts her hand on Nefise's head, lying there so submissively, and touches her forehead. Click . . . Toby . . . Toby, where are you? . . . Toby doesn't exist any more . . . The War goes on.

This must be love. Is not love sharing each and every memory, each and every thought, even if only in a brief encounter lasting no more than a moment? A moment as endless as infinity and as large as the heart . . . Nobody can take Nefise's place. Nefise was the first person to sense the burden of misery borne by a Vicdan who seemed mature enough to tackle any setback, and who in fact had never learnt how. Vicdan had sealed up the fiery essence of her being in a crystal jar. The flame was reflected in the crystal, a fine sight, but cool to the touch. Nefise was the first, and perhaps the only, person to break the jar, to touch the flame and to be burnt. Nobody can take her place.

When Vicdan woke from her dreamlike stupor, her body was still clinging to Nefise's, her cheek still on Nefise's.

Nefise was cold . . .

Raik was waiting for his wife in the hospital forecourt. Vicdan took refuge in his warm arms like a small wounded bird. The earth beneath her feet had given way . . . Still, Raik would always be by her side to guide and protect her, at each of the moments which trumpet 'the end of the world'. For neither of them would there ever be such another closeness, another love. Raik and Vicdan, orphans of a worn-out nation, they, the makers and witnesses of the miraculous resurrection, will always support and lean on each other.

Today Nefise has gone and the world has ended for Vicdan.

(It is not your first experience of this, Vicdan. Ever since you were a child, the world has ended, again and again . . . Remember your father's death, Vicdan, remember the invasion, remember the treachery of your fellow Muslims, remember the man hanging from the rope, remember your uncle's mansion, brilliant with jewels and dark with hidden intrigue, remember the day Mustafa Kemal died, remember September the first, 1939.)

A ship in the middle of the Black Sea, sailing from Trabzon, Raik's home town, to Istanbul. A small orchestra is playing tangos, Turkey's favourite dance tunes after the War of Independence, in the dining hall, 'La Cumparsita', 'Daisy May', 'The Nights I Spend Without You'. See how the Kemalists dance the tango, so seriously, as if performing some national duty. See, Raik's feet are not very comfortable in his shoes, but he does not complain, not wanting to disappoint his wife who wishes to dance. Suddenly, a vast silence hits the dance floor. Crash! Germany has invaded Gdansk in Poland! France and Britain have declared war on Germany! September 1st 1939. The music stopped. Vicdan took refuge on Raik's broad chest, like a young bird. The floor beneath her feet gave way. Childhood memories that had lain dormant, in all the cells of her organism, stirred. In that instant, Vicdan's inner self lost its balance, slipping off the varnished floor, and for a moment her tiny feet were fluttering down into the turbulent terror-filled waters of the Black Sea. She hugged Raik tightly, not to lose her husband whom the War could well wrest from her side. The six dark years of anguish had just begun. (This is not the first time . . . Worlds have been ending ever since you were born, Vicdan. The distress of Nefise's death is not the first.)

> Raik, she told me everything, why she used to torment me . . . But I didn't tell her that I talked to Mustafa Kemal, the Gazi, in 1935, that I saw him, heard his voice, that when I touched his hand, I touched the light . . . I couldn't . . . I didn't want jealousy to stir in her tranquil

heart, like a snake lifting its head. I know why she was so ambitious; she must have sensed that her life would be short. Nefise, where are you?

The time for black-out is approaching, they have to get home quickly. Raik has been called up for a second time because of the war, and will leave for Gallipoli tomorrow, to join his regiment. Vicdan will be left alone in their small flat in the Sıhhiye quarter of Ankara. A German air raid is expected at any moment. The government is still trying to remain on good terms with Germany, in a desperate effort to keep Turkey out of the war's reach. Pressures on antifascists are increasing. The Marxist poet, Nazım Hikmet, is in prison, as is Raik's cousin. Farmers have become soldiers, and farms and villages have been left to starve. Everyone is silent. Bread is rationed. Raik sometimes supports government policy, and sometimes is critical of it. 'President İsmet Pasha is trying to keep the boat afloat,' he says, 'he changes course according to the winds; he is trying to take the waves on his stern so as not to capsize. The boat is rolling, taking on water. One moment İsmet Pasha is cracking down on the rightists, at another on the leftists. He has one single aim which is paramount: to keep out of the war. All other issues are irrelevant to him at the moment. If he fails to concentrate on one single target, he won't have a hope of success. You will see, he will succeed.'

My husband, my Raik . . . My brothers,
My Burhan, my Reha . . .

'Don't worry,' says Raik, 'none of us will die. What an old sea-wolf he is, İsmet Pasha! We shall survive the storm. You, me, your brothers. Take my word for it, the war will soon be over, we and our country will survive. But our salvation will come at a price! What's that? Difficult to guess, but the price will be high. We shall live, and we shall see.'

Nefise has gone. Raik is leaving tomorrow. Burhan and Reha have already been drafted. The nights when we can expect bombers have begun. Far away, the England I have known and loved is perishing. London is in ruins . . . Ankara is being evacuated.

Vicdan remembered Nefise's letter: 'Ankara looks like a German town, not an Anglo-Saxon one.'

Husband and wife, seeking warmth from each other's bodies, walked in silence along the dark, cold, quiet streets of an Ankara that resembled a German town more than ever. A sullen town that had become a stranger to their hearts.

AT THE SUMMIT

Mother Cybele, squatting on her heavy haunches and suckling, for thousands of years, the child – both husband and son – pressed to her ample bosom! . . . Oh, Mother Goddess, Daughter of Anatolia, called Artemis on the Aegean islands, Demeter where the sea opens into the Mediterranean, Isis at the Nile delta, Lat in the Arabian desert! Mother Earth, symbol of endless life and of endless death . . . Mountains, plains, plateaus and hundreds of husbands are yours! You set up home on the summit of Uludağ, our Anatolian Mount Olympus, and fed the rich Mysa plain. Your eyes have searched the blue horizons of the Aegean and Marmara seas for millions of years, from the time when the earth ceased to emit savage fumes and cooled down, until the middle of the twentieth century, when an air filled with flecks of soot and industrial gases blurred your vision.

The things you have witnessed! Churches were carved out of rock, minarets rose from the plains, galloping cavalry horses trampled the fields. Spring rains splashed down. Peasants harvested golden corn and honey-tasting peaches. Centuries flowed by. Did you shed tears when, as the nineteenth and twentieth centuries met, your children on both shores of the Aegean – their roots entangled – strangled one another? Did you recall that ancient slaughter, when the dauntless Agamemnon, insidiously – in a way unworthy of his valour – sneaked the wooden horse into the city of Troy, suffocating the noble Priam and his queen, Hecuba, a mother in deepest mourning for the loss of her gallant son, Hector? Did your heart burn, Mother Cybele, when Troy was destroyed nine times?

Thousands of years later, a poet forged from fire like Homer, yet different as well, said 'We have taken revenge for Troy.' A poet who wrote his poems in deeds, he was the one who said this, thrusting his roots into Anatolian soil and drawing sustenance from its thousands of years of history, while he ended the throes of vengeance for his people's wounds, still so fresh, with an apt solace drawn from antique legend.

See, those who have faith in him are climbing, mother Cybele. Can you make out the young Kemalists climbing our Mount Olympus, Uludağ, from the foothills to the summit, on a hot day in July 1935? Some young Turks are coming to claim their homeland. Have you ever seen anything like it? Turks like these used to wander as nomad tribes, scattered and despairing; were driven from plateau to plateau, from one camping ground to another, from one border to another, disheartened, rueful, and resigned. Bandits would cut them down and malaria would deplete them. They were quite unaware they had an empire . . . they bore their burden silently. Now their heads are up, their faces smile as they climb to the summit, to the fortress of the god Zeus. Can you believe it, mother Cybele, Turks are coming to make peace with father Zeus! . . .

There are three of them. The young woman in the middle wears a suit of Irish linen, a broad-brimmed white hat shading her face, and white patent leather shoes. Take a good look at her, mother Cybele. She is Vicdan Hayreddin, and beside her are her brothers, Lieutenants Burhan Bey and Reha Bey.

They thought, 'How can you visit Bursa and not climb Uludağ?' and resented the prudent older people who wanted to stop them, and started out on their expedition in that Irish linen suit and the uniform of army officers . . .

The climb was Burhan's idea. How handsome he was, standing on the wind-swept deck of the boat as they crossed the Sea of Marmara from Istanbul to Mudanya. His pose recalled the statues of gods on the Ion ruins. His hair, tossed by the wind, was a streaming mane. Reha, docile as always, agreed to the proposal. Would Vicdan be likely to refuse to climb a mountain when two young officers of the Republic were going with her?

They were visiting some relatives in Bursa. Part of their childhood had been spent in this town with its plane trees and porcelain. The mountain used to be unbelievably far away then, the summit, so inaccessible, reaching up to the clouds . . . But now! . . .

Both the brothers and their sister were filled with self-generating energy. They could demolish the world and build it all over again! They, the young intellectuals of a Republic which was only twelve years old! Reha and Burhan had graduated from the Military Academy. Vicdan had been assigned to her institution, and was about to marry Raik. And . . . she had recently seen and spoken with Kemal Atatürk, with 'Gazi' himself! For these brothers and this sister there was no goal that could not be reached, no peak that could not be conquered, nothing unknown that could not be discovered!

Burhan and Reha unfolded their maps at once, made calculations, and decided on the route they would take. The southern face of the mountain was sheer, but the northern face, looking over the Bursa plain, rose in a series of slopes. After crossing a number of plateaus, you reached a place covered with small chalky stones. There were a number of peaks, about fifty metres high, rising above this place. They could reach the Kirazlı Plateau by car, then walk across the stretch of chalk, and climb one of the peaks. No, no need for a local guide; maps, a compass, hats and strong staffs would be sufficient.

Puffing and snorting, the Ford they had hired took them up to the Kirazlı Plateau, which greeted them with golden gentians spread over its rich green turf. Paradise should have been laid out here!

Reha picked a flower and fitted it into his sister's lapel. Vicdan smiled warmly at him. Reha . . . as gentle as ever . . .

Look, mother Cybele, they have begun their ascent. A difficult task when it is so extremely hot! They are in no hurry, and are climbing slowly as their eyes and hearts absorb the view. See how Vicdan Hayreddin, in her high-heeled shoes, jumps the chalky boulders on her way up, like a mountain goat, but without spoiling her poise. She isn't even sweating . . . Is she climbing? She might as well be flying! On either side of her, her brothers climb steadily, placing their staffs firmly between the boulders.

As the slope gets steeper, the green turf of the plateau below disappears from sight. They are in the heart of unadorned, untamed nature, far from the plains cultivated by human hand.

Even wild plants are nowhere to be seen. Only the bare rock and the sky! A blue-yellow light pours over the limestone like a hot shower. The air is growing thinner as the ascent continues, they are breathing with difficulty, but are determined to go on. 'Need help?' Burhan asks his sister. 'No,' she replies, smiling. All the same, they take their sister's arms and fly her up like a bird. They don't talk any more; they have to preserve their breath and their strength. Weariness is like drunkenness; they have crossed the threshold, and are no longer aware of inner restraints or pressures. They feel their togetherness strongly, yet each is on his own, on the naked rock, in his inner world. What they sense most intensely is the texture of the stones beneath their feet and the thin blue air they inhale. And those images tossed up suddenly from the memory, those forms animated by imagination . . . always there, as natural and as real as the rock they step on or the air they breathe – yet mysterious also.

Burhan and Reha are aware of their bodies, agile and strong. The images of women they have touched or dreamed of touching appear and vanish. Reha sees the slender, supple body of Yıldız, that beauty of beauties; scents the smell of the women he visits in Beyoğlu brothels, in Istanbul. Burhan thinks for a moment of the young girl, daughter of his mother's neighbour, who is in love with him. A quiet, placid girl, very suitable for the wife of an army officer whose demanding life would be full of hardships. Then he thinks of Vecdet. Is he in love with her? Vecdet is not one of those women created to complete a man; she is already a wholeness in herself. Vecdet is not for Burhan.

Vicdan thinks of the Gazi . . .

The afternoon sun, reflected off the pier of the Dolmabahçe palace in Istanbul, was shining behind the Gazi. Vicdan could not see his face. What she saw was a silhouette cut out of light. The silvery shimmer of the sun's beam turned to a golden halo round his head and dazzled her.

She had been flying on the eager wings of youth drawn to deeds of daring while in the official black car that took her from

8 Sakızağacı Road to the Dolmabahçe Palace. But now, all her courage had left her, as if her heart had stopped.

She stood awestruck on the threshold of his Excellency the President's office, in her muslin dress and her mother's single string of pearls, her body numbed, her mouth dry, her hands cold.

The Gazi rose from his seat, came towards Vicdan and held out his elegant, slender hand. He was wearing a neat grey suit. A faint scent of lemon cologne wafted round him.

Vicdan's first impression was: What a well-groomed man!

She was taking in all these details about him at great speed, although her body was still incapable of moving. How could she manage to walk towards the President? As if under the spell of a powerful magnet, she could not stop staring into the Gazi's eyes, deepset and clear, lit from some inner source. The Gazi's probing, solemn gaze, which cut through outer layers and tapped the essence of people and events, was on Vicdan. Observing her keenly but not unkindly, he said:

—Welcome, my child.

His voice was soft, his accent unaffected. He took Vicdan's right hand in his own and clasped it lightly but warmly. He held on to her hand neither too long nor too briefly. His grip was neither too weak nor too strong. It was a kindly, reassuring pressure and then a release . . . Not a rejection . . . A letting-go of a young bird, up and away into the sky.

As she shook hands with the Gazi, blood pulsed through Vicdan's veins.

—Please, take a seat, my child, he said, indicating the armchair to the right of his own.

As soon as she sat down, she felt more relaxed, and a surge of pleasure filled her.

—Does your esteemed self live in Makriköy? asked the Gazi, and he had used the formal mode of address, as if she were his equal!

Vicdan felt like laughing. The great President, Mustafa Kemal himself, addressing her, only a young woman, like this! Incredible! And to say 'Makriköy'! The President's unaffected way of referring to Bakırköy by its former Greek name seemed rather endearing to Vicdan at a time when the younger generation was eager to use the newly-formed Turkish names of some districts, not without a touch of pomposity.

She smiled at him. God only knew if it were true, all those rumours about how, although he disapproved of monophonic Ottoman music being played on the radio, every evening he sipped his rakı while listening to and even joining in the 'alla Turca' chorus!

—Yes, my Pasha, she said, my family lives in Bakırköy, and she emphasised the 'bakır'.

She was no longer frightened of him, and did not realise that the indulgent expression she assumed, when she noticed some mischief of her brothers, had just appeared in her eyes.

—You were born in Salonika, weren't you? asked the Gazi.

—Yes, my Pasha.

—You see, we happen to be compatriots.

The charming smile round his mouth grew, almost reaching his eyes; he had an air of playfulness.

—Yes, said Vicdan, a ghost of a laugh escaping her.

So the President had taken the trouble to do his homework on her.

—Your late father was a veteran of the Balkan War; I presume you must have suffered as we all did during the occupation years.

She felt once more the old lump in her throat, that choked her whenever she remembered her father; her eyes filled with tears.

—Yes, she murmured.

—Thank heavens, those dreadful times are over.

—Thanks to you, my Pasha.

Vicdan bowed her head as she did not want the Gazi to see her tears. Would it not be unseemly for a person whom the Gazi had deigned to receive, to show weakness?

—Not to me, thanks to our nation, he went on. We have all suffered, my child, believe me.

He sighed.

—I have fought battles all my life. I have never liked it; I fought when I had to, but never enjoyed it. War always brings suffering, my child.

Vicdan raised her head, she no longer hid her tears from the Gazi's eyes.

—We have lost a part of our homeland, my child, and losing a home is like losing a part of oneself; it can never be replaced. But one learns how to live with the loss and how to teach other parts of the body some of the special skills, some of the functions of the part that was lost. Fine exploits may spring from pain and suffering. Our homeland is Anatolia, our beloved Turkey. We have to transform the bitterness in our hearts, my child, into love for our dear homeland.

Vicdan forgot about her sudden attack of sadness, and listened carefully to what the President Gazi Pasha had to say.

—Our country has been saved thanks to the nation's endeavours. But victory by itself is not as important as it may seem. Our homeland will prosper by the endeavours of young people like yourself; then it will really have been saved. Other nations are by no means our enemies. No nation is better or worse than the rest. World politics is a bloody fight for spoils, my child. Whoever pursues personal gain or privileges for minority interests or cliques, is destined to be doomed within this bloody rivalry, and to bring disaster on those close to him. We have to consider what is beneficial for Turkey above our petty personal aims. Simply because, in the long run, this is the most rational route to take. Now, my child, tell me about England, and about your life as a student there.

Vicdan was glad that the solemn atmosphere had dissipated. She had been overwhelmed by an exhausting intensity of emotion while the Gazi was speaking. She felt proud that Mustafa Kemal had honoured her with his reflections on world politics, and at the same time she strained every fibre of her being, not to risk the slightest mistake – the wrong word, the wrong gesture or facial expression – that might end the Gazi's confidences; and as well as this, she was absorbing the significance of the ideas his words conveyed, quite independently of the unexpected intimacy that flourished between them, something which had developed quite spontaneously, unwilled by either one of them. This triple concentration wore her out.

Now, cheerful again, she started to tell him about the years in England. The foolish details she confided in the great Gazi! He listened to her, a pleased smile playing round his mouth, and signified his approval by nodding his head; at times he raised his eyebrows to show his astonishment.

Vicdan sensed he was relaxed and enjoying what she was telling him. Or was he only listening to her voice, the voice of a young woman, quivering with pleasure, excitement, and earnestness? This possibility thrilled Vicdan. She had never experienced such profound and complex sensations even when Raik proposed to her. Her strongest emotions were often entangled with pain. But now she felt clever and appealing like a naughty little girl, and simultaneously beautiful and alluring, exceedingly feminine. There must have been some enchantment, radiating from the Gazi's being, that sharpened her intellect, flushed her cheek, caressed her body and laid silken overtones on her voice.

She sensed that the Gazi could be relaxed and vibrant at the same time, and realised that this encounter created a tension almost as exciting for him as it was for her. She was amazed and proud. She absorbed this new mood of his at once and went on with her story. She could contain the shifts and switches of his moods, as she realised that a harmonious partnership of contrasting reactions was his natural mental climate.

His many-layered response had evoked a similar range in herself, or rather helped her to recognise a hidden part of herself unacknowledged until this meeting. For a moment she imagined that the Gazi would reach out his slender, elegant hand with its tapering fingers, pale as wax, and that he wanted to touch her flushed cheek. What would that touch express? The feelings of a father caressing his child, the yearning of middle-age for youth, or the burning desire of manhood? Perhaps all of these things, and also some element different from them all, an ineffable composition. But the conversation with this young woman had exhausted the Gazi – his face grew sad.

—My Pasha, I am sorry if my chattering has given you a head ache.

At once the Gazi shed his sombre mood.

—Not at all, my child, he said, on the contrary, I have thoroughly enjoyed it. You have made me very happy. I have listened carefully to you and come to a decision. I shall ask a favour of you, if I may.

—Of course, my Pasha, anything.

—It will be for our country. The people most suitable to represent our young republic abroad should not be elderly diplomats, but those young ones like your esteemed self who have managed to combine the Western way of thinking with the qualities of our own nation. It appears that, thanks to contacts made by our Ministry of Foreign Affairs, the broadcasting corporations of the Western world would like to have information on our political and social reforms. One of the corporations showing an interest is Britain's BBC, which intends to devote a programme specifically to the women's rights aspect of our metamorphosis. I think it would be entirely appropriate if you could bear to undertake a second journey to Britain, a country you know well, and give a talk on the BBC. I should be most grateful, if you would be so kind as to grant my request.

—Oh, my President, I should consider it an obligation.

—No, not at all. It is just a humble request. And after your return from England, I shall make a personal request as well.

—Please tell me what it is, my Pasha.

—I should like you, while you remain in Istanbul, to give English lessons to my adopted daughter.

—Certainly, my Pasha, anything you wish.

Mustafa Kemal sighed, and closed his eyes for an instant. In a weak voice he said,

—Very well, please discuss the particulars with my aide-de-camp.

He was pale and his breathing was shallow. Vicdan, realising that the interview was over, rose to her feet. The Gazi forced himself to stand. At that moment he looked like a very old man. Vicdan made a move to kiss his hand; The Gazi stopped her with a gracious gesture and they shook hands. He held Vicdan's hand in his a little longer this time. Vicdan noticed that his face had grown as white as his fingers. Her instinct told her that The Gazi was a sick man. Suddenly all her satisfaction changed to sheer panic! She blurted out,

—My Pasha,

as, without intending it, she reached out a protective arm towards him. What could she say? From whom or from what could she, just a young woman, protect the great Gazi? He slowly raised his white hand and put it between them.

—Goodbye, my child, he said, go with my most sincere wishes for your success. I hope you will always be healthy, happy, and cheerful.

—For an instant Vicdan hesitated, torn between her personal happiness and the anxiety she felt for the Gazi. But the sadness on Mustafa Kemal's face had vanished, he was smiling. Hope flowed from him to her. Vicdan's anxiety evaporated and, in good spirits again, she hurried out.

The particulars were discussed with the aide-de-camp, and soon Vicdan was aboard the *Théophile Gautier* again, sailing through the Mediterranean. After reaching Marseilles, she crossed France by train and boarded a boat at Calais that would take her across the Channel. The angry waves rocked the boat as if it were a mere nutshell. Who cared?

Nearly all the passengers were seasick, but Vicdan resisted as if she were made of steel! She is on deck in her thin raincoat, defying the cold wind that scours her face! The Gazi has chosen her, has believed in her, treated her with respect, entrusted her with a mission. Mustafa Kemal has talked to her, has exposed his thoughts and his suffering to her. Raik is in love with her; Burhan and Reha admire her, their sister, who has graduated from the great Cambridge University with honours, just like a man, and who can still remain graceful and fragile . . . Oh how they wish they could meet such another young woman. If they did, they would fall in love at once and marry her. But how and where to find a girl just like their sister? Vicdan is unique! Let's hope to God Raik will realise how precious she is! Vicdan smiles at the storm. The love her menfolk cherish for her enfolds her like a warm coat of fur, impenetrable by wind or rain. After the meeting with the Gazi, a whole new, liberating vista has opened before her: the world of men and the range of responses it arouses within her.

Vicdan had lived for so long with anguish and anxiety, that tunnels for trouble had been hollowed out within her inner being, through which the sufferings of the outside world could reach her heart unimpeded. Fresh instances of sadness and distress could travel easily to the core of her emotional life. But now a blissful sense of security has blocked all these routes. She will be married soon, and begin teaching, she will represent her country in the capital of the British Empire! The responsibilities on her shoulders, instead of wearing her down, make her soar higher and faster, as if flying with the wind. She is free of foreboding, and no longer remembers her uncle's mansion in Istanbul, no longer recalls the insidious darkness pervading its recesses. She no longer questions her relationship with Nefise. She has abandoned the old world of women and moved on. How suffocating it had been there! Her mother's domineering, all those sombre years of secondary and higher education in girls' schools and colleges! And her fraught relations with Nefise. The effort of analysing the complexities of their friendship, which used to claim all her leisure hours, has almost ended. Vicdan has no intention of going back to that old world of women! She has not yet learnt that what she is abandoning is a sanctuary, somewhere to run to and take refuge in, when you are battered by other forms of life.

Vicdan is drunk with happiness . . . If it were not for that sad image appearing like a question mark . . . The pallor of Virginia Woolf . . . The face of an emancipated and creative woman in a most liberal country . . . But the Channel wind has blown Woolf's image away! . . . Vicdan has reached Dover free from anguish . . .

She is once more in her beloved England! . . .

Vicdan gave a talk on the BBC about the women's rights movements in Turkey. She heard that Western countries had started to call her homeland 'the feminist republic'. She met the Foreign Secretary, and on that auspicious day wore the white suit of pure Irish linen which she had bought in Oxford Street. A prominent daily published an interview with her.

—Did you ever fall in love during your six years here, Miss Hayreddin, and consider marrying an Englishman?
—No, never.
—Didn't you like Englishmen?
—Certainly, they are true gentlemen.
—Well?
—I and my friends were in love with our country.
—Do you think so?
—What great will-power.
                    (Perhaps . . . caution . . .)

What about Hugh Eliot, the sacrifice to Vicdan's will-power or to her prudence? He is no longer relevant . . . Raik is in love with Vicdan . . . The Gazi has honoured Vicdan, and she has been liberated from remorse.

On her way back, while she was crossing the rough waters of the Channel, Vicdan did not realise that she had done her country a substantial service. She was not hungry for success, having always been a student whose efforts brought her achievement. Her hunger was for the love of men, had been so ever since her father's death. She had pined for the love of men at her schools for girls; for the love of men which she could not satisfy with her brothers' company, as they were always away at boarding school; for the love of men which she could not savour in England during those circumspect years. Now at last the lack was replenished. As for the country . . . It was only natural that she should serve her country which had given her the chance of a free education.

After her return to Istanbul, during the period before she started to work in an education college, an official black car took

Vicdan on certain days of the week from 8 Sakızağacı Road to the Dolmabahçe Palace, to teach English to the Gazi's adopted daughter – a task for which she was paid generously. She was told that the Gazi had followed her successes in England, that he was extremely pleased, that he sent her his grateful thanks. She never saw him again.

The reflections of sun and sky dance on the hot white stones, in a flush of gold and sparks of blue. And once again he is there! The Gazi's head rises above the peak . . . Watching over her, supporting her. The breeze brings his kindly, soft voice: 'Turn the bitterness in your heart, my child, into love of your homeland.'

Look at them, mother Cybele, see, they have succeeded. They are at the summit . . . of integrity and youth. They have climbed right up and relaxed against the poles marking the height . . . and have taken pictures . . . as souvenirs of that day . . . in the summer of 1935. Do not forget the day we climbed Uludağ. They have savoured their country's air, breathing deeply, their hair streaming in the wind . . . They have scanned the horizon with Cybele's thousand-year-old gaze, until their eyes were sated.

Vicdan Hayreddin lay on the hot chalky stone, no creases marring her Irish linen suit, planting her hips firmly on the summit of Uludağ.

She surrendered her whole being to the delicious exhaustion flowing from her body into the stone, surrendering to the silence in which every cell of her anatomy was dissolving. Her brothers Reha and Burhan lay on either side of her, their heads resting on her breast, while it rose and fell as accompaniment to her deep breaths; they are almost asleep.

The young female body they are resting on rouses part of the young men's inner being, a deeply slumbering part, causing ripples of secret remembering; without fully realising it, they recall a time when they were tiny, on the migration road, in a mosque enclosure, a time when they took refuge in a sweet-smelling body resembling their sister . . . Now only happiness and warmth radiate from their sister's. What they had lost, twenty-two years ago on the migration roads, is being restored to them. Reha and Burhan will always remember this day, remember the infant joy they tasted on the summit of Uludağ, their adult minds not really comprehending the mysterious ecstasy. They will always remember that hot summer day when their sister, stroking the dark head of one, the fair head of the other, told them the legends of Uludağ and of Mother Cybele who had made her home on its summit, of Troy on the Sea of Marmara, and of Hector, the brave martyred son of Priam of Anatolia. They listened to her soft voice, relating all those ancient legends, of Troy stabbed in the back, and of Kemal Pasha taking revenge for Troy.

Vicdan remembers as she speaks . . . the old days when she used to press her brothers' uniforms for the military academy. Reha is only eleven months younger than she is, Burhan only two years younger, but she enjoys being the elder sister. She remembers her brothers' lost childhood, when they were separated from their mother to be sent to the dormitories of the Kuleli military academy. She hugs them tenderly. Reha looks up at her, childlike, drowsy. He only hears the music of her voice as if it were a lullaby, as a plant listens to the wind. Her voice reaches Burhan's ears like a lullaby also, but he listens to her words as well. Burhan, dear Burhan, listen to my voice, understand my meaning. The story of Troy sends electric charges through Burhan's brain, building bridges between his young body and the ancient legend – bridges that earth themselves in the Anatolian soil he is lying on with his brother and sister.

Why does Vicdan love Burhan more than Reha? Is it because the sparks of blue in her brother's eyes link Burhan with the man she adores? Burhan's physique resembles the Gazi's, a fact that will prove both auspicious and disastrous for him. He will climb high, imagining his soul is like the Gazi's as well; and there . . . On this hot July day of 1935, Burhan's soul, snuggling up to the body of the only woman he really loves, his sister, still preserves its innocence, and Vicdan loves him very much.

Vicdan could die of bliss; Reha's touch is as carefree as a gentian's, linking her with the rocks; and Burhan's unfurls the world of myths and possibilities for her.

What magic spell hovers in the air of Uludağ, Mother Cybele, distilling a mysterious elixir from the recollections and dreams of human existence? Vicdan's tale of Troy is over.

Now her inner self is a place of shadows, where the vibrations of violin strings ebb and flow in her memory.

It is a melody she heard in England; she cannot recall the composer and does not force herself to remember. Burhan and Reha feel drawn to the tune their sister is humming, and which they are hearing for the first time. Tired and satisfied, they absorb the music.

Why, what is this clamour that suddenly explodes through the rapid flow of the concerto? Isn't it a Thracian air? (Are your memories of the old country you were the gazing at but not seeing, the land you had forgotten. Are those memories stirring, Vicdan?)

The monotonous melody of the Thracian folk-song slices, like a sharp blade, through Vicdan's heart, and, like a violin bow, sets her emotions, now taut as strings, resonating. Fantasies take shape in her imagination, nourished by her skin's contact with her brothers'. The gazi Mustafa Kemal and Lieutenants Burhan and Reha Bey, are at dinner together, at ease, feasting at a table replete with rich delicacies and glasses filled with rakı, drinking relaxedly and sampling the excellent food with relish. The winds of freedom blowing from the mountains of Macedonia ruffle their hair.

Oh, these geese winging away from Mount Maya
Oh, these girls with their white skins and pink heels,
Oh, the Vardar plain, the Vardar plain

And Raik appears, he ought to, he must . . . Raik, her darling, her fiancé, waiting for her at the mountain's foot to walk the road of life with her. Steady, reliable, faithful Raik . . . No, Vicdan simply cannot imagine him sitting at her fantasy table, cannot get him to join in the licentious song.

Poor old me, who can't earn enough money for rakı . . .

Please, gentlemen, make room for Raik. No, Raik immediately disappears after all Vicdan's efforts to place him at the table, and returns to his post at the foot of Uludağ. Vicdan gave up the idea of organising her fantasies, surrendered herself wholeheartedly to the promptings of nature . . . and thanked heaven that Raik existed, that he was not at the summit now, not experiencing the moment she was sharing with her brothers, this sacred moment when the sister and brothers were rediscovering what they had lost, a long time ago . . .

A sense of security enfolds Vicdan, as her brothers' voices join in the melody. All three of them sing the song of the Vardar plain, while the wide plain of Bursa, whose edge reaches the blue mists of the Sea of Marmara, listens . . .

> . . . *Vardar plain,*
> *I am the star of Mount Maya*
> *I am my mother's only daughter*

Our bodies have dissolved into voices passing through the stones into the earth which still cradles the groans of Troy. Uludağ has absorbed our song, the ballad of Mount Maya. We have now become part of Uludağ, like rain formed in the Macedonian mountains, and falling on the arid Anatolian land. We have been dispelled into the lucid blue air, Uludağ will be ours to eternity. Our dear sister and ourselves . . . The only daughter of our mother.

> *I am my mother's only daughter.*

Oh, Vicdan, dear sister, Fitnat Hanım's daughter. Raik will soon take you away from us. Hope he treats you well.

> *I am my husband's right eye*
> *Oh, the Vardar plain, the Vardar plain.*

Oh these geese winging away from Mount Maya
Oh, these girls with their white skins and pink heels

Oh, how my lover's heart weeps
Don't try to deceive me, don't delay me,
I can no longer loiter here.
How I long for Mount Maya
And that Vardar plain.

The arid soil, the red-hot stones, the lizards and snakes are listening. The grass and water listen. The deep blue sky listens.

We have listened to the earth embracing us and to the distant sounds it holds in its bosom. No, we have not heard the groans coming from the East.

AN HONOURABLE OFFICER

They were waiting for the blizzard to end so they could move on. A heavy silence had blanketed the company since they passed the checkpoint. They stamped their feet and flexed their fingers. The capote was a thin, wet bark covering the trunk. Did he want the waiting to be over? Neither yes nor no. The fear that had invaded him on leaving headquarters had turned to ice with the rest of his emotions. He would face whatever came. Neither he nor the company had any choice, not after the checkpoint. The training he had received at the Kuleli academy on the Bosphorus had at last sprung to life in his veins and muscles. The relentless concentration of the hunter!

The checkpoint had loomed up with its frozen bodies while they were scouting ahead. The corpses seemed to belong to a species other than man. He could feel no pity. He could only perceive the crystal-clear inevitability of the combat facing them. For one single moment he was piercingly aware of the vitality of his young body, felt his penis growing.

One single moment . . . The sensation was ended instantaneously by his awareness of the inevitable. The company were staring, dull-eyed, at the spectacle: the exhibits stood in lopsided jars of ice. Icicles hung from some of their fingers. If it had not been for the colour of their flesh – ranging from a crimson to a purplish hue – the sight might even have been considered beautiful. They were stark-naked, and their penises had shrunk.

Later a soldier the company rescued would tell them how the rebels had raided the checkpoint, how they had stripped his comrades and his commanding officer, how they had poured buckets of water over the naked men, had dragged them, all wet, out of the checkpoint and had left them to freeze in the open air. He was the only one to escape. The blizzard began immediately after that, wiping out his footprints.

The soldier was half-frozen himself when the company came across him. The men rubbed his body with snow, while they poured warm tea into his mouth. After he recovered his senses, he told in short bursts, stopping and starting, what had happened at the checkpoint, while the men of the company held their breath and listened. He watched, as if behind frosted glass, the flashes of anger burn in the eyes of his audience, then like a young animal fell asleep and snored before he could satisfy the curiosity of the men, hungry for horror.

Reha watched his brother. Burhan's eyes, like blue lightning, threw out bolts of vengeance, as the soldier spoke. Reha envied his brother. How could Burhan, under any circumstances, whip up such depths of self-justifying emotion? Whereas Reha could feel neither rage nor resentment! He was lost in a perplexing maze, having slipped into the mood that seized him when performing tasks he disliked. What he was experiencing could not possibly be happening! How he missed his mother, his sister, and Yıldız . . .

Reha would only be able to feel the pain of that raid on the checkpoint long after the campaign. In later years, the purplish crimson flesh of the murdered soldiers would very often appear before him, as the most incredible, intimate, and revolting scene he had ever witnessed, and he would be overcome with nausea. Sometimes he would be seized by an apparently causeless fit of weeping; and after the fit was over, he would imagine frozen hands, arms, legs and penises. Long years after . . . the blizzard stopped, the company attacked.

In the spring of 1937, after the orders had been carried out, the operation successfully completed, Lieutenant Burhan, his brother Reha, and First Lieutenant İzzet sat by the fire at their headquarters near Dersim. The crackling of the wood produced a sense of security, wiping all thoughts of bitterness from their minds. Now was the time for nostalgia for loved ones, for the years before Dersim.

First Lieutenant İzzet said, 'Nothing will be the same. We've lived through an unforgettable experience here. The rebels and government troops have inflicted wounds on each other which will never heal.'

Lieutenant Burhan said, 'No, everything will be exactly the same, it must be. We are not the first army that has ever fought. Our fathers and brothers fought for their fatherland and fell. Now it is our turn. We have done our duty. There's no need for anyone's conscience to carry a burden of guilt. What happened was an emergency situation.'

'Perhaps,' said İzzet. His fastidious face was thoughtful. His wire-rimmed spectacles rested on his pointed nose, accentuating the sad, yet sardonic expression he wore. 'Still, how justifiable is it, from the point of view of history and the individual as well, to dismiss what's happened?'

'You can't live looking back at the past,' said Burhan, 'life always lies ahead.' His face was alight with enthusiasm, a fiery sincerity blazing in his eyes. 'As soon as we leave Dersim, the experience will be consigned to the past. We are officers of a young state. The foundations of our nation and our country are still not complete. Dark war clouds that threaten the whole world are gathering on Europe's horizon. It's absurd to get entangled in the past, when new deeds await us.'

Reha sat silent. From time to time, Burhan cast anxious glances at his brother. Reha, his eyes fixed on the fire, looked as if he was not even aware of the conversation. He was murmuring a song:

Come, sing my song with your voice of love

In Reha's memory, the image of Yıldız merged with that of his mother. His fever was rising. The melody of that song had echoed from the gardens beyond, when he had kissed Yıldız; the air had smelt of magnolia, and the moon had been a silver tray floating on the waters of the Bosphorus. It had been one of those nights that made you almost swoon, relieving the earthbound body of its weight, and setting the spirit soaring towards the stars.

The milk-white body of Yıldız was veiled by a white muslin evening dress. 'My bride,' he had said, 'be my bride.' Yıldız was warm and not unfriendly, not pushing Lieutenant Reha away even if she had not returned his kiss. Didn't that mean 'Yes'?

Then visions of his childhood returned, his beautiful, beautiful mother sitting on the divan in her white dress, her feet bare, her silky hair rippling down to her shoulders, like an angel of grace. His father was circling round his lady who was playing a lute, and singing in her fine soft voice.

Come, sing my song with your voice of love

He wanted to come close to his mother's body but dreaded his father. His mother kissed and caressed Reha, calling him 'my son, my lion son, the pillar of my home.' He did not grasp her meaning. Was his father alive then? He only wanted to bury his head in his mother's hyacinth-scented bosom, to hide himself in the folds of her long skirt, and never be parted from her again.

Then the images suddenly vanished. Emptiness . . . the same bitter scene always returned after these serene, enchanting visions. His mother on her sick-bed, pale as wax . . . Her silky black hair spread over the blue satin pillow like dark tidings . . . She was moaning. Silent glances, whispers, hot water jars, cloths which were spotlessly, immaculately white, and a peculiar, frightening smell which he could not define as a boy, but which in later life he was to encounter in hospitals, filled the house. Terror turned his little heart to stone.

The wooden staircase, ascended and descended by anxious, hurrying feet, creaked wretchedly and groaned. The whole house was in mourning. The usual Armenian doctor, Vartan Efendi, examined his mother and shook his head, deep in thought. Reha felt that his father, who was all but invisible, was linked to what was happening. But what was the connection? He could not solve the riddle. Reha remembers that day clearly, however. Burhan was too young. And their sister? No, she did not recall it either.

Reha could not understand why his mother did not approve of Yıldız. She found all kinds of reasons for opposing the marriage. When had the graceful fairylike creature of his childhood turned into this haggard witch? He longed for his mother when away from her, but once they were together, he could not stand this nagging old hag.

'You will ruin my relations with long-standing neighbours'; she had made her mind up, and refused to change it, not believing in the love Reha claimed he felt for Yıldız. She goaded him with, 'What number is Yıldız in the list of your love affairs? I have lost count, and I'd be surprised if you can remember.'

Yes, true . . . he had been sincerely in love every time. Such an ardent fire blazed within him! It was thanks to that fire that passionate words poured from his lips and poems from his pen. He never worked on them. Then all of a sudden, the fire went out. How many times had his mother rescued him from some ardent woman still hot on the trail of an old affair's fading spoor?

From the Greek girl Marika, the Bulgarian Evdoksia, the Armenian Madam Hayganus, the Jewish Esther . . . sometimes with gifts and money, at others with anger and threats . . .

'If you seduce Yıldız, I shall disown you! You tramp, you can't keep the ties of your underpants done up!' she raged.

He could not admit to his mother that it was impossible for him to seduce Yıldız, that he had extinguished his flesh's fire in Beyoğlu, Istanbul's place of entertainment, that he seduced women who pursued him with his fiery words and not with bodily fire.

With Yıldız . . . everything was different. For the first time he truly wanted to propose to a woman. He would not dream of touching Yıldız other than on her honey-sweet lips before their wedding night.

Then . . . well, God would help him . . . he did not worry about it.

Burhan disliked Yıldız whom he took to be an excessively 'modern' girl, and did not think her a suitable future wife for an army officer who must do his duty for his country out in the wilderness. Burhan was one of those kinds of men who rate their profession more highly than women. Reha could not get to the bottom of Burhan's grudge against the opposite sex. Could it be that Burhan would not forgive their mother's remarriage? This seemed ridiculous to Reha, when the misery of the occupation years was so obvious. What was their mother supposed to do, be driven into direst poverty with her three children? Reha had not grieved deeply when their father died. He could not recall a single instance when his father had embraced him. The dead man was almost a stranger. Reha was repelled by Burhan who took refuge in the backyard, roaring and weeping, as the coffin was leaving their house. Anyhow, he did not feel much affection for this younger boy who was born to share his mother's and sister's love. From then on, their mother and sister would belong to the two of them, Burhan and Reha. But look! Their mother wore black for the man who had made her lose torrents of blood in an atmosphere heavy with the smell of lysol; and her beautiful face lost its smile.

Reha perceived that he had lost his mother as well, and felt deeply grieved. This did not last long, however. His instincts found the way to a remedy, which was to fall in love with the honey-eyed girl living opposite. He could only see her at the window, while there lived in the very same house an orphan servant-girl, who would step into the garden to put the linen out to dry while her eyes, hungry with desire, gazed at Reha in his uniform of the military academy. When he was thirteen, Reha caught the servant-girl, who was slightly older, under the willow tree, and managed to touch her breast.

His long list of sweethearts had begun. When their mother Fitnat Hanım remarried, Reha, whose affairs of the heart were in full swing, was not much concerned. External events could not affect him much. The Aegean towns under the occupation, their uncle's house in the Istanbul of the Amnesty years, could not leave any deep impression on his consciousness. He forgot easily. His stepfather was a true gentleman and cherished a sincere affection for the children of his wife's first marriage. Reha approached the new master of the house like a docile cat who sensed it was loved. He never approved of Burhan's surly behaviour and was greatly perplexed by it. He would never be able to account for Burhan's violent temper when they reached adulthood, and never allowed himself to realise that Burhan felt the same dissatisfaction with Reha which he himself had felt for their father. A secret defensive reflex always drove the relationship between his brother and their mother out of Reha's mind. Their mother had hoped for a baby daughter during her pregnancy; Burhan came as a disappointment, and Fitnat Hanım disliked disappointments. She let Burhan's fair curly hair grow like an infant girl's, down to his shoulders, until he was three. Who knows, perhaps she was unhappy with her colonel husband, years older than herself. The eldest child, Vicdan, was her father's favourite. Fitnat Hanım was emotionally rather distanced from this daughter who had been named after Hayreddin Bey's mother. Vicdan belonged utterly to Colonel Hayreddin Bey. Perhaps Fitnat Hanım dreamed of another daughter after Reha, just for herself, a close friend, a confidante, a loving embrace for her later life. She longed for Burhan to be placid and docile like an infant girl, just as she wanted Reha to be brave, reckless, and full of initiative. Her wishes were not granted.

Their stepfather decided on boarding-school for the brothers, the Kuleli military academy. They had been enrolled before the wedding ceremony, a fact Burhan never forgave . . . On their first night at Kuleli, the brothers wept together, without trying to hide their tears from each other. From the domain of women, filled with the rustling of silk, melodies on the lute, and mouthwatering recipes, they had passed into the monochrome, khaki world of men. Their childhood was irrevocably over. Their weeping together was the most intimate moment in the brothers' lives. From then on, Burhan began to conceal his suffering from his brother, while showing an amazing affinity for the school he had joined so unwillingly to begin with. He grasped the principles of life within the institution very quickly, and turned into a being for whom 'to hear is to obey' with the speed of a forest fire. Whereas Reha could only see a huge, unfriendly stone edifice, with barred windows obscuring a view of the sea, and predefined, non-negotiable hierarchies within this establishment he had entered in the hope of impressive uniforms, the clatter and clash of swords, enchanted as he was by daydreams of heroism and martyrdom. How he longed for the mother of his childhood! He could only bear this place, where no sign of a woman was to be seen, by developing an imagination potent enough to fall in love with every woman alive on earth. And so he grew into an incurable dreamer.

The brothers' closest friend was İzzet. But even before they joined the military academy, İzzet had already begun to move away from them in spirit. For him, neither soldiering nor the fair sex had any real importance; he was engrossed in books and ideas.

While Reha pursued his fantasy relationships with the girls of the neighbourhood during the vacations, Burhan kept away from women and studied hard. His aspiration was to become a staff officer. Burhan's determination, his ability to wrest from life whatever he wanted, disheartened Reha, and nearly drove him to melancholy. He respected Burhan and was ill at ease and hesitant in his presence; and he disliked the way Burhan dominated and moulded life to his liking, as if he were God – as far as the restrictions of the academy allowed, of course. Reha knew every one compared the two of them, and took Burhan for the elder, although he was actually a year and a half younger than Reha.

The self-confidence his bearing exuded made Burhan seem older; he was, in their relatives' estimation, an efficient and brave officer with a strong sense of responsibility, while Reha was a little bashful, a little unreliable, too much inclined to changes of heart.

Their mother was sick with grief when the brothers' regiment was posted to Dersim. Reha was completely silent, his lips clamped shut. He was not disturbed by the idea of fighting, did not in fact give the matter much thought; his anxiety was over how he would cope with the ache of his longing for Yıldız. Burhan was also silent, but his thoughts dwelt on entirely different matters: he was enthralled by the thrill of becoming one of those who fashion history, and fully grasped the serious and likely chance of death involved in that fashioning. Reha, until the moment the company left headquarters on the day the raid on the checkpoint took place, dreamed only of Yıldız, of her honey-coloured eyes, her muslin dress, and the curves of her body glimpsed through the white fabric.

He realised with deep distress, after they had set off, that the expedition might lead them into combat. Yıldız floated away from him through the air, her white dress streaming in folds . . . An earthquake! The peak of Uludağ was shaking violently. The cherished memory of that wonderful summer day, when Reha was able to burrow into the love between Vicdan and Burhan and be nourished by it, that memory was in tatters like an old photograph. Then the sweet mother of his childhood flew into the sky, deserting him in this desolate, snow-shrouded land, this cruel and treacherous land . . . He felt the freezing cold, his eyes were moist. How he pitied himself! Burhan's face was set, his bright eyes gazing straight ahead. How Reha envied him, how proud he was of his brother Burhan, that unflinching officer!

The company started singing. Burhan joined in so lustily as they marched that his vocal cords were all but shredded. Suddenly, Reha realised that Burhan was more frightened than he was, and all of a sudden remembered:

their mother used to punish them for their naughtiness when they were little. Burhan used to dread being beaten and would shout that he hadn't done anything wrong; whereas Reha adored their mother even when she hit him. It was as pleasurable for him to hear the rustling of her lovely dress, to smell the delicious odour of her body when he was being beaten, as when he was being caressed.

Reha thought it was pitifully funny that his brother should hide his dread under the rhythm of the march, but his heart could not possibly sustain such negative feelings for long. It was only for an instant that he thought himself superior to Burhan. Next moment self-pity reigned supreme, and he felt ashamed of the tears once more filling the corners of his eyes, and bent his head to hide them from his comrades' sight.

As he gazed at the fire, and daydreamed about his mother and the woman he loved, Reha found İzzet and Burhan complete strangers to the preoccupations of his soul. Their ability to devote themselves to a cause beyond the reaches of their personal concerns was a quality Reha could not identify with. The future of the Turkish republic had lost its glamour very quickly for him, and had changed into an obligation as narrow and grey as a corridor in a boarding-school, stretching on and on. Reha seldom envied men devoted to causes. He sensed that such men had no notion of what moved him. If he had opened his heart to them, they would probably have laughed at him, and then forgotten his secrets and his confidences. Only women, only they could sympathise with Reha.

Burhan saw the signs of fever in his brother's swarthy face, in his fine-drawn, pensive features, and grew uneasy, whereas İzzet was listening to the song Reha was murmuring. It was a lyric composed by Bimen Şen. İzzet started to ponder on what it was like to be an Ottoman. What was the impulse stimulating Bimen, the son of an Armenian priest, to compose one of the finest pieces of Turkish music? How much of the Ottoman had the Turkish republic inherited? What fragments of those Ottoman qualities that formed a kind of sympathetic synthesis could have survived the destructiveness of the Great War, and the cruelties the Turkish-speaking population both suffered and perpetrated? İzzet suspected that many things that had happened had been consigned to decay and oblivion, and did not consider this secrecy to be justified. He suspected that what they had experienced in Dersim would be consigned to oblivion under the weight of a deafening silence, and did not think this justifiable either.

Burhan was inclined to explain everything by the fever; Reha's confession was nothing but the hallucination of typhus fever. Before they had left headquarters, Reha had come up to Burhan, and said with some embarrassment,

—I want to confess something, brother; just for a minute I wasn't able to restrain myself and did something dreadful. I don't want to enter eternity with such a weight on my conscience, if I'm shot during the fighting.

Burhan looked at him with some reluctance. What could he possibly have done, Reha who was too sentimental for an army officer! . . . Burhan always feared – although he never admitted it even to himself – that sooner or later his brother would get involved in some muddle that would bring trouble to both of them. Reha, his head bowed, spoke hesitantly. The previous night, when he had gone out to relieve himself, he had heard a rustling. His heart leapt into his mouth, as he mistook the sound for a wolf and, with his soldier's instinct, immediately felt for his gun. Two eyes were shining like burning coals in the dark. It was a woman! A dark woman with long black hair and thick black eyebrows. Reha caught her wrist. Her skin felt hot in the icy weather.

—Who are you? he asked.

She mumbled some words Reha could not understand.

—What are you looking for?

She looked straight at him, silently, fearlessly. Reha grabbed her by the arms and shook her. As she tried to scratch and kick him, a force he hardly recognised began to spread through his body, compelling him to surrender all inner resistance. He found a strange pleasure in the sharp throb of the scratches on his face, fingered by the frosty night. The Armenian prostitutes he had known in the back streets of Beyoğlu began to cavort in the dark, rough sea of his imagination, like swarthy mermaids, coming and going. Then all was quiet . . . as Reha dissolved in a dark, deep pool of delight. He had never felt any female body to be so completely his.

Anger was choking Burhan. That Reha could still shape fine phrases, even in his moment of shame, got on Burhan's nerves. Reha was gripped by a fit of laughter that showed signs of growing hysterical. Burhan found his elder brother completely despicable. They used to tell each other dirty stories back in Kuleli, in their early teens, and explode with laughter in exactly the same way as Reha was doing now. Reha would never grow up.

Reha had been deeply ashamed when he began his confession, but now that his brother was scolding him, uncomplicated relief started to replace the fading shame. Burhan's mind was utterly confused. Could Reha's story possibly be true?

Childhood memories flashed like streaks of lightning in his brain. Reha used to fabricate imaginary peccadilloes and, when struck by their mother, would subside into tears, but would be comforted. Burhan too sometimes confessed to imaginary misdeeds, but for quite different ends: he loved to be a self-sacrificing hero. What a child Reha still was! He would never understand the deeper significance of events.

—And you let her go, roared Burhan, it never occurred to you that she might work for the rebels!

Reha was genuinely astonished.

—You never thought what her purpose might be, being so close to headquarters in the quiet of the night! Oh dear God! dear God! She must have been sent to find out how we stood. She must have been one of them! Oh, my God! At any moment we may have a raid on our hands!

Burhan sprang from his seat and started pacing up and down.

—Just a woman, Reha whispered, what harm could she do?

—We have to tell the commander what's happened. We have to take measures at once in case there's a raid.

This was bad news! How could Reha admit his moment of weakness to the commander? It might have been possible with a guilty conscience, but how could he do it now, when he felt himself absolved? A sense of frustration overwhelmed him. Meanwhile Burhan kept up his nervous pacing, while his mind was busy devising and revising tactics.

—No, no, Burhan said, despairingly, you would be courtmartialled.

Reha started back. —Courtmartialled!

Burhan asked uneasily, in a voice full of exasperation,

—You haven't mentioned this to anyone, have you?

—No, said Reha at once.

—And you won't mention it to anyone! Nothing happened last night. You saw no woman, no one.

—I saw no one, no woman, not a soul, repeated Reha, like an

obedient child.

—Well, said Burhan, the matter is closed.

After their expedition was over, Reha was to make a second confession concerning the woman. But for the time being, Burhan considered Reha's story was the result of the effect typhus fever had on the imagination. Burhan's conviction was so strong that, as time went by, Reha also started to attribute everything to the typhus.

Throughout the night, İzzet, Reha and Burhan sat in front of the fire, while İzzet and Burhan debated their country's problems, and when Reha murmured Bimen Şen's song, the revelations of the second confession had not yet been made. The confession to Burhan of this new aspect of the affair would burst out during Reha's convalescence, and would finally end all emotional ties between the brothers. The talk beside the fire, even though he did not take part in it, was the last time Reha found peace in the company of men.

After this campaign, when the brothers were on leave in Istanbul, Reha stayed in bed for a long time. The typhus attack had left him very frail. He felt powerless and worthless; he could not express what he felt in words. He sensed that if he could have embraced Yıldız or his mother, buried his head in one of their kindly laps, he would have found relief, would even have been able to discover the words to convey what he was going through. But he could not depend on . . . he dreaded the possibility of being misunderstood. It was a very difficult task for him, in fact quite beyond the capacity of his fragile nerves, to begin tentatively feeling his way with the women, ready to retreat if it proved that they were in no state of mind to accept his story, in short, to plan, just like a military campaign, the narration of what he was experiencing or the withdrawal of that narrative. So he retreated into suppositions . . . What if Yıldız had thought him too soft to become an honourable officer? What if his mother had exclaimed, 'Alas for all my toil and effort! My eldest son, whom I have raised in the face of so many hardships, crying like a woman!' It would have been quite likely. His mother and Yıldız had not seen that frozen flesh, had not sensed the changing moods of the men marching steadily, freezing but determined, towards their fate, in that desolate land where only God existed, and the unending carpet of snow. It was probable that his sister Vicdan could have sympathised with Reha, but she was far away and very busy, engrossed in the task of founding a new educational institution.

It slowly dawned on Reha that from now on, he would not be able to find peace even in the presence of women.

Yıldız's refusal of his proposal, although it grieved him, was at the same time a relief. He did not consider himself worthy of her. He was so overwhelmed by the love flooding his heart, and by the image of Yıldız, that he was unable to fathom what the flesh-and-blood Yıldız might feel. But was it likely that he could have been so mistaken? The delight shining in her eyes, the soft touch of her hand on his brow . . . could all this have been only his fantasy? Burhan refused to speculate on the reasons such a whimsical young woman might have for refusing an officer's proposal. And their mother said,

—My foolish son, Yıldız's heart belongs to you, but her eyes are on the social high ground. An officer's modest income wouldn't satisfy her. How many times do I have to explain to you? Who cares for my opinions? You may have become a captain, but you haven't grown up yet.

Reha was glad that he had not opened his heart to his mother. His mother, ever since she had ceased to sing as she did in her young days, had developed a strange stratagem of explaining facts in the the most shorthand way possible. Her views were so one-dimensional that they could not possibly represent the wholeness of reality. Reha was absolutely sure of this. But what was missing from his mother's diagnosis? He could not decide. Fitnat Hanım was extremely proud of both her sons' promotion to the rank of captain, and thoroughly enjoyed describing to her neighbours, turning bitter aloes to honey, the tears she had shed when her sons were away on campaign. Reha no longer adored his mother but was in dire need of her, in a more subtle way, especially after Yıldız turned down his proposal.

The promotion to captain was no cure for Reha's nauseating sense of his own worthlessness. Naturally he desired to be a hero, but promotion did not achieve that. Nobody treated the fighters on that particular campaign as heroes. It seemed they had performed a distasteful service to safeguard their country and now they must keep quiet, for it was best for everybody to forget its bitter savour.

Reha did not debate in his heart whether what had happened was good or evil, but wished the benefit for his country had not come at so high a price. He wondered whether all veterans felt as desolate as he did. The heroes of the War of Independence remained self-assured, whereas he felt empty, drained . . . Was the emptiness he felt peculiar to those taking part in internal upheavals? But yet, look at Burhan, more efficient, determined, and confident than ever!

Reha was posted to Erzurum after he had recovered. He was there throughout the Second World War; and later in Kars, Ardahan, Çorum, Konya, Gaziantep, and Bolayır; he moved among the military units based in the small towns of central and eastern Anatolia and Thrace, feeling almost a stranger. He would come to Istanbul, every few years, to visit his mother, and sometimes travelled to Ankara to see his sister Vicdan. He did not like Ankara, and constantly yearned for the mirage of an older Istanbul. The Istanbul he returned to after each posting was more alien than the one he had left on his last visit. During the fifties the non-Muslim population migrated from Istanbul, Greeks to Greece, Jews to Israel. Armenians had already become scarce when he was a lad. He used to find the non-Muslim citizens of Istanbul closer to his heart than the rough provincial crowds replacing them. People who were remote – in place of origin and so inevitably in their tastes – from the drinking of rakı with white cheese and water-melon, while listening to some lyric by Bimen Şen, people who did not enjoy the taste of dolma as thin as your little finger and cooked in olive oil – such people frightened him.

The high concrete buildings rising from the vacant lots of lost gardens and lost yalis – those old villas on the Bosphorus – crushed his spirit.

For him, the American soldiers from the NATO bases, together with their rock'n'roll music, were distasteful, and he kept yearningly humming those tangos that no one else seemed to remember. The stench of burnt fat, rising from heavily peppered kebabs and invading streets once redolent with honeysuckle, did not suit his stomach.

His youthful infatuation with women had been reduced to ash by the typhus fever. He was shy and clumsy with them, could not stop himself succumbing to a nervous laugh that was quite out of place. His diffidence, that once enfolded women like young ivy now seemed to them more like a thorny growth, assailing them.

During the fifties, he married a young widow his mother had chosen for him. Though the loves of his daydreams were pink-and-white girls, he was drawn at first sight to the smooth olive complexion of this woman from an eastern province. She had an inner fire that set his blood racing as soon as he set eyes on her. He was tired of living on his own. Having been a confirmed bachelor, he might have been expected to weave any relationship with meticulous care, selecting the threads with precision. But no! He married in haste.

Fitnat Hanım was taken in by her wealth, and in any case . . . times were changing, daughters-in-law no longer respected and cherished their mothers-in-law as they used to; the young women of the big cities tended to be more and more independent, whereas a bride from the east should make an obedient wife.

The disharmony of the marriage grew as the years flew by. Reha had simply been frightened of marrying a virgin; but now he could not help tormenting himself, could not break free from jealousy; the ghost of the dead husband haunted him. In bed, he pressed his wife whom he called 'my black tulip' to swear that she loved him better than the dead man. The poor woman found it hard to be patient with Reha's insistence. In any case, she disliked being called a 'black tulip'. Reha was courteous in ways she was unfamilar with, and she mistook his kindnesses for unnecessary display. When she travelled to the east to visit her family, she received letters like this from her husband:

> *My black tulip, dearest wife, my only love,*
> *ever since you have gone*
> *my loneliness is vast and desolate.*
> *Nothing can fill your empty place, not even the*
> *emeralds of Shah İsmail, or the treasures of Croesus.*
> *Light of my eyes, my fragile flower,*
> *why do you not write to me? Do you not*
> *know that I yearn and weep for you?*
> *Your skin like dark velvet, your hair*
> *cascading like a waterfall are*
> *always before my eyes.*
> *The fire of your pomegranate blossom lips*
> *condemns my wretched soul to the flames.*
> *Your breasts like dark cloves . . .*

They made her feel ashamed, she blushed with embarrassment and tore the letters into pieces in case anyone should find them and make fun of her. She had dreamt of an entirely different marriage. She longed for quarrels full of mouthed oaths, even if they could only end in violence.

That was the way of life she had been accustomed to in her parents' marriage and in her first. But now Reha would at once adopt a conciliatory position whenever the slightest disagreement arose, and would try to soothe her.

Marriage for Reha was a piece of Sèvres porcelain, whereas his wife was accustomed to earthenware jars.

Reha's graciousness made her curt and irritable, although her nature was not basically cantankerous. Who knows, perhaps she was secretly aware that her husband's gracious manner was meant for an imaginary being, and not for her actual self.

After a few years, she got into the habit of insulting him. Reha survived in this marriage like an animal crouching in a corner.

During working hours loneliness penetrated every fibre of his being; and at night he longed to escape this never-ending desolation by the touch of her body. But she was tired of his asking her to make love night after night. His tenderness was insufficient to kindle passion in her flesh. She pushed him away, hurt his feelings, but alas, his desire grew ever more demanding. She began to scratch, which strengthened his desire, but could not exhaust his kindness.

In the meantime, they had two children. He thought he was a loving father, but the children did not feel loved and sided with the 'black tulip'. And the wife got the quarrels she longed for in plenty, in her relationship with Fitnat Hanım, her mother-in-law. The discord between them seriously distressed Reha.

His military life went monotonously on and on. Dersim was so incredibly far away. During the last days there, Burhan had an accident, breaking his ribs when he fell off his horse.

He was unwell for a long time, and had to retire from military service at a very early age, due to some complication to do with his lungs which resulted from the broken ribs. Burhan's aspiration of becoming a staff officer had turned out to be written in sand. But he was undaunted, began to study law, and after a time became a successful lawyer.

When the military coup of 1960 took place, both Burhan and İzzet, who had resigned as soon as their compulsory terms were at an end, had been retired from the army for several years. But Reha was still dragging his way through the service, and would have idled his life away in the army supply depot of an obscure base if the military regime had not set about clearing incompetent elements out of their overcrowded profession. When in 1960, the uniform he had never identified with, but had grown used to, was stripped from his body, Reha's soul ached; he felt as if his skin had been peeled off and his naked flesh had been left bare.

It was during those years that he started to brood on the past. Dersim . . . the almost obscene sight of soldiers left to freeze in front of the checkpoint . . . days of a remote past . . . moonlit nights on the Bosphorus . . . Yıldız . . . his lost dream . . . that reckless day when he and his sister and Burhan climbed up to the top of Uludağ . . . the emerald plain of Bursa lying beneath their feet . . .

Vicdan, where are you? Where is your sweet-smelling body? The breast I laid my head on? Vicdan is in Ankara, living a well-ordered life with her husband and little daughter; she is teaching and translating. She is tranquil and neat, and completely ignorant of what Reha has been through . . .

Reha wept secretly as on those cold nights at the Kuleli academy. His childhood, his mother's illness . . . that unforgettable day when Fitnat Hanım returned from the threshold of death after a miscarriage. Incidentally, where was Burhan that day? Someone must have taken him away from that house filled with the smells and misery of illness, as he was very young then. Well, was Reha old enough to face the crisis? Where was Vicdan? Their father must have taken her under his wing. Reha was forgotten, as always. No one seemed to remember that dark day except Reha. Once he tried to talk about it to his mother. She said, 'Oh my son, the things you remember! What disasters we went through in those days, your father's death, the invasion! What you are recalling is simply not important.'

Reha and Burhan almost never met nowadays. Burhan was a director of an important bank on top of everything else; there was no room in his well-regulated life, full to overflowing with his law practice, his clients, his wife and mistresses and his sons, where he could fit in brotherly love. What about their youngest brother, Cumhur? Well, neither Burhan nor Reha could feel much closeness to the product of their mother's second marriage.

After their mother died, Reha was, to all intents and purposes, left without a family. Retirement intensified his solitude, and his wife's aggressiveness. Reha was frightened of her. He had not called her 'my black tulip' for a very long time. He had to plead with her and put up with her profanities in order to have one single moment of sex.

On a spring day in the seventies, the retired colonel, Reha

Yurdakul, was walking idly through the streets of Istanbul. He had left home with the intention of seeing a doctor, but halfway there had changed his mind. He gazed at the spring opulence that surrounded him, but he could not feel it. Because of the perpetual state of gloom that had settled on him in recent years, life passed him by without touching his body, worn-out at too early an age.

During recent months, he had lost weight, and had lost his appetite. His wife thought he might have cancer. So did Reha . . . He dreaded the disease, while secretly longing for it. He had two reasons for giving up the idea of seeing a doctor on that particular day: he might descend into a clinical depression after learning that his condition was diagnosed as cancer; or he might descend into a clinical depression after learning that it was simply malnutrition as a result of loss of appetite, and that he was condemned to the life he had been dragging his way through for God knew how many more years . . .

As he walked along streets sheltering under green shadow on that lovely spring day, he grew more and more convinced that he was a victim of cancer. By the time he reached home, he had completely forgotten that this was only something that was suspected, and the illusory situation had already been transformed into the ruling reality of his life. He could imagine all the stages of the disease in vivid detail – operations, radiotherapy, treatment that left you bald, pain, torment . . . His eyes filled with tears. What a tragic end it would be, waiting for death on an uncomfortable mattress at home, or in a remote corner of some hospital, the only saving grace being the attentions of his unrelenting wife! How bitter it was to close the book of life, without really performing one single action worthy of honour, without tasting even once a heady draft of heroism's charmed potion, to end your life with a feeble, tottering, miserable death . . . How he cursed his unhappy fate! . . .

The illusion of illness affected him in a very extraordinary way. He suddenly felt young again. Even his posture changed, and acquired the graceful strength his body once knew, before going to Dersim. His spine grew straight again, and his step was almost as if he were dancing the tango.

He had lived up to that moment as an honourable officer, so he would die, standing proud.

He murmured a song as he made his preparations. He pulled his pistol out from where he had hidden it and, handling it tenderly like a lover, cleaned it. He oiled it, inspected the barrel, inserted the bullets. He put on his uniform and scribbled a short note for those he was leaving behind: 'I know that I am suffering from an incurable disease. I want to die in an honourable way without being a burden to anyone. Nobody is to blame for my suicide.' He took his pistol in his right hand, stood before the mirror, and put the muzzle to his right temple . . .

At that very moment, his courage was shaken . . . The beautiful mother of his childhood . . . Yıldız when he kissed her in the moonlight . . . His sister-mother on the summit of Uludağ . . . His heart ached with a searing pain. The past was resurrected in all its glorious beauty, and he desired to live with a passionate desperation. Then suddenly he remembered his disease. He had never been good at coping with physical pain, ever since he was a child. A sob was torn from his chest and rose up in his throat. He lost the strength to stand and collapsed on his bed. It was only in God that he could find sanctuary. He murmured a prayer, an *elham*. He faced the inevitability of the situation, stood up again and moved in front of the mirror. Yes, he was ready. He brought the pistol close to his temple, the muzzle touching his skin. The training he had received stirred within him like a distant echo, and he focused all of his concentration on the target.

At that very moment they appeared before him! A pair of eyes, glowing embers, challenging him!

He closed his own eyes, and pulled the trigger.

They had finally spotted the cave where the survivors of the rebel force had taken refuge. Snow had covered the entrance, concealing it. Snow enveloped whatever there was to remember, to comprehend and to hope for, annihilating place and time. Snow existed before words and deeds . . . And afterwards . . .

nothing else did . . .

They crowded into the mouth of the cave, and kindled the strips of cloth which had been soaked in petrol; after a little while, they could smell the poisonous fumes of the smoke. They kept this treatment up until they started to hear muffled coughs from the cave's inner reaches. Then they waited.

Human shapes began to emerge from the sooty smoke. Those coming out would have to pass between two lines of soldiers.

Then the order was given. Because of the shortage of ammunition, the operation would have to be performed with bayonets. The soldiers hesitated for a moment. To encourage them, their officers took up positions right in front of the entrance, their drawn swords in their hands. Reha felt nauseous; he looked at his brother. Burhan wore an iron mask of determination instead of a face; İzzet had a profoundly sad, disturbed expression on his. Reha felt like weeping, his legs were shaking. 'I can't . . . ,' he whispered to his brother. 'Bullets or swords, what's the difference, be reasonable,' Burhan hissed back, and Reha saw his brother's firm blade rising swiftly.

The sibilant sound of steel cutting through bone broke the silence of the snow.

Then everything was quiet.

'I am freezing,' thought Reha. He was unable to move a muscle, unable to hear a sound; it was like watching a silent film. 'I am dying,' thought Reha. This was the last dream he was ever destined to have. Arms rose and fell, the blue gleam of steel flamed and died, blood froze on the snow.

Burhan struck for the motherland; İzzet struck, feeling the bitterness, the absurdity, and the compulsion of that moment when history reduces the individual to the point of nothingness.

Reha could not . . . All of a sudden he saw her. A pair of eyes like burning embers! Staring at him dauntlessly, challenging! It was she, the dream woman he had made love to, on the snow! . . . But was it she? What was she doing here? Was Burhan's suspicion right? Was she one of the rebels? Of course not, it wasn't her! It looked like her! It looked very much like her! No, not in the least!

It was exactly like her! No, no, it wasn't a woman! Only a pair of eyes! A pair of coals kindled by revenge! But why? Though she had resisted at the outset, she had opened up . . . yielded . . . taken him . . . held him . . . had caressed . . . Blood surged to the muscles of his body, his virility stirred, his right arm found its former strength. The training he had received, its keen precision and electric speed sped from brain to eyes, then to the neck and artery, via the nerves and muscles of the right arm to the hand gripping the steel.

He struck.

MISUNDERSTANDING

Sister, please steel yourself. I have bad news. Reha has shot himself.

Why? But WHY? . . . WHY???

Disaster after disaster. Starting with my mother, then Raik, now Reha . . . Ahh . . . Raik, my husband, where are you? How I wish you were at my side . . . and could tell me, with your never-failing logic . . . could tell me, step by step . . . why my brother Reha shot himself . . .

Vicdan is shaking with anguish at the entrance to the morgue, on the arm of her youngest brother, retired Captain Cumhur Özgecan, who has been invalided out. She has heard the news from Burhan.

She is now in her early sixties. It is exactly thirty years after Nefise's death. The year the war ended, Vicdan's heart was filled with the joy of a new life; she had a daughter. The years rolled on, one after another, tranquil and orderly. Then suddenly deaths began to occur. Her beautiful body had remained erect until this latest news, in spite of the griefs of loss coming one after another, the deaths of Fitnat Hanım and of Raik.

Being a woman, she was not allowed into the morgue to see a male body; she could not see Reha for the last time.

My eldest brother Reha has died. He was a retired army officer like myself. Well, it wasn't an untimely death. He was quite elderly. Wish he hadn't shot himself. It's a sin. My duty, to break the news to relatives . . . Tough job . . . Especially when everybody is on their summer holidays.

My uncle Reha has died! . . . He has committed suicide . . . Wrong diagnosis . . . He thought he had cancer . . . Mother says in her letter, 'Don't interrupt your holiday, there's no need, we have already buried him.' My poor, poor uncle . . . I think he actually died a long time ago . . . He would drift, like a phantom, across thresholds, and then drift out again . . . I think he was suffering from a nervous breakdown. He was old. My heart is breaking with the pain of this love affair of mine that's ended . . . The wound inflicted by my father's death hasn't healed yet . . . I can't handle another tragedy, let me finish my holiday first . . . Uncle Reha, after my grandmother and my father . . . How will mother cope with this new loss . . . Wrong diagnosis.

Reha committed suicide! He shot himself. All right, did he die? Reha died! Because of a wrong diagnosis . . . A very big mistake! What bad luck!

Burhan arrived, arrogant and angry, armed with his encyclopaedic knowledge of the law. He made enquiries like a detective inspector, put the case for the prosecution, sentenced like a judge. He acted as defence counsel for his brother Reha.

Who is this incompetent doctor who made the wrong diagnosis and gave it straight to his patient's face?
(There was no such diagnosis . . .)

How did his wife and children treat my brother, to make him commit suicide?
(Are all lawyers suspicious, or do those who are suspicious by temperament become lawyers?)

Burhan, you can't do this! You can't have an autopsy performed on Reha's corpse! Especially without his wife's permission! It's forbidden by law, or it should be!

Well, I've already had it done!

He has already had it done . . . Burhan rose to defend his brother Reha, armed with all his professional skill and contacts.

But why? . . . Why are you behaving like this? How can you suspect his wife? Our sister-in-law may be a little sharp, but she's no monster! How will the children feel? Don't you have any regard for our nephews? Burhan, you are breaking hearts, damaging relationships, decimating lives . . . Do you imagine they will ever be able to forgive an uncle who has made such accusations against their mother?

Reha Yurdakul's widow and children are weeping and clinging to each other in a corner.

> Life repeats itself, Burhan. Once upon a time, we were hugging our mother and weeping in dark corners when our father died. Please Burhan, give up this crazy idea, let's embrace them, our sister-in-law and our nephews, hold them close to our hearts.

Reha's wife is having intermittent fits; she keeps losing consciousness. She had been invited to a party by a woman from a neighbouring apartment on the day of the tragedy. Returning home, she found her husband lying there. She is in shock! And now there is her brother-in-law Burhan Bey's grave accusation!

> You have no idea, sister! The incidents one comes up against in the law courts! The kind of women who put pistols in the hands of husbands they have previously poisoned – they do exist!

> It's impossible! Burhan, what you're saying is quite absurd! Cumhur, Cumhur, why are you keeping quiet? Say something!

What can Cumhur say to his brother Burhan who has the law at his back? Obey your elders . . . This is what he has been taught! . . . And even his surname is different! Cumhur Özgecan . . . Only a half-brother . . . son of Burhan's stepfather . . . The law would not even consider asking his opinion.

> Well, there's the note Reha left behind, 'Nobody is to blame' . . .

> Handwriting can be imitated.

> Burhan, you're a religious man. Our religion decrees that bodies should be buried intact.

> Bodies can be mutilated on a battlefield.

> Are you satisfied, Burhan? You attack, feigning defence! Nothing has been found! No cancer, no poison . . . Why did my brother shoot himself!

He would drift silently across thresholds like a phantom . . . Sometimes he would travel to Ankara, and stay in the home of Vicdan and Raik for a couple of days, then depart as quietly as he had come. He seemed to be content, haunting the shadows, without partaking in what was going on . . . He never complained.

What is wrong, brother? Is it your wife? Is she worrying you?

Everything's fine, sister.

He used to drop in at inconvenient moments. When I was in my office . . . very busy . . . I could never manage to make him understand that I was busy. He wouldn't go away but would stand there like a piece of furniture. Brother, I can't see you now! I'm busy with a client!

Never mind, I will wait.

I HAVE WORK TO DO!

Well, it was quite obvious he could find no comfort in the family home. I warned him, told him to divorce that woman. And if he insisted on keeping his marriage going, he had better see the eminent psychiatrist, Rasim Adasal, and have his nerves seen to.

When he came to Ankara to see our sister, he used to pop in to see me. We didn't talk much. No, we never mentioned the army or our mother . . . If you ask me, retirement exhausted our brother Reha, and our mother's death finished him.

He would drift across thresholds, silently.

May I never set eyes on that woman or her children again ! They made my brother miserable! From now on, I disown them!

May I never set eyes on my brother-in-law again! He had my husband's body desecrated! Damn him!

From now on this uncle no longer exists as far as we're concerned! He had our father cut to pieces! He suspected our mother! When our parents were such a happy couple!

Have you heard . . . Reha Bey's elder brother Burhan has disowned his sister-in-law and nephews. He holds her responsible for Reha Bey's death! Good God! Unbelievable!

Didn't Reha Bey shoot himself because he had an incurable disease? Of course . . . How sad . . . And what is even sadder is that he wasn't even ill . . . Really?! . . . Yeees! . . . Well, what a mistake, what a mistake!

The quarrel between our sister-in-law and Burhan is doing the rounds, it's on everyone's lips, neighbours, friends, all the relatives. The actual incident has been forgotten. Burhan is still not satisfied. Neither the autopsy nor the breaking off of relations has been enough for him . . . He's demanding that Cumhur and I should renounce our sister-in-law and nephews. He must have gone crazy with grief.

Don't press me, Burhan. I can't abandon my nephews and she's a sister to me. I can't part with them – have you ever seen flesh and nail separate? Whatever you choose to think . . . don't interfere with us, Cumhur and me.

So you will turn your back on us. Suit yourself! . . . You are mistaken, utterly mistaken. Oh, how I wish you could see how mistaken you are!

I didn't stand up to my brother Burhan, but I certainly don't approve of his attitude. I am an uncle too. It doesn't matter that I'm a half-uncle, I refuse to renounce my ties with our sister-in-law and nephews. So he'll turn his back on us if we don't turn against them! Well, that's what I call a joke! Has there ever been a moment when Burhan was close to me?

But he was to me . . . Was it very long ago . . .

Dear sister, our brother Burhan has grown very high and mighty ever since he got rich and settled in Istanbul. He only loves himself.

That isn't true. He loves me.

—Oh, Burhan, we have lost Raik. My darling died suddenly this morning.

—Sister, dearest sister, I'll jump on a plane and be with you in next to no time.

Burhan has always been close to me. Yes, true, he did turn away from us, from his brothers and sister. But when my husband died, I found the brother I loved again. Now, when I've lost my Reha, is Burhan going to turn his back on us again?

He has never been close to me. He has always been a bully, my brother Burhan, and will always remain one. Why we go on discussing the matter I really don't understand. Let's drop the subject. My brother Reha died needlessly. He thought he had cancer . . . That's all . . . We never mentioned the war or our mother . . . I was with him when they washed his corpse, the remains of the autopsy. No matter how I try not to think about it, that scene will always haunt me . . . His body . . . like the bodies of those killed in war, torn to pieces . . .

THE VETERAN

The sound of a bullet splitting the air . . . The sound of tissue, cloth, skin, muscle, encountering metal . . . The gush of a broken artery . . . the gushing, warm voice of blood .

We are damned to a cold, dark hell.

Mortar shells exploding in a bunker . . . The sound of fragments of bone marrow pattering down.

A night in May, 1953 . . . Severe wintry conditions prevail over the thirty-eighth parallel. Darkness and voices are all there is . . . Voices advancing in waves through earth and sky join those already echoing there. Joining the voices of the Yalta Conference, the voices of Churchill, Roosevelt and Stalin . . . joining the sound of a world splitting apart . . . joining the sounds of dread, distrust, and foreboding.

Communists, communists, communists! They will confiscate our property! They WILL! (What is life without property but a naked breast without a shirt?) NO! NO! NO!

The sound of the gavel sealing the death sentence! The Rosenbergs must die! The sound of the electric charge; the snakelike hiss of the current searing flesh. The creaking voices of bolts locking jail cells . . . The heart-rending screech of pens trying to voice protest! . . . The clamour of printing-machines as they engrave brains with the daily headlines . . .

Forget the atom bomb! Think of Stalin's labour camps! The executions of the Thirties in Moscow! Those of Prague in 1952!

The sound of the neck the rope breaks . . . The sound of silence weighs as heavy as lead on one half of the world, while feverish, furious, panic-stricken roars from convulsed throats fill the other half:

Communists, communists, communists!

Rage sweeps across Turkey! . . . The sounds of the boots of the Tzarist armies mount, wave on wave, from the depths of the earth to the upper regions of the memory . . . Hatred and apprehension as Stalin makes demands . . . anxiety and precautions against Soviet bases . . . the voice of the President on the radio: 'Our Dear Friend America.' It is İsmet Pasha speaking, General İsmet İnönü, second president of Turkey. The siren of the battleship *Missouri* in Istanbul harbour . . .

Girls on the outskirts of the city wear nylon underwear, souvenirs from their American boyfriends; the electric hiss of synthetic fibre crackles as it links up with 'Hey Joe' rhythms echoing from the seven hills of Istanbul.

Who are these men chewing gum, whose baby-like, carefree faces smile all the time? They have broken into the twilight, dull life of the Turks, in the aftermath of the Second World War! These Joes, Sams, and Georges . . .

Raik's questioning voice, full of anguish . . . What do they want from us? Burhan's confident, complacent voice replies: Brother-in-law, the world has changed since the war.

From now on, no country can possibly stand alone and make progress! We must enter NATO! NATO!

Into NATO! Into NATO! How? Where is the road to NATO? Reparation is necessary! Reparation? Reparation for what? Compensation for the War of Independence must be paid to the West!

What is Cumhur's opinion? Silence . . . He is an army officer . . . He may think but keeps quiet . . . He carries out orders in silence . . . He, Lieutenant Cumhur Özgecan . . . son of Fitnat Hanım and an Azeri father . . . his mother's last child, and his father's first . . . one of those Turkish soldiers who, on the thirty-eighth parallel 'are on the watch everywhere, at home and in Korea', as the old marching song put it. He is fighting against North Korean and Chinese communists. The voices are there, above his head and beneath his feet, in space and deep in the earth, those voices radiating to infinity, echoing and lingering, always. Endlessly murmuring, if there's an antenna sensitive enough to pick them up. Cumhur Özgecan hears nothing! . . . No, this isn't true! He does pick up some of the reverberations: horses rear up in the Caucasus Mountains; their valiant young riders, Azeri men slender as twigs, vibrant with the fresh potency of life . . . the year is 1920 . . . the sickle of the Revolution mows down the valiant riders, who fall like ears of corn on the Caucasus Mountains. Horses neigh in anguish . . . Horse-shoes slip on the slopes, roll over the precipice . . .

Survivors of those valiant troops escape to Turkey . . . the year is 1921 . . . one of them, Nizam Bey, is Cumhur's father . . . Fitnat Hanım's last husband, he has been silent since arriving in his new country, the crossroads for migrations. His heart is heavy . . . he will never forgive the Revolution . . . How he longs for the golden crocuses of the Caucasus Mountains . . . He drinks . . . his silent rage is absorbed by every cell of his organism . . . Cumhur's flesh hears the potent energy of rage massed in his father's nuclei, and like a powerful antenna tunes in and listens.

The enemy is melting away like snow in sunshine. Still they don't retreat. How ruthless the cruel power must be that still keeps them at the front!

Vicdan lays aside the letter her brother has sent from Korea. Vicdan, a child of the War of Independence, cannot comprehend how Cumhur can harbour such hatred for the North Koreans who are struggling to unite their divided country. How can she know that it is impossible to fight without anger?

She is distressed, anxious. The Second World War had not succeeded in sentencing her to what she dreaded most, had not touched her husband or brothers.

Vicdan is grateful to General İsmet İnönü . . . but Korea . . . How is it that this faraway land has crossed her path! . . . A fresh, unanticipated disaster has snatched from her arms that young brother whom she loved like a mother – he used to climb on to her lap at the dining-table, when he was in short pants, snuggle up to her breast and fall asleep, his head resting on her shoulder.

Vicdan waits for letters . . .

Gaziantep, 1 April, 1952

Dear Sister,

Tomorrow I shall leave Gaziantep for Seferihisar, where I shall join the Turkish Korean Brigade. I am not sure whether I shall be able to write to you from any of the halts on this journey.

Please stop worrying. I am not worried. War is the natural environment for a soldier.

I have been meaning to write to you for the last few days, but have not had the chance. We have been getting ready for a general inspection by the Army Commander. I had applied for a few days leave, but it turned out to be impossible because of the said inspection. You see, in the army, duty is the one thing you can depend on. Probably it is best that I go without seeing you and mother, as otherwise parting might be too painful.

As a last souvenir . . . I mean the last before Korea, I am sending you a recent photograph of me in uniform.

I kiss your hands, and your eyes; give my niece a hug, and kiss brother Raik's hand.

Your brother,
First Lieutenant Cumhur Özgecan

How handsome he looked! Vicdan had the picture framed and put it on her tallboy. She kept her brothers' letters in a drawer of that tallboy.

28 April, 1952
Seferihisar

Dear Sister,

At last I have joined the Turkish Expeditionary Force

destined for Korea. A support unit made up of all sorts – infantry, artillery, and so forth. I am sending you my address at once. I am very well, and continue to do my duty. All soldiers and officers are accommodated in tents. No chance of leaving for a month. We are having exercises every day.

The son of Eşfak Bey, our neighbour in Sakızağacı Road, is also here: Mehmet Açıkalın. He is an officer in the reserve.

If you are worrying about us, you are worrying pointlessly. This business will reach a satisfactory conclusion. Whatever must be, must be.

I kiss your hands,
First Lieutenant Cumhur Özgecan

12 May, 1952
Seferihisar

The first batch leaves on 10 June. Most likely we shall leave with the second batch which is scheduled for 27 July. However it's not certain. Well, that's the army for you, nothing more important than duty.

In Korea, our company will be on exercises fifty miles behind the front, so no need to worry. Hope everything works out well.

Commanders come, commanders go, one inspection after another, we are very busy. Last time we were inspected by the Commander of Land Forces, Şükrü Kanatlı Pasha.

She could pick out two different tempos in the letters. One consisting of a short, decisive, staccato rhythm, like the sound of marching boots; and then there were the long flowing sentences with a slightly wistful tinge.

15 July, 1952
Seferihisar

Dear Sister,

This is my last letter from Turkey. We shall start boarding on *the 28th. Departure is on the 30th. I am sending brother Raik a warrant, so that he can draw my monthly salary. Bearing in mind the leave we shall be spending in Japan, we are all asking friends and relatives what they would like. Please write to me without any reservations, telling me what you would like to have. It seems that you can find your heart's desire in Japan, from the latest domestic appliances to the newest fashion in clothes, everything. I have informed mother of this fact in my letter, and have written that her request shall be my command. Imagine, all the items unobtainable in our paradise of a country are on sale in Japan! Toys of all shapes and sizes . . . I shall buy a big geisha doll for my niece.*

I kiss you all on your hands and eyes and entrust you all to God Almighty.

Your brother Cumhur

> *14 August, 1952*
> *On board the General Nelson Walker*

My dear Sister,

I wish you were here, pensively gazing at this beautiful view with that poet's mind of yours. We are cruising between North Malacca and South Sumatra. The sea is quite smooth, like a great sheet; its colour is like your eyes, a shade of turquoise . . . Islands like emeralds are dotted all around us, and mountains have begun to appear on the far horizon. Since 8.30 a.m. (3.30 in Turkey, there's a time difference of five hours), I have been on deck, admiring the view and reading Kerime Nadir's 'The Road to Faraway' – very romantic! At this very moment what is clearly a luxury cruise liner is sailing past on our port bow. Today I am full of beans and optimism. A little while ago we performed the manoeuvre for rescuing a 'man overboard', just as an exercise. It was very interesting and fun as well.

As we draw closer to Singapore, the channel grows narrower and the view of the coast gets clearer. Right now local canoes, holding one or two people – like the ones we have seen on films in the cinema – are gliding alongside us.

Today we are, to all intents and purposes, living in a film. After a stormy and tedious crossing of the Indian Ocean, this beautiful scenery and pleasant part of the voyage has cheered us all up; and suddenly I feel like writing to you. Soon I shall record this wonderfully splendid day in my journal.

Now the sun is setting. As we move closer, Singapore, with its multicoloured lights, rises like a miraculous vision above the fading horizon. Even though our ship is sailing on a route five miles from the coast, for exactly two hours we have been gazing admiringly at this enormous city which appears to be made up entirely of swathes of electric light.

An hour after we left Singapore, planes appeared and guided our ship with their flares, flooding the whole area with broad daylight.
Goodbye for the time being,

Your loving brother Cumhur

Such enthusiasm will never again appear in his letters.

Pusan, 21 August, 1952
Finally, at 8.00p.m. (1.00p.m.Turkish time) we arrived at the Korean port of Pusan. It was good to land. After Singapore, the tedious voyage out in the mid-ocean swell, without the faintest sign of land (every day the same faces and the same food), had bored us all.

A greeting ceremony lasting one and a half hours was put on for us in Pusan. I hope to God, as I land on Korean soil, that everything will turn out for the best. I feel positive and optimistic that we'll be together again with God's help.

We wandered around Pusan for about two hours. It is an enormous port. There are factory chimneys sprouting everywhere. But the people are poor. They live in brick houses with thatched roofs. Those whose homes have been destroyed are housed in rickety shelters, hastily constructed out of pieces of cloth and cardboard. Well, I don't know what to say . . .

Ch'unch'on, 23 August, 1952
We have reached the military base of Ch'unch'on after a twenty-six hour train journey. The camp is ten minutes (by truck) away from the town. The railway runs along a valley beside a stream. Roundabouts are covered with emerald green turf. The whole of the plain is cultivated. We have passed wheat and rice fields, and gardens full of fruit and vegetables. Well, the same vegetables we cook at home. There isn't so much as a hand's breadth of land that is unoccupied. What an industrious people! The villages look like ours. Children run out of the houses and wave to us. We passed the towns of Tegu and Seoul on our way here. Buildings, factories, all demolished.

Ch'unch'on has a large airfield from which the planes fly on bombing raids over North Korea. We are fifty miles behind the front line. The company that is going back to Turkey has arrived from the front and gone on to the port of Pusan. The front is quiet. Nothing has happened for five months. The distance between positions is about ten to twelve yards. We officers are billeted in sheds, and the soldiers in tents. Don't be misled by the words 'shed' and 'tent' and so on, they are even more luxurious than our barracks at home – like high-quality hotels! Well, we might just as well enjoy our leisure time.

His sentences were growing shorter. The teasing tone began with this letter. Her young brother's sense of humour, which until now had been subdued by the sadness of leaving, had emerged again. It caught Vicdan's attention.

5 September, 1952
Dear Sister,
Our company has settled down as 'reserve' beside the Turkish

brigade, at a distance of twenty miles from the front. I have been appointed 'Company Commanding Officer'. Hope to God for the best. There is not much going on other than inspections. Our gunners are busy. Before we came here, we had seven months' training as infantry reserve. We are comfortable and enjoying ourselves.

In October we shall probably be at the front; we might continue to operate as the reserve force as well. Our planes are bombarding North Korea like cotton carders scattering cotton wool! Bravo! The news agencies report that the fighting is hotting up – is that so! All of us here are greatly amused by such exaggeration. I tell you what: it is exactly like a Boy Scout camp over here. I heartily recommend partaking in this kind of war to all my friends. Our only complaint is that our heads ache with the noise the planes make. But we have got used to tank noises; they don't bother us any more than the buzzing of mosquitoes. On a more serious note, sister, it is absolutely necessary for an officer to experience this kind of war, fought with such a wealth of equipment.

If you have huge numbers of men, and any amount of equipment, fighting is no problem. The communist planes can never enter our zone. Our planes are on the alert the whole time. Helicopters take the wounded away to tent-hospitals. Oh sister, those tents! So luxurious! Believe me, sometimes I so envy the patients lying in those comfortable beds that I almost wish I were wounded . . .

Cumhur uses the word 'our' when referring to the American planes. 'Luxury' and 'luxurious' are new words he often uses now. His letters are getting short . . .

5 October 1952

We had a 'morale-boosting' evening. Mickey Rooney put on a show. We laughed heartily. We may be in Turkey by the end of April. Six months' duty, two months' voyage.

Our company – as the reserve for the American Fifth Infantry

Regiment – is a mile and a half from the front. The weather is cold. But our tents are comfortable; there are twenty men to each tent; heating supplied by two gas stoves. It is warm and cosy. The stoves don't give out the nasty smell of paraffin.

15 October 1952
Nothing of interest to report. Our company is moving away from the front. I wish we could come home without so much as a nose-bleed . . .

20 October 1952
Let me tell you about the bunkers. At the front, we call the dugouts for two or three people, which have been reinforced with sandbags and planks, 'bunkers'. Each bunker is divided into two parts: in the front there is the mauser hole, at the back are two beds. Two soldiers are on watch while one is busy digging and the other is taking a nap.

Behind the lines there is the mess, where food is served. This place can hold a whole company. While two soldiers stay in the bunker, the other two go to the mess for lunch; everything is regulated in this way, by turns.

The bunker is so strong and durable that even if a shell scores a direct hit, it won't damage the inside. From this point of view, the front is preferable to the zone immediately behind it. Am I boring you with details? But I know you want to learn . . .

This thing called a 'bunker' – is it right at the front line, or behind it? True, he gives a lot of details but he skips the crucial bits.

30 October 1952
Celebration of the anniversary of our Republic. We imagined we were back at home. We officers went by jeep to brigade headquarters. A Korean general, four American generals, the commander of our division, Williams, a woman captain, and a black first lieutenant had come to congratulate us. The commander of the army corps flew in by helicopter. The children of a primary school in Suvon sang a Turkish marching song.

Well, that was it . . . Being so far away from our homeland on the anniversary of the Republic left us heartbroken.

There is the possibility of our drawing back from the front. The American division has been pulled back as the reserve for the army corps. The nights are cold; there's heavy rain. Remind brother Raik not to forget to draw the fuel allowance with my salary.

Our leave in Tokyo is drawing closer. I have not forgotten my promise to my niece. I shall buy a geisha doll for her. Recently we have covered a distance of one hundred and ten miles. Not on foot or horseback as it would have been in Turkey, but in vehicles! To cut a long story short, we are living here like English lords. I am afraid we will have difficulty readjusting ourselves to Turkish conditions after our return. It seems to me it is better to be a sergeant in the USA, than a 'pasha', a general, in Turkey! Don't repeat the last sentence to anyone. I was only joking. The peasants are desperately poor, although we live like 'beys' . . .

Sentences unrelated to each other. Paragraphs incorrectly divided. The letter is written as if to cloak what is being experienced, not to reveal it.

A question arises in Vicdan's mind . . . How to capture reality? She is a woman of letters, and knows that what we experience oozes between lines and verses, in spite of all the writer or poet can do.

Vicdan turns to poetry. Her new hobby is to search for poems on Korea, in newspapers and journals, and to analyse them. Disappointing . . . she will not be able to find what she is looking for. She will only be able to keep grief and anger at bay by dissecting the poems with her relentless criticism. Raik watches his wife anxiously . . . Here, Vicdan is analysing those poems on Korea with obsessive intensity . . .

Vicdan's notes

'Our commitment is worthy of a nation and state
Whose honoured forebears fought the whole world(a)   (a) Chauvinistic
Now our borders reach out to Korea (b)   (b) What about our
Long live the motherland   National Oath, which
Long live our nation   promised no further
War is the Turkish heart's desire (a)   movement of our
Our songs once exulted over Yemen (b)   borders after World
But today we are taking on Korea (b)   WAR I
The Turks' most honourable decision
Is approved by all except the
Russian bear (c)   (c) Anti-communism
Support for freedom
Support for peace
The Turks will never stoop to refuse' (d)   (d) Empty pride

'Kill the infidel for the love of God   Exploitation of
Mehmet, your faith gives you the right   religious feeling
'Brave' is a word unworthy of you
Let the world find you a finer title

Your fame has spread throughout the world   In praise of violence
Your battle-cries ring across continents
For you indeed the field of battle
Mirrors the finest wedding feast

The fame of the Turks spreads as they fight   Racist feelings
Bayonet your enemy, the infidel,
You have quenched the red fire in one day
You, Mehmet, tornado of the Turks

'The mighty son of great Atatürk
Our motherland's medal of true honour
The foe can't resist when your blood is up
Your Turkish blood, my Mehmet'

'Judgement day will be crowded with martyrs
The devious foe will tear his hair in hell'

'Words will not suffice to describe this battle
Mountains and rocks spoke in their language
First a voice crying 'Charge' was heard
Then my Mehmet called "Allah Allah"

Neither home, nor mother, nor his lover
He dreams of none
Come, see the raging Mehmet
He does not blink an eye
When exposed to the hail of shells, my Mehmet   Masochism

Tonight the stars look pale and wan   Beautiful lines
The weather is wintry, the hills shudder   Sensitive image
It's as if one mountain crowds out another   Brotherly feeling of
To give a supporting shoulder to Mehmet, my Mehmet.'   solidarity

'The ground shakes when the Turks fight
May God support them, and the prophet   Primitive racism and religious
A holy light shines down on the martyred   fanaticism linked
The star of power gleams on our breasts.'

'You have died, and your death like a nearing to God   This resembles Mehmet Akif's
As if leaping a thousand bars at once   'Martyrs of the Dardanelles',
Offers fresh goals like a new Koranic ayet   from the point of view of
Mighty Turk the world tries to match your daring'   form; but . . . racism, religious
fanaticism and an inferiority
complex go hand in hand!

'Our flag led the way on the battlefield
You have soared to the sky embracing the flag   Racism and religious
While the Koran and Prophet give you their blessing   chauvinism
Angels weave you wreaths of crescents and stars'

'Those who once scorned the Turkish nation   Who could have looked down
Calling her barbarous, nowadays   on us during the Gazi's
Wear us like a crown; those who refused   lifetime? Would Atatürk's
The loan of a penny give billions to aid us   country beg for alms from the
West at the cost of her citizens'
lives?

Korea enhances the fame of the Turk
Dear Mehmet sheds his blood over there
The Security Council acknowledges his rights
The Atlantic Pact admits him today

Don't find fault with the party or with Bayar   Returning to the fatalism that
Seek the answers in God's commands   wrecked the Ottoman ship!
When our dear Mehmet was felled in Korea   Everything is crystal clear!
God granted him victory and he has risen.'   No need for comment!

Vicdan's final note: The message common to these poems gives rise to the question, should the aim of a Commander-in-Chief of military forces be victory at whatever cost, for the sole purpose of supporting the allied armies? Without the slightest consideration for the lives of his men? Did not this particular habit of mind destroy the Ottoman armies on the Galician front, in the Yemen, and in the Caucasus, during the First World War? If so, are the military forces of the Republic of Turkey being Ottomanised?

The grief in Vicdan's heart grows. What creates beauty in literature is the harmony of words and sincerity. Whereas these Korean poems consisted of two different currents of feeling moving in diametrically opposed directions, one concealed under the other. They made her think of a frightened child singing in the dark, and lacked the reality of individual experience. Vicdan thought that the verses she had noted as 'crystal clear, no need for comment' cried out a historical truth. What a pity that the one who cried out wasn't aware what his words actually meant! Her spirit, that had twined itself round the concept of 'country' like flowering ivy, ever since her days in the teacher-training school for girls, now wilted and drooped. She did not, definitely did not, want to bend with the wind blowing all round her, but withered under a searing insight into what was happening. In those days, she began to cut reports on Korea from newspapers and keep them.

She was unaware that a time was coming when she would receive letters from her brother that reflected his true feelings . . .

7 November, 1952

Dear Sister,

An overwhelming, suffocating sensation has possessed me for the past few days. How I wish we might come home without so much as a nosebleed . . . I am keeping myself busy so as not to sink into despair. I have begun to learn how to take photographs.

I don't know why, but recently I keep remembering our aunt's house in Bursa, and the garden. Do you remember that evening, when you, brother Raik, and my brothers Reha and Burhan sang songs at the dining table? My mother wanted to put me to bed, as I was very young, but brother Raik asked a special favour for me, and my mother could not refuse her son-in-law's request. My brother Burhan recited a poem. What a beautiful evening that was . . . How life has flown past . . . How I miss you all . . . My dear sister . . . Why don't my brothers Reha and Burhan ever write to me? I am afraid they have never felt for me as a 'brother' . . . not even after my father's death . . . Inwardly, I am really annoyed with them. I was not affected by their indifference before, but nowadays it is always on my mind. Do you think I am exaggerating?

I kiss your hands, my dear sister, do not leave me without your letters.

Cumhur

Vicdan wept when she received this letter, the lack of communication in those earlier letters had tied her nerves in knots, which now gradually eased, and returned to normal . . . Later, more letters would arrive, ones that rendered her earlier state of mind darker and more permanent . . .

15 November 1952
The 110 miles I mentioned previously was the distance we had to cover in order to reach the advance front line. After switching locations four times, we settled in the Kumua area, and took over

the positions at the front from the Americans. We admired their discipline and organisation. We are right in the front line. We are firing all the time and enjoying ourselves. Here, it is just like a fair with fireworks and Roman candles, we feel as if we have returned to our childhood days. The enemy melts away like snow exposed to the sun. They will never be able to mount a major offensive, and small ones are of no effect anyway. In any case, the communists lack planes and cannon; they are using mortars, poor things! Mostly, the mortars only hit people who are wandering about outside. We here (in the bunker I mean) are lying down and enjoying ourselves as if we were on holiday, relaxing on our fathers' estates.

First Lieutenant Cumhur Özgecan

18 December 1952

Our brigade has been at the front for a month. We have lost a few men. We have had no casualties for a week. The Turks are good at war: even the thickest soldier's mind works as if a genie inhabits his brain. Recently the Chinese surrounded one of our detachments which was on reconnaissance, and our soldiers broke out by using their bayonets! My lions!

Sister, you are a thinking person, it isn't necessary for me to warn you, but nevertheless I shall: please do not go round discussing news of the war. This is a matter for our country, and duty is far more important than anything else. And don't believe all you hear on the radio, especially any rumours. You have heard that Mehmet Açıkalın has been wounded! A complete lie! He is standing right in front of me, fitter than ever. I wouldn't lie to you, would I? No shells have hit our company, we are six or seven km. from the front. The shell that could travel a distance like that hasn't been invented yet. I am fine, I don't have a headache, I don't feel the cold, there's nothing whatsoever wrong with me. What more could I wish? You know nothing about war, sister, so stop worrying. You think shells fly like magic carpets. Well, no, sir! The object called a 'shell' is made of metal, weighs a lot, and falls easily . . .

25 December 1952

Sister,

I shall be brief . . . I am fine, and continue to do my duty in the best of spirits. Our boys are having the time of their lives in the bunkers . . .

30 December 1952

We have been withdrawn to the reserves. We are 25-30 km. from the front. The front is even more comfortable than where we are. We are not exposed to any danger. Everyday we hold exercises. We work until 2.00 in the morning. I am keeping a record of things – well, you know, my 'war journal'. The front is quiet. Mehmet Açıkalın has been wounded, very slightly, a mortar shell just grazed his arm. There is nothing to worry about, nothing dangerous. I have often hurt myself, on my hands or arms, while using a saw for repairing woodwork at home.

The letters ran on like this for months . . . Then suddenly they stopped . . . Was Cumhur in Tokyo, on leave? He never wrote, God knows why, when he was on leave. Raik used to say, 'He's having fun with geishas or American strippers'. But he had not written that he would be on leave.

24 May, 1953

Dearest Sister,

Two months ago I was appointed commander of the Fifth Company. I did not let you know, in case you worried. We suffered a lot of casualties as soon as we reached the front. On 29 April, the Chinese attacked the advance guard of our brigade. 115 dead, 10 missing, altogether 400 casualties including the wounded. I have been told these numbers in confidence, so please keep them secret. My wound was quite honestly slight. After a few days for recuperation, I was sent back to the front on the double, and I was there during the Vegas fighting which you people at home heard about on the radio. For two days and nights the battlefield bubbled like a hellish cauldron. Afterwards we were withdrawn to the reserve. I had been wounded again. We were in the bunker, and a mortar shell exploded 50 metres to the right of our position. Shrapnel caught my right calf. Thank God nothing happened to my trunk. If I had not been wearing a bullet-proof vest, I would have been blown to atoms, and would have been elevated to the sublime role of martyr! Thank God, I have saved my ass for the sublime role of veteran! What else could I ask?

25 June, Tokyo
American Military Hospital

Well, I really am astonished! Rumours fly faster than planes! There isn't a wound or anything the matter with my arm! I don't understand how these stories get started! Mere scratches must have been mistaken for wounds! The shrapnel penetrated my right leg; the bone was broken so it was put in plaster; some muscles had to be stitched, and they have never been better, once the stitches were removed.

Tell my niece that her 'hero uncle' is being reconstituted; and what is even more important, he hasn't by any means forgotten about the geisha doll.

As for you, my dear sister, do stop worrying. My duty is over, and soon I shall be home. But our men will not be able to leave Korea unless the relief force now grouping at Seferihisar arrives. I am in good health and my morale is high. There are Turks everywhere! We chat all day. Our men are pouring in here from the front. Most of them have wounds to the legs or arms; not very important. Casualties are few, as we have been protected by our bullet-proof vests. Believe me, it is much better to be in this luxurious hospital than toiling away at the front, on an empty stomach, and covered in dust and dirt.

1 July 1953

The new Turkish force will arrive at the port of Pusan in a few days' time. This means that our return is imminent.

No really, madam, the way rumours spread! No, there isn't

the slightest probability of my leg being amputated. Well, my wound isn't that unimportant, but still we have to thank God. Oh, sister, you have no idea of the casualties in our detachment! The dead number between 150 and 200, whereas the wounded number more than two thousand. Only yesterday two lieutenants fell! On my steel vest there are traces of three or four shells that could have done fatal damage. You and my mother should be thankful I have been wounded and so have had the chance of leaving the front early. That filthy front will take God knows how many more lives.

Vicdan did not see the last letter.

Brother Raık,

My state of health offers not the slightest chance of my remaining in the infantry. Could I transfer to personnel? Probably. But I should feel frustrated when I compared myself with my pals back in the infantry. Besides, how many years can you serve in a department like personnel? I bet it's no more than ten. Can a man adopt another profession at that age? If rumours are true, two hundred officers mean to resign from the army. What I mean is, before they pension me off, I want to present my application for retirement. I am not sorry. A local grocer or a village headman is more respected than an army officer. Why the surprise! How could an officer supply the number of votes in general elections such people guarantee the party in power? Some of my friends are so furious, words can't describe it. I am writing exactly how I feel as officers' letters are not censored. And even if they were, I shouldn't care any longer. The government sent us here, and forgot us! Not the slightest notice has been taken of the wounded! How bitterly disillusioning it is that we Turkish men would have been destitute if it weren't for the American authorities.

I do not know whether the authorities at home are doing anything for the families of casualties, other than holding a 'mevlit' for the souls of the dead – I bet they aren't! A political power that abandons the officers of its very own army which has unhesitatingly shed its blood for the motherland in a distant country, and then reduces them to poverty on their retirement . . .

Well, anyway, if my health allows me to marry, why should I let my children suffer on an officer's ludicrous salary? Keeping my physical condition in mind, could you try to find any suitable job for me, without letting anyone know for the moment . . .

Raik is waiting at the port of İzmir. The ship of the American navy, *General Nelson Walker*, is slowly docking. The disembarking from the huge ship will take hours. Flags are waving frantically. Those meeting the passengers are clearly impatient – parents, wives, children on shoulders, fiancées.

Raik would accompany Cumhur from the port to the Mevki Military Hospital in Ankara. On the train journey from İzmir to Ankara, Cumhur would rest his head on his brother-in-law's shoulder. Burhan wasn't able to come and meet Cumhur; he is very busy . . . Vicdan could not bear it.

I should prefer to postpone meeting my mother and sister for a while; I don't think I could stand women pitying me.

That is what he wrote to Raik.

Raik's head lolls forward . . . Is he taking a nap? An agonisingly heavy pressure is crushing his chest from within. It is too hot! From time to time, he raises his head and fans himself with his felt hat. The band is playing, an excruciating blare of trumpets erupts, journalists in short-sleeved shirts and loose neckties dash about, pushing their straw hats to the backs of their heads. Flashlights, like great lamps compressing the heat, explode.

The atmosphere resembles a wedding celebration. The survivors have come home.

Raik looks at the heroes in American-style uniforms. Who are these men? Their chewing-gum is missing. Are the ones coming back the same people as the ones who left? What festival is being celebrated? Turkey has donned make-up and finery, adorned herself with cheap jewelry, and is dancing the mambo after all these grim postwar years, oppressed by silence and poverty; but her mambo still resembles belly-dancing.

—Colonel, what have you to say to the papers?

—And you, Major?

—And you, First Lieutenant?

—What about you, Mehmet?

All the men reply loudly, in chorus:

'The motherland is our life, we would willingly shed our blood for her. We would sacrifice our lives for our motherland.'

And the people shout:

Brr-a-vo . . . Long live the Turkish soldiers!

Raik, in the second half of the twentieth century, hears the cacophony of discordant voices as a huge drop of silence . . . Silence . . . it has always existed . . . Discretion . . . ever since Raik has come to know himself. Before the Great War and after the Republic . . . before the Gazi died and after . . . When he was young, silence was a jar filled with fertile leaves fermenting very slowly into meaningful words. The Second World War, like a vice, jammed it between merciless jaws. Then, with the second half of the century, just as words were maturing, the jar cracked! The contents have been wasted . . . words have been scattered, dissipated, before the meaning was fully distilled.

Silence has even seeped in between Raik and Vicdan . . . In the old days, when they were engaged, in the first years of their marriage, and even during the War, they used to recite poetry to each other in private, political poetry, and secrete it between the lines of their letters . . . the hope-inspired verses of Nazım Hikmet, the great Marxist poet, that embraced the whole world . . . How long has it been since they dropped this shared habit? They were well aware that silence was meant to safeguard them both. They were waiting in silence, side by side, for the day they could use their voices again. No, such a day would never arrive

. . . Could your homeland betray you like this, like a faithless lover? She could . . . The longed-for day would never dawn . . . Prose was hushed, verses were shattered . . . they shot the Marxist writer, Sabahattin Ali on the border, Nazım was forced to flee, at the precise moment when hostility towards the Russian bear was rearing its head . . .

Clashing fragments of broken words collide . . . 'Homeland'. 'hero', 'war' . . . The meaning linking words, syllables, sounds with the minds of the heirs to the War of Independence has drifted away . . . Some are attempting to join the broken fragments using artificial, imported gums, and say, 'Well, it's better than it was' . . . Some, Burhan for instance. 'It's not real, not genuine,' thinks Raik, meditatively.

Words flap convulsively to the rhythms of mambo or chacha on the surface below which silence begins; meaning masses ominously in the depths to which it has been driven; have the police forbidden all attempts to reach it? Words and meaning are drifting in different directions . . . Raik stands wretchedly between the opposed currents, feeling as if he's exposed to a draught . . . his heart aches like an old, rheumatic joint . . . if only he could sleep and forget . . .

He really fell asleep for a while and, in the August heat of İzmir, dreamed of mountains covered with snow. A dream that changed into a nightmare of cold . . . He saw his elder brothers in that snowbound hell . . . the soldiers of another army . . . of the Ottoman army massacred on the Caucasian Sarıkamış front. Horses stumble on the icy slopes, his brothers roll down over the snow-covered precipice . . . leaving their grief-stricken mother behind . . . Raik learnt as a child what it meant to lose loved ones to death . . . He likens loss to a snowy mountain; when the summit is reached, the breath-starved heart will all but stop . . . then the sweat of exhaustion bathes the aching body . . . and from there, from the peak a brand-new, broad horizon can be seen.

He has not lost Cumhur . . . He has acknowledged Cumhur as a son, and has survived Cumhur's losing a limb, like a death blow. And now, very soon, Cumhur will be standing before him . . . Raik has prepared himself for this encounter. The whole experience has been like a difficult, painful ascent; now Raik is at the top; but why can't he see the view? The horizon has been obliterated . . . fog has covered the whole land . . . syllables devoid of meaning echo through its blanket of darkness, hoarse as the howling of wolves . . . Wolves tore to pieces the valiant men lost on the Caucasian mountains! Wolves are worrying at the soldiers! Which soldiers? Which? Packs of wolves run from the mountains to the plains, enter towns, infiltrate schools, and in the primary school Raik's and Vicdan's little daughter attends, form fresh packs of wolf cubs . . .

We had learnt how the wolf of legend was a nurturing mother, an agile and vigilant companion of the heart, showing the way to the ancient nomadic tribes. When was she transformed into this fierce monster, bearing off lumps of bloody flesh in her jaws, her eyes raging with vicious intent, her savage breath snarling?

Wolves overran the soldiers of the Turkish Republic, bit them and turned them into wolves!

Raik jerked awake in anger; in his rage, forgetting that Cumhur had turned into one of these wolves, he stood up, and with all the embittered force of his fury, raised his right arm for all the oppressed peoples of the world! He felt the sickle of revolution bond with the veins and muscles running along his arm to his heart. For an instant he was infinitely strong!

Then suddenly he saw another blood-bath with his mind's eye, those brave young men of the Caucasian mountains who had been mown down, Cumhur's father among them . . . His heart couldn't bear it. He nearly collapsed back into his seat . . . and realised that no heart alert to the century's accursed destiny would be able to last long . . .

Vicdan cut out all the information – of whatever kind – that appeared in the press concerning the Korean affair, and stuck the cuttings on a wall in her home.

'Reds attacking the Turkish Korean Brigade were fiercely repelled with bayonets.'

Akşam, *15 May 1953*
'*A Chinese force of two thousand men fled, leaving fifty dead, after a struggle lasting only five minutes. The Turkish contingent has won another victory.*'

Milliyet, *16 May 1953*

She stared at the newspaper cuttings and thought about them for hours.

'*There will be a mevlit for the souls of the martyrs in the Sultan Ahmet Mosque. The premier has given Istanbul radio permission to broadcast the service.*'

16 February 1952

'*Twenty-five thousand Muslims congregated in the Süleymaniye Mosque, Istanbul, at a solemn memorial service for the martyrs.*'

21 April 1952

Raik keeps an eye on his wife; he is worried. At first he was relieved when Vicdan, refusing to be overwhelmed by the painful process of awaiting her brother's return, directed her attention to reports and poems on Korea; he had been scared that Vicdan would mourn and grieve throughout Cumhur's tour of duty. The memory of Vicdan's interminable forebodings during the second World War led Raik to expect this. Vicdan was indeed deeply depressed in the months between Cumhur's posting and throughout the forty-five day sea voyage, until his arrival in Korea. Then she underwent a sudden metamorphosis: her tears stopped, and she busied herself with cutting out and sticking up any news items or poems appearing in the dailies and journals. She searched out reports and articles in newspaper archives concerning the period before Cumhur's posting, and included them as well in her exhibition.

'*The gallantry of our army has proved that our men are not lacking in the calibre or skills of the most advanced nations in the world.*'

Nihat Erim, in **Ulus,** *12 February 1951*

Raik began to dread the way Vicdan externalised and objectified her grief, and to wish that she would weep again. Besides, the dense array of newspaper cuttings underlined the absurd contradiction between the appalling fact of man's annihilation of man that ruined the whole meaning of life, and the vacuous applause of those on the sidelines of the battlefield. Absurdity loomed over Raik like a huge, unassailable monster that would swallow his whole being and grind him to dust.

'The Turkish flag flying in Korea has taught the whole world what it means to be a Turk. The free world has discovered the Turk.'

İsmail Habip Sevük, *in* Cumhuriyet, *5 December 1950*

'The Turkish soldier with his bayonet attacks and charges across the Chinese corpses, has won victory after victory.
Hürriyet, *29 January 1951*

Then Raik also began to analyse the newspaper cuttings. As time had gone on, a new meaning had emerged from within the absurdity. In the summer of 1953, if the period since 1950 was to be viewed retrospectively, what had not been obvious while it was being lived through became obvious, like a sea-bed which was murky while you were swimming, but limpidly clear when viewed from the shore.

The Minister for External Affairs, Fuat Köprülü (Democratic Party): *'Our whole-hearted and sincere commitment to the decisions of the United Nations constitutes the unshakeable foundation of our policy.'*
Cumhuriyet, *1 July 1950*

Hikmet Bayur (National Party, in opposition): *'The government has decided to send our troops without the approval of the National Assembly.'*

Cumhuriyet: *'The decision to send troops outside Turkish territory is strictly a matter for the National Assembly, in accordance with article 26 of the Constitution.'*

27 July 1950

The Republican People's Party (leading the opposition): *'The sending abroad of our troops is strictly against the Constitution.'*

Cumhuriyet: *'We would remind our government that our young men who are under arms are only responsible for the defence of Turkish territories'!*

7 July 1950

Bülent Nuri Esen (Professor of Constitutional Law): *'The requirements of the laws of the Constitution, dictating the conditions under which armed forces may be sent abroad, have not been fulfilled.'*

Ulus, 3 August 1950

Prime Minister Adnan Menderes (Democratic Party): *'The sending abroad of our men is not an act of war, but for the preservation of peace. I implore our nation to think positively.'*

Hürriyet, 29 July 1950

'Turkey has been elected to join NATO by an unanimous vote.'

Hürriyet, 4 August 1950

'Our commitment of 4500 men to the war effort rejoices General MacArthur!'

Hürriyet, 7 August 1950

'Turkish troops cheerful and optimistic!'

Hürriyet, 9 November 1950

'The Turkish contingent joins the American Eighth Army!'

Ulus, 8 November 1950

'*MacArthur congratulates Turks on their success!*'
Hürriyet, *19 November 1950*

'*Sixty of our officers and men have been decorated by the American Military Command.*'
Hürriyet, *22 November 1950*

'*KUNURI*'
Cumhuriyet, *29 November 1950*

'*Casualties are not as heavy as first reported.*'
Akşam, *4 December 1950*

'*The American Eighth Army sent a message of thanks to the Turkish Brigade for their brave and costly action at Kunuri*'
Akşam, *10 December 1950*

'*Those of our wounded who died in Tokyo have been buried there with full military honours.*'
Hürriyet, *11 December 1950*

'*The list of the soldier martyrs.*'
Hürriyet, *16 December 1950*

'*Another military decoration ceremony: Turkish soldier is number one!*'
28 March 1952

'*The Turkish Brigade has lost 5 officers, 3 sergeants and 300 men.*'
Milliyet, *26 April 1951*
Hürriyet, *28 April 1951*

'*The American 'silver star' medal has been awarded to three martyred Turkish officers.*'
Hürriyet, *8 June 1951*

'President of South Korea awarding decorations.'
Hürriyet, *20 September 1952*

'24 killed, 32 wounded!'
Hürriyet, *14 August 1951*

'10 dead, 24 wounded!'
Hürriyet, *21 May 1952*

'Another soldier dead!'
Hürriyet, *23 May 1952*

'4 martyred, 30 wounded!'
Hürriyet, *4 June 1952*

'A colonel and a soldier martyred!'
Hürriyet, *10 June 1952*

'Eight killed, seven wounded!'
Hürriyet, *27 July 1952*

Total casualties
721 killed
175 missing
234 captured
and
2147 wounded

official cease-fire: 27 July 1953

Cumhur was wounded at the battle of Vegas by a mortar shell exploding close by his bunker, on the night between 15 May 1953 and 16 May 1953, two months and twelve days prior to the official cease-fire. A short time before, he had written in his journal, 'We are damned to a cold, dark hell.'

Waiting was the worst. Waiting for the enemy attack in the cold, dark confines of the bunker . . . The body, its movements restricted, in some strange way exuded longing and anxiety.

Sometimes they played cards, sometimes backgammon. Some wrote letters, some made notes in their journals. The committed, aggressive tone of the conversations at headquarters was not – for some reason – heard in the bunker . . . They cherished an indisputable conviction, when at headquarters, that 'they were defending world peace against the lousy communists'. Even though that conviction did not entirely disappear in the bunker, the strong current of shared emotion dissipated, leaving their certainty stagnant and diminished. You thought of home, of your mother, your sweetheart, your children . . . Snapshots kept in pockets over the heart were taken out and looked at, furtively. Officers cared for the men who would be shot in this alien land and would remain here forever. Only nineteen years old when they were called up . . . lieutenants, first lieutenants, they too were very young. Nevertheless they were officers, 'father-figures', and acknowledged the men under their command as 'sons' . . . They had to be the first to confront any danger they would ask their men to face. The men were entrusted to the officers, and officers to God! All of them had assimilated completely, with or without being aware of it, this unspoken rule, this chain of trust that keeps an army brave and soldierly. God would aid the Turk! The commissioned officers cared for those who were non-commissioned, sympathising with those who had been granted no time to grow accustomed to the morbid emotional bonds within the military. Especially since very many of the men conscripted with them were at home, safe. . . It was hard for the reserve!

What drew together both commissioned and non-commissioned officers was their shared responsibility and affection for their men, all of whom were conscripts. How innocent these crowds of They did not have pin-up pictures above their beds. Those who were married sometimes put up photos of their wives, and usually of their children; the unmarried ones put up pictures of parents, brothers.

They could hardly bear to look at the half-naked American girls dancing on 'morale-raising' evenings, and hung their heads in embarrassment; although there were some who managed to cast furtive, cagey glances. How shy they were! They ignored their own bodies meticulously, and clung to their celibacy with alarming determination. They dreamed of the hazy face of the 'sweetheart', remote as a censored letter or a faded snapshot; they had forbidden themselves any private moments, the intimate reminiscences and fantasies of the flesh. They could not possibly reach martyrdom status without a well-washed body. They had to be alert and ready to die at any moment, and to enter paradise, the home for martyrs! Without realising it, they saved their virile energy for mortal combat with bayonets, that potent strength which was locked inside their flesh and which, finding no escape through reminiscence or dreams, transformed their physical being into an explosives warehouse, filled to the brim with devastating violence.

Obscure young dreams, the longing for the smell of their mothers (how many years has it been since they parted from their mother's body?) sometimes hit on a path winding through all the savage single-mindedness and leading to the heart; then some voice would be heard singing a poignant song, striking a chord in the tough landscape of the thirty-eighth parallel, deep under its snow. 'Home' was the symbolic name given by the Turkish soldier, unused to the process of analysing and sorting out his feelings, to every particle of life beyond the battlefield. 'Home' was a warmly welcoming embrace.

Then what about God? God was of course present everywhere and always. But God's existence and omnipresence did not suffice, on the thirty-eighth parallel, to transform the endless encircling land into a warmly-welcoming embrace for the Muslim peasant spirits which tended to be veiled, diminished, and concealed within the soldiers' outer husks when they were left on their own. The omnipresence of God only manifested itself in their souls when they inserted their bodies into the living, moving organism of the mass.

When he was waiting on his own, within the narrow confines of the bunker, God was as far away and as foreign as the stars for the Turkish peasant, whose thoughts could not get beyond the limits of his own physical self! He longed for the enemy to attack, for his company to move as one, like the organs of an animal . . . Then the warm, protective hand of God would stretch out from the distant, frozen stars, and touch him! . . . And when the counter-attack began, then the icy, alien reality of the thirty-eighth parallel would turn into a warm and bloody vision which he knew well. A vision promising great things, such as Paradise, God, the quintessence of Turkishness, the flag, and – for the officer – Mustafa Kemal!

Ever since his days at the Military Academy, when the cadets at morning inspection shouted as one the response, 'He's within us' to the number '1283', the number which had been Atatürk's, ever since then, First Lieutenant Cumhur has felt the presence of Mustafa Kemal within himself.

The commander of the Anafarta front in the Dardanelles! The soldier, Atatürk himself, against whose chest a shell exploded, and who was saved from certain death, by the watch carried over his heart, a watch that bore his mother's blessing! This same man, a general by then, who directed the defence on the Conk heights for three whole days without even a moment's sleep, on horseback, so ending the allied occupation. Then again, the commander-in-chief of the 'Great Attack', ending the Greek occupation. During the latest assault, in Cumhur's imagination, it was Mustafa Kemal mounted on a red horse, his golden hair streaming, who ordered the Turkish Korean Brigade towards a horizon stained crimson with mortar fire.

Cumhur Özgecan has a quality most soldiers lack. He has a well-developed sense of humour. He has inherited this trait from his father. He is on very good terms with his brother-in-law Raik who, just like Cumhur, loves a joke.

A sense of humour is entirely lacking in his older brothers and sister Vicdan, immigrant children of Fitnat Hanım from Macedonia, whom she conceived with her Salonikan husband. A strange sadness shapes their inner worlds. Cumhur is different. His letters from Korea usually carry traces of the humour which help to make the front tolerable for him and for his friends. Cumhur has the ability to view his circumstances and experiences objectively; and he starts to reflect on them whenever his sense of humour prompts him. But there are matters an officer should never question, such as foreign policy, government decisions, and so on. Cumhur the joker sometimes wonders whether or not the government should have found some other way of inducing the West to accept Turkey than by partaking in the war. And he is exasperated. Anger is close to treason and does not suit him, must be suppressed, must not, under any circumstances, be revealed to others! He may pour out his rage against the communists as much as he likes, but must hide his indignation, his grudge against the government. He will not allow himself to make a synthesis of his two angers. He tries to escape the dilemma he is trapped in by clinging to humour; he falls willingly into humour's embrace, which detaches him from his feelings!

During the years that follow, he will not talk about Korea or, if he cannot take refuge in silence, he speaks of her smilingly. The lucky ones who returned from the war with whole skins will sometimes boast about their bravery; but Cumhur will only smile:

Come on, imagine a ward full of men. Some have lost arms, some legs, and others their minds. Piece them together, and then you'll get a whole man.

Uncle Cumhur, don't make me laugh. I don't want to laugh at tragedies.

The moment when he was wounded divided his life irrevocably in two. In the second part, the hero and the suffering man within him were silenced for ever . . .

He was twenty-nine when he was posted to Korea, thirty when he returned. He had fought for almost one year, and received medical treatment for nearly five. He was promoted to 'captain', was awarded a medal, and resigned as a disabled veteran because of his lost leg. Years passed before he could really adapt to civilian life. He married, had a family, became a father.

What else is there in life, anyway?

Thirty-five years later, his heart suddenly stopped, while he was resting in his armchair.

In his last days, he had often thought of his brother Raik, who had his first heart attack on the İzmir quay, while waiting for Cumhur to arrive. Raik had tried not to reveal his condition to Cumhur, quickly slipping a trinitrine tablet under his tongue. Some years later an infraction finished him off. Cumhur thoroughly enjoyed brother Raik's disquisitions on politics, though he did not take part and only listened. It had been hard for Cumhur to come to terms with Raik's absence . . .

On a wall in Cumhur's flat hung a portrait of himself, Cumhur Özgecan, in those brave days just before his voyage to Korea, a young lieutenant as bright and keen as a sharp knife. On the opposite wall hung another soldier's portrait, that of Cumhur's hero, Mustafa Kemal Pasha, veteran of the Anafarta front . . .

These two men stared distantly from their frames at Cumhur Bey who was now over sixty years of age. He loved them, probably more than anyone or anything, but could not reach them . . . He could not understand them any more . . . Still he felt very close to them . . . But was he really? There did exist a fragile bond between the three of them, linking those who had been exposed to identical wrongs . . . That was all . . .

Cumhur Bey's being was sinking slowly into the sea of forgetfulness. He was forgetting and being forgotten by everyone.

For a long time he had been living like a prickly bush right in the middle of a tranquillity created by women. Here was his daughter clearing the dining table; his wife was in the kitchen, she must have been heating the washing-up water; he could smell the soap. Ever since he had started to spend the greater part of his days at home, he had been watching their domestic chores like a shadow-play. Without being aware of it, he had come to know their ways in minute detail. At this moment, his daughter was wiping the breadcrumbs off the table into a teflon container, using a synthetic yellow sponge. Such doings must have some significance! He, Cumhur Bey, had never been able to grasp this meaning: the idea that he himself might explore what domestic tasks were about had never even crossed his mind.

It had gradually been dawning on him, as a troubling perception, that the women's shadow-play was the sole reality, solid and reliable, of his existence. At the least he, the retired, disabled veteran, Captain Cumhur Özgecan, lived at the mercy of and dependent on this solid, reliable form of reality, so close to him, yet so remote. This revelation displeased him.

He did not imagine that his wife and daughter were perceptive enough to see through him. Such an insight had to be completely out of the question, he thought, just as it was impossible for him to fathom the reactions of women. So he kept silent. In any case, he had never been in the habit of expressing the disquieting reflections of his mind in words.

He did not often remember the war, indeed, did not want to remember. His forgetfulness was not only due to the ache in the vacant space where his leg had been; but rather to the fact that his mental frame was painfully strained by any attempt to build a bridge capable of crossing the abyss which separated his time at the front and his present life-style. So it was better to forget the far side . . . Sometimes, through this queer numbness, anger – about something he was no longer sure of – stirred. A feeling of having been betrayed . . .

Recently, an altogether different shadow-play, which he was unable to control, ran through his mind, with images – no, not of the front – but of the wounded and dying in hospital wards. Just as he was watching his daughter clearing the table, the image of the wounded soldier who had died on the ship bound for home, returned to Cumhur, and he remembered the lad's last word. His very last word had been 'mo-ther-land'.

'Mo-ther-land,' repeated Cumhur Bey in a weak voice, below the threshold of hearing.

His daughter turned round, thinking she had heard a whisper. No, she was wrong, there was her father sitting in his armchair, quietly engrossed with his own thoughts as usual. She went on with her household task.

'Na-tion,' said Cumhur Bey. 'Home-land . . . Na-tion . . . the F-lag,' broken fragments of words . . . The meaning that had tied the syllables together and to the mind was sliding through the cracks . . .

His head drooped . . . He was dead . . .

YOU HAVE FORGOTTEN SALONIKA

Carbon, oxygen, hydrogen and nitrogen . . . Protein and lipid molecules, formed out of miniscule units in spirals, metres long . . . The endless string, within the cells, of proteins and enzymes, precipitating within the honeycomb of the organism . . . the cells respiring, through the structuring of the spirals . . . differentiating tissues from one another . . . Arteries, blood circulation, the brain . . .

In which protein spirals, in which cell nuclei of Burhan Yurdakul, aged eighty-one, have the immense collection of images, emotions, and impressions been stored like reels of film?.. The Salonika quay, with its elegant Beyaz Kule, the work of Sinan . . . the avenue running alongside the Aegean . . . the breeze blowing from the sea. Oh, beautiful city, how you resemble İzmir . . . The sea, the breeze tempt a man to a glass of rakı, making him break his pledge . . . Mustafa Kemal must for sure have sipped his drink here in his young days. Burhan Bey had left Salonika long before he was old enough for rakı, in fact he was a baby, on his mother's lap. His eyes had never rested on the avenue by the sea with any awareness. It's impossible, he can't remember . . . Well then, to which sea town does the view that appears before his mind's eye during the final days of his life, belong? No, it isn't İzmir. It certainly isn't Istanbul. Where is it then?

Is there anyone who knows to which layer, deep in a protein spiral, perceptions, impressions, penetrate? Do molecules completely disappear when they are dispersed, or do they leave their mark on atoms, and deeper still on electrons? Does an impression of any human being, in any place on our earth, reverberate to infinity, like a pulse of universal awareness?

When someone is in their dotage, have some of their brain cells died? Or has some cell, while retaining its internal organisation, consumed the memories stored within it, destroying them?

Or do all perceptions stay where they are? And has the link between perceptions and the state we call consciousness been broken? Or was this consciousness demolished, pulled down like a wall deprived of its support when the link snapped? Who has destroyed the mechanism that animates the pictures stored in the memory? And the equilibrium between proteins and enzymes? Who has shuffled the atoms?.. Time?.. God?.. Or was it the so-called electricity, or let's say the 'feelings' between the positive and negative poles of impressions and perceptions, and between them and the protein spirals on which they have been collecting?

Burhan Bey is expiring like a candle . . . First of all, the glinting light of his steel-blue eyes grew opaque. Then a bitter expression settled on his face. His features drooped. He rarely spoke. He grew shorter and his spine bent. He became thin . . . The tissue between skin and skeleton has dried out. The whole organism is insufficiently nourished . . . so is the brain. Cells are not receiving sufficient oxygen, the circulation is poor. The loss of tissue means loss of proteins . . . the process of dying has begun. Perceptions, knowledge, memories . . . Have they mingled with the air, puffed out in laboured breaths, together with dissolving proteins; or have they been poured out in splashes of urine?

The news of Cumhur's death is the final blow ending the process! Now a new phase begins, speedier, going downwards precipitously towards the 'end', towards death and, in some strange way, towards the beginning, towards infancy and perhaps birth . . . The city of Salonika, the seashore . . .

Seagulls fly round the Beyaz Kule, Colonel Hayreddin Bey drinks a single glass of rakı on the avenue by the sea. He is already late getting home; Fitnat Hanım will be annoyed. She is still housebound, having recently given birth to their third child, Burhan. She expected and wanted a girl, and will for the time being dress her little boy in girl's clothes. Hayreddin Bey is extraordinarily lenient with his young wife, never crossing her wishes, even the absurd ones. A happy family, in a way. But peace will soon be at an end . . . The hurricane is approaching . . . The Balkan War will snatch Salonika away . . . Little Burhan, Burhan the baby, will tread the migration road.

Burhan Bey aged eighty-one, in the last days of his life, remembers Salonika, forgetting that he erased the name of his birthplace on his identity card!

My mother descended on my room like a blue gleam of sunlight, her dress rustling. I dared not touch the fabric, in case I creased and spoilt it. They are going to my uncle Burhan's; why don't they take me? I shall be left with Nanny Faika, and be put to bed early. My mother never changes my routine; wish I could go with them, the hall at my uncle Burhan's is vast, with glittering lamps on the walls. His sons – I call them 'big brother' – always talk about amusing things; they are doing badly at school but they don't care. There's a great variety of things to eat. I love my aunt, she is always laughing, and isn't at all reserved and sedate like my mother. Mother doesn't approve of her, I know. She thinks my aunt isn't good enough for my uncle. The other day I overheard a conversation between mother and father:

'He should have married Vecdet,' said mother.

'I wonder where İzzet is,' said father.

'He will treat Handan exactly the way he treated Vecdet,' said my mother. 'Is this man the brother I loved?'

My uncle has a mistress called Handan.

'Indirectly, you prevented his marriage to Vecdet,' said my father.

'Whatever are you talking about, for God's sake,' exclaimed my mother. 'He broke up with Vecdet, such an ideal woman, and got engaged to this girl, this motherless waif, then regretted what he'd done, and tried to break the engagement so he could go back to Vecdet! How can anyone condone such a foul way of behaving? I can't believe he is my brother!'

'That's men for you,' said father.

'You're not like that,' said mother.

Then they embraced. Then I think they kissed. I feel jealous when they kiss. Why don't they include me in their embrace?

'You did a good deed, when you took pity on her,' said father, meaning my aunt.

'You're wrong. People used to look down on girls who were jilted. And now, there's no one to match the high and mighty lady; she's so snobbish, she's trying to trace her ancestors back to our sublime Ottoman dynasty.'

'As if those sublime Ottomans deserved the slightest regard.'

They laughed scornfully. Does my aunt really have royal blood? It's like a fairy tale . . . Like the five-hundredth anniversary of Mehmet's conquest of Istanbul – you know, we shall celebrate it in our school very soon. My parents don't approve of this business either.

'Imagine a country which, instead of priding herself on the level of civilisation she's attained, needs to boast about a military conquest that happened five centuries ago so as to boost her self-esteem!' says father.

'Ah, Atatürk,' says my mother.

Still, I love my aunt, she is not serious like my parents. As for my uncle . . . well, I am afraid of him. His eyes flash like lightning. He looks so like the picture of Atatürk hanging on the wall of our classroom. Atatürk's face never smiles; he is so upright and so unimpressive in his sombre attire. He doesn't rouse my curiosity. Whereas the Sultans in pictures are adorned with jewels, silken robes of state, and variations on the turban, coiled, pleated, or wound into intricate shapes with well-balanced hollows and protrusions. There's the sultan who used to string pearls through his beard. Isn't that intriguing and attractive? My mother and father love Atatürk very much . . . My mother saw him once, and talked with him . . . What a long time ago . . . I don't like the ceremonies on the tenth of December, commemorating Atatürk's death – my feet get cold in the damp school yard. I am frightened of Atatürk as well; was he as fierce as my uncle? Did he beat children?

'He was love itself, from top to toe,' says my mother, and then she asks my father, suspiciously: 'Raik, what do they teach our children in the schools?'

My mother was shocked and indignant when we learnt the poem 'The Altay mountains, my beautiful homeland' by heart, at school, with all its racist implications.

She complained to my father, 'They don't teach our children to love our own Anatolian land and those who live in it.'

'If they're going to justify involvement in the Korean war, an imaginary homeland and imaginary borders are exactly what our government needs nowadays,' replied my father.

'We are teachers as well,' my mother says, 'but I don't think we have anything in common with those who prepare the teaching programme for primary schools.'

'We must admit it's natural,' says father, 'It's the way history works, counter-revolution follows revolution.'

Whatever that means. Sometimes I think my parents are fonder of Turkey than they are of me. Never mind. Nanny Faika is coming to take charge of me. I'll pretend I'm asleep.

My mother was like a blue sun. I risked one fingertip on the fabric. Will my mother and father dance at my uncle Burhan's? I wonder . . .

Jezebel . . .
If ever a devilish plan
Was made to torment man
It was you
Jezebel it was you

A tango stirs the flesh. Is Burhan's wife leaning a little too closely against her partner? Vicdan does not approve of the lyric comparing a woman to the devil. The seductive voice of Frankie Lane is silenced. Now it is Nat King Cole's turn. The velvet-smooth, soft melody affects Vicdan, but she does not like the lyric that stresses the uncertainties of love.

If you really love me say yes
And if you don't dear, confess
But please don't tell me, perhaps
Perhaps, perhaps, perhaps.

With each repetition of the word 'perhaps', Burhan's wife sways her fat hips to the right, then to the left . . . Smiles wreathe the face she lifts up to her tall partner, a flirtatious light in her eyes twinkles 'perhaps'.

Vicdan thinks, 'She knows about Burhan's infidelity.' Ah, Burhan, how can you inflict such pain on your wife! Burhan swears fervently, she doesn't know, dear sister, hasn't the faintest idea, will never know. That is what you think, Burhan.

Couples are now cheek to cheek . . . Burhan is dancing with the wife of one of his clients. Is he pressing his cheek against a married woman's face? Oh God! Isn't he supposed to be in love with Handan?

And the mambo . . . The rhythm is hectic . . . Bodies move one step forward, then back, furtively discharging the energy the tango has generated . . .

Hey mambo, mambo Italiano
Go, go, go.

The contractor, Burhan's client, who comes from Raik's hometown, is twitching his body about in a novice's jerky movements to a hybrid rhythm, half mambo, half horon folkdance, and singing with a strong provincial accent,

Jo, jo, jo

Vicdan surveys those gyrating bodies, stamping feet. This is not dancing, it is devoid of grace or skill, just a game for naughty adults (So what is wrong with that, Vicdan?) I don't know . . . Everything the body does is serious and significant to her (Perhaps you have never been a true child, Vicdan).

Does any individual have the right to behave irresponsibly, regressing as it were to childhood? My brother is an irresponsible father and husband!.. He goes in for free enterprise, blinded by his greed and ambition. Where is Burhan the idealist, with his shining eyes? Now a dangerous fire, stoked by a single-minded pursuit of material wealth and power, blazes fiercely in those eyes. He burns, destroys, oppresses, and succeeds! A new type of person for Turkey!.. Years of short commons have given birth to his ruthless ambition. Or there may be other reasons.

As soon as he got back from Dersim, Burhan had married their neighbour's daughter. His sons were born one after the other. He was a young army lawyer; his salary was very small. There was a posting to Konya after Elaziz, and then to Adıyaman, all military bases in very small towns. On an impulse he resigned, and started to work as a lawyer in Ankara. He had changed, was distant with his mother and brothers; only with Vicdan did affection endure. Meanwhile Burhan's wife is aware of Handan, but is helpless. The only price she can ask for this infidelity is that Burhan should see his mother and brothers, whom he has already deserted emotionally, very rarely. It is a pitiless power game . . . The wounded wife needs to believe that she has succeeded in tearing her husband away from his family, and imagines that this will repair her damaged self-esteem. She is angry with Vicdan, the sister-in-law who has always supported her, because she cannot share the matching concerns and enthusiasms that have kept Vicdan and Burhan together. She is jealous, because Burhan idealises his sister Vicdan as a unique icon of womanhood. Her bitter resentment of Handan has intensified ever since the rumour reached her ears that in some ways Handan resembles Vicdan. Her flirtation with her partner while dancing the tango is in fact a petty act of revenge against Vicdan . . . She knows how to wait; patience is the only weapon the powerless possess. And indeed, Burhan and Vicdan now have different priorities; life will soon part them . . .

Vicdan, knowing nothing of her sister-in-law's private thoughts, is contemplating very different matters, such as their brother Cumhur's involvement in the fighting in Korea. No letters for a long time now. She cannot conceive how Burhan remains on good terms with the politicians who sent Cumhur to this unjust and unnecessary war.

Wasn't our motto 'peace at home, peace in the world,' Burhan?

Certainly, dear sister. And our soldiers are members of a United Nations force striving for the preservation of world peace.

No, Burhan, they are there because the USA insists on a government under her control for the whole of Korea. This isn't our cause, it's the Americans'.

Sister, the USA is our ally. Communism threatens world peace. It has to be stopped.

What devastating contempt and disgust contort Burhan's face and voice as he utters the word 'communism'! Vicdan used to be anxious for him when he was in the army, in case he was discharged for being a Bolshevik; his friendship with İzzet had strengthened Burhan's leftwing commitment. Vicdan used to worry about İzzet too . . . İzzet, where are you? Since Burhan broke off with Vecdet, they have not seen İzzet, only hearing later that he had resigned from the army. Probably İzzet had never forgiven Burhan's jilting of his sister for the girl next door. Once upon a time, Burhan and İzzet would read Nazım's poems in secret. Burhan wrote poems as well – about hunger – verses seething with rage and resentment, brimming over with revolutionary zeal!

What a long way you have come, Burhan! Your anger and hatred are the same as ever, only their targets have changed.

Communism . . .

Sister, have you forgotten Stalin's demand for military bases on the Bosphorus, as soon as the War ended?

Vicdan doesn't approve of communism. She has not forgotten Stalin's demands, but she doesn't approve of the American army invading Korea. Relying on another country, being under another state's control, trying to curry favour with her, all of these things seem dishonourable to Vicdan. There should be another way!

If Atatürk had been alive, he would never have pursued a foreign policy of this kind.

You are wrong, sister, he would have behaved in exactly the same way.

I tell you 'No', Burhan! I was abroad at that time. We used to be a respected country. And now! We have become the buddies of American sergeants!

The war has changed the world, sister! You must get used to it.

That damnable Second World War! Vicdan remembers the first of September 1939 whenever she hears dance music.

A ship rocking in the middle of the Black Sea: Vicdan is on the dance floor with her husband, her darling Raik, dancing the tango. She is so happy; she is on wings . . . The news strikes like a thunderbolt: war has been declared! The music stops . . . it seems to her that the silence beginning at that precise moment has remained ever since, and will go on for ever. The thunderbolt scorched the sprouting happiness, the stirrings of security and *joie de vivre* in the arid soil of her bitter childhood, and kindled embers of foreboding in her being which would glow internally, from then on. This house of Burhan's, why is it associated with that other one she prefers to forget, their uncle's mansion, filled with wealth and shamelessness, during the years when Istanbul was occupied?

Nobody cared about the war in that house, and nobody cares here about Korea . . . The master of the house has a brother, First Lieutenant Cumhur Özgecan, in Korea, who could be wounded or killed at any moment . . . No letters . . . Please, God, protect my brother . . .

How can you be on such good terms with politicians of the Democratic Party? They have sent our brother to the front!

Dear sister, remember, we all fought in the past.

That was different.

How different, exactly?

It was to put down a rebellion by reactionaries.

Is Burhan secretly pleased that Cumhur is in the firing line? Can he really be so?!

Sister, do you imagine that the reason for the fighting has any meaning for men in the front line?

But it should!

That meaning only exists for those who are safe at home. It only exists for you.

Resentment in Burhan's voice that he cannot hide! Vicdan stares at her brother in dismay. And thinks that she knows nothing about this brother to whom she feels so close.

Where do men conceal the other side of their personalities?

Only death exists. Killing or being killed. That's all. So whether it's Dersim or Korea makes no difference. Either you obey orders and murder, or you are murdered. If you survive, the faces of those you killed come to stay, always before your eyes; if it's the other way round, your face lives on in someone else's memory, until he dies! That's all.

Vicdan's heart ached. She touched her brother, gently.

Dearest Burhan . . . You shouldn't think this way. In private life we're sometimes forced, in spite of ourselves, to do things that hurt other people, on the grounds that, if we don't act now, the problem we're faced with will do even more harm, and it's the same for nations that are sometimes forced to use violence. You can't separate violence from its cause. You're splitting life up, when in fact it's a whole, and then you're concentrating on the violence, and suffering pangs of guilt.

Do you think I cared whether the cause was right or wrong? The only thought in my mind was that if I didn't obey orders, I would be shot.

'You were wrong,' replies Vicdan's clear voice. 'My dear brother, please get your thoughts in better order.'

A deal of scorn in this sisterly love of hers! She seems so self-confident, that Burhan doesn't feel able to accuse her of being a conceited fool, pedantically pronouncing on something she's never experienced. How very much he would like to accuse her, so freeing himself from her criticism, strengthening his conviction that the weight on his conscience is inevitable, and totally erasing from his mind any hope of restoring his peace of mind.

Could Vicdan kill? A woman could, if she believed it necessary for her children's salvation! Then how would she cope with the sense of guilt? She would endure the pangs of conscience, and close the book, saying, 'I've paid my debt.' Then go on with the housework, as if nothing had happened. Burhan shrugged irritably. They possessed such power, these women! They had the knack of countering injury with injury, suffering with suffering, uniting them, absorbing them, and then starting afresh! Thank God this vitality, such an inescapable part of their being, was unrecognised by most of them! Probably wealth, position, respect, weren't as attractive to them as they are to men, because their thirst was quenched by that refreshing, secret spring of theirs that feeds their vital functions from within. Burhan was driven into a savage state of awe and resentment whenever he came upon this ability to regenerate and develop, his own lack of which he was painfully aware of. Women refused to be crushed! They would never admit defeat! His mother, who had survived the Great War and the War of Independence with three children; his wife, fighting to the bitter end not to lose her husband to her rival; Handan, determined not to lose him to middle-class respectability; and Vicdan! For the first time he admitted the probability of Vicdan's having lived through an agonisingly painful period in England! One of her friends had committed suicide, hadn't she? It was dawning on him for the first time that his sister might have quietly drawn back from the brink of self-destruction . . . If so, why didn't she ever mention it? Because she was through with the mood of that time . . .

Women don't talk about what is over and done with, and

men don't discuss what is still going on. Strange . . . for the first time, in a very oblique way, Burhan was thinking about his reactions to Dersim . . . for the first time in his relationship with his sister, for the first time in his life . . . He would never ever touch on the subject again. Was it women's fecundity that provided them with better ways of coping with the sensations evoked by the deaths of others – and of their own selves?

Vicdan's maternal feelings were certainly not confined to the child she gave birth to. Burhan could never really identify with his half-brother Cumhur, whereas Vicdan loved him dearly. Cumhur's posting to Korea was nothing out of the ordinary for Burhan, and he knew his insensitivity annoyed Vicdan. The fact that her brother's life was in danger sharpened her anger against the Democratic Party then in power.

> They have compromised Atatürk's principles!
> They are having the call to prayer, the ezan, in Arabic again!
> They don't give anywhere near enough importance to women's rights!

To all these faults of the party in power was now added 'putting Cumhur's life in danger for a cause which has absolutely nothing to do with us . . .' Vicdan was wrong, of course. The Democratic Party was simply pursuing a pragmatic policy in both internal and foreign affairs.

> We are no longer living in Atatürk's era. My sister and brother-in-law Raik are incapable of understanding that to repeat Atatürk's principles like articles of faith for all time is nothing but fanaticism!

A coloured portrait of Atatürk used to hang on a wall of the drawing room in Burhan's house. Vicdan looked at this portrait and thought, 'He's an outsider here as well, like me and Raik.' Why did they put you up on the same wall that their vulgar, showy furniture stands against? The portrait gazed sadly at its surroundings with a rueful expression. Vicdan and Raik are sitting at the table; they do not feel like dancing, but they are trying to look cheerful. Burhan wants to involve them in the entertainment.

'I know the sort of music you like.'

He puts the record of 'La Cumparsita' on the gramophone. Now they have to dance. Raik and Vicdan dance gracefully and skilfully to the tango (Vicdan, you are in the arms of the man you love, wipe from your mind all perverse thoughts, forget about your surroundings, just enjoy the present moment!)

Finding perfect harmony in their dancing is far more important for Vicdan and Raik than any sexual gratification they derive from their movements.

They have stopped dancing and are back at the table.

'Eh, real nice, the way you spun round and round . . . Real nice, real nice! Give us another one, eh . . .'

The contractor is speaking. He is a powerful figure in the Democratic Party. Burhan is keen to keep on good terms with him, as his ambition extends to politics. He wouldn't refuse if offered the chance of being a deputy. The contractor is very talkative this evening.

Local features that used to be suppressed during İsmet Pasha's time are tolerated nowadays. That is the way it should be. Isn't it the fact that the contractor, Temel Tonyalı Bey, speaks uninhibitedly, without any sense of embarrassment, in the accent of his region, freedom itself, a symbol of democracy?

'My brother-in-law comes from the Black Sea region. He's a great guy, very typical of the area. Aren't you, Raik?'

'You from Trabzon, eh? Tell us about your folk. From the town itself, or from thereabouts?'

'I come from the city. My people are called Mıhçıoğlu. And where do you come from?'

'Me, I'm from Tonya. What's your job?'

'I teach mathematics. What do you do?'

'I see . . . You're a bookish bloke; well, I got my learning from the school of life. I build apartment blocks and sell 'em. Build and sell, build and sell. Make a pile of brass, mind you . . . Thank God.'

'How nice. I wish you the best of fortune.'

It was no doubt fortunate that the contractor from Tonya did not take to the American businessman, Mr. Walker, the guest of honour on that evening, and the reason for Vicdan's having been invited.

'There are some mistakes that, no matter how you try to put them right, can only lead to other mistakes.' Such would be Raik's answer to his wife's question on their way home. 'This entire evening was that kind of mistake. Who is this American fellow? What does he do? What links these people together is very unclear.'

Clouds of suspicion have gathered in that atmosphere of sham cordiality. 'What does Burhan hope from contacts like these, what does he expect? Are they worth it?'

'My brother doesn't even have the time to bother with his sons. It's too bad,' said Vicdan.

Raik was in no mood to be interested in Burhan's teenage boys.

'He even tried, all for the sake of advancing himself in the party, to use the fact that I come from the Black Sea coast! A provincial accent? Damn it all, he wanted me to play a part in that contractor's farce!'

Raik was wildly indignant.

'A provincial accent!' he repeated, 'when we try so hard to get the younger generation to speak good Turkish!'

'Do you think we went too far, making people feel embarrassed about their backgrounds?'

'By no means! What can be more ridiculous than the pomposity of a fellow who can't speak his own mother tongue correctly, and all through his own fault? The only rational way forward for him is to improve his command of the language.'

Vicdan looked at her husband. Raik had always shown more interest in literature than could generally be expected of a mathematician. Had his inclination anything to do with Vicdan's being a woman of letters? Although the pronunciation of all the people Vicdan knew from the Black Sea coast showed some characteristics of the accent of their home region, Raik's did not have the slightest trace of the local dialect – yet he too had certainly started life with the Black Sea accent on his lips. Vicdan wondered whether her husband had been terribly embarrassed by his pronunciation when a student at the teacher-training college in Istanbul. The possibility made her shudder. Or did he have to exercise self-control so as not to make a mistake in front of his wife who came from Istanbul and had been educated in Western literature, in case he should lapse all too easily into the Trabzon dialect? Could it be so? Could you remain a stranger to the one who is closest to you? Burhan . . . Obviously she had never really known Burhan. Could there be a similar invisible wall between her and Raik? Agitated, her eyes searched her husband's profile. Oh no, I'm thinking nonsense. Trying to laugh, she said,

'You were invited for the contractor, and I for the American.'

Burhan was always proud of his sister who spoke English fluently.

'That American,' said Raik, 'another clown! Burhan was quite wrong to imagine the American had as fine a mastery of the English tongue as you do.'

'Why do Americans try so hard to make themselves agreeable by telling such stale jokes?' asked Vicdan.

'Because they don't have secure roots, they lack historical and cultural background. Yesterday's cowboys have gained control of almost the whole world. They don't possess the cultural wealth to shore up the power their government has laid hands on.'

'Would I seem paranoid if I confessed to the impression that our government has granted them certain rights, such as permission to search for oil and minerals?'

'Certainly not. It's as obvious as a geometric shape in black ink on white paper that our government is handing them some of our sovereign rights.'

'In return for what? What will we gain by it? Our country and us?'

'Nothing for our country or us, but a certain clique will make huge gains.'

'Burhan belongs to that clique then, doesn't he?'

Raik was silent. Vicdan sighed.

Wish Cumhur would come home safe.

'He will, my darling, he will, everything will be fine. Didn't I tell you during the War that our country would survive the blow, that none of us would die, but that we'd have to pay a price for our survival? Well, didn't that turn out to be right? Now, mark my words: Cumhur will return.'

Husband and wife drew closer together as they walked along the streets of an Ankara that day by day grew a stranger to them.

That night Vicdan jerked suddenly awake. What woke you, Vicdan? Was it something to do with your body? The sexual energy your body didn't use up in the swift movements of the dance? Her husband was sleeping peacefully beside her. She thought of Cumhur. The time must be 8.30 a.m. in Korea. Perhaps Cumhur was murdering someone at this very moment – or were they murdering him? Burhan had killed, Reha had killed, Cumhur had killed!

She lived in a country supposed to have been at peace for thirty years, and only Raik's hands were clean, only his! She embraced her husband thankfully, taking care not to wake him, as he slept like an innocent babe.

Is he asleep or in a coma? Difficult to tell. Blood-pressure is too low, heartbeat too slow. Adjust the drip of the serum. The blood test cannot explain the drop in blood-pressure. Burhan Bey, Burhan Bey, can you hear us? Strange . . . It's as if the patient is withdrawing into himself. Doesn't he want to live? Burhan Bey, the levels of vital ingredients in your blood are normal, you can live, please make an effort. He is too weak, obviously must have been starving himself lately. He will not make it, I'm afraid. He is too old.

The memory is ebbing – this is low tide – from conscious purpose, from what is accepted as reality to the primary state of matter; from the shores of the sea town, from the shrieks of seagulls, to the beginning, afloat in the warm maternal waters. The memory ebbs, tracing a huge, undulating spiral in the emptiness of space.

I learnt to love my uncle after my father died. But not immediately. Right after father's death, my uncle's efforts to mend the broken bond with mother alienated me, as he seemed to be seizing an opportunity made by death.

I was on my way to Istanbul. The seventies. What was the purpose of my journey? I have forgotten. My uncle met me. Where? I don't remember. It was a grey, wet day, yes I do remember that; I had not come to terms with the loss of my father yet, I remember; a fine sliver of emptiness throbbed within me. My uncle was wearing a grey raincoat, a grey felt hat, and a smart scarf.

He took my cold hand and tucked it under his arm; it was warm there, I remember. He could have been considered old then. His blue flashing eyes were greyish and weary. His shoulders drooped. I noticed it for the first time that day. His sons caused him pain, I knew that. He had grown thin. I was no longer afraid of him. He held his umbrella over my head, his other hand clasping the handle of my suitcase; his arms were still strong. We walked for some time close to each other, my hand under his arm. Evening was falling.

I thought everything was wrong with his life. His marriage, his mistresses, his relations with his boorish sons, his view of life, the wealth he had accumulated, his opulent but loveless domestic surroundings . . . the hell he went through after Uncle Reha's suicide, his cold treatment of Uncle Cumhur . . . his furious temper, his arrogance, his self-confidence verging on vanity . . .

Yes, they were all wrong, his political opinions, and his antagonism to the left, which intensified as he grew older and wealthier, manifesting themselves sometimes as hidebound states of mind, and sometimes in bouts of convulsive rage. He was devoted to Atatürk with a love almost verging on fanaticism, or at least, he asserted such devotion. Mustafa Kemal's portrait kept its place in his drawing-room even when all the furnishings were changed in the course of time. My uncle thought Mustafa Kemal the greatest man who ever lived. I certainly respected the revolutionary who fought against imperialism; but from whatever angle you viewed him, he was a leader of the petty bourgeoisie! I found it strange that he was almost worshipped, and difficult to grasp that, for my parents' and uncles' generation, Mustafa Kemal was one of the central pillars of their existence. All the same, I knew that the devotion and love my parents felt for Mustafa Kemal was demonstrable in their simple lifestyle, whereas my uncle and his family exhibited theirs in the pomposity of their language. It was wrong. My uncle's life . . . was wrong from start to finish.

Still . . .

I had begun to love him. And sensed that he loved me too. By that time we lived in different cities, but my uncle was playing a part in my life for the first time.

I began to examine him from another angle, before writing him off as a capitalist on the grand scale, swimming in dirty money.

On a number of occasions, I watched how he prepared a case file and organised his defence. An electric charge emitted by his brain seemed to stir the whitening fairness of his hair. His eyes grew huge and shone with a strange light. He prepared the defence like a commander drawing up battle plans, taking into account all possible factors. Then . . . he attacked. Watching him was for me equivalent to hearing the sounds and seeing the colours of that wonderful symphony which so enchanted me – of genesis, of the biochemical formulae you come across in academic works, of all those vital fluids, of compounds of stress and excitement, of the molecules of tension-effort-caution-warning-and-attacking. He homed in on his subject with the whole of his being, his tensed muscles like a hyena's as it lies in ambush; he smelt his opponent's weak point, soon he would spring and attack and, like a lion, seize him in his claws. After tearing the opposition to pieces, he would feel replete for a while and would walk away with a tiger's grandeur. He would not deign to gnaw another bone. The moment he was satisfied, he would become infinitely merciful. He would grow like a noble hero, like a saint in his wisdom, to greater heights than ordinary mortals. Perhaps mother loved him so much because of these sublime moments . . . Then . . .

He had filed the laws and their interpretations in court, and had stored them away in that extraordinary memory of his. He recalled any one of them with ease; he used his legal knowledge, like a skilled surgeon his lancet, to cut to the heart of the matter. His conduct of a case was fluent and impressive. He was indeed a punctilious legal practitioner. To what end did he take his profession so seriously? Was contributing to the realisation of justice the chief justification of his existence? No! Did the sheer power of that passionate bond of love and anger that was at once established between himself and a case attract him? By no means . . . My uncle loved to win! He had an insatiable appetite for rivalry and for beating his opponent! The reason? A lack of affection reaching back to his childhood? And there I stopped. What lay concealed in that childhood shared by my mother and two of my uncles? Evaluation of uncle Burhan's oppressive behaviour as a subconscious reaction and an aspiration to masculine identity, linked to the fact that he had been dressed in girl's clothes until he was three and a half years of age, seemed to me too facile a form of explanation. Life is both too complicated and too simple to be contained in such clichés.

By the bye, why did grandmother keep uncle Burhan's hair long and dress him up as a girl? I don't know. The human spirit is like the barn with forty doors in the fairy tale! The fortieth door always remains locked! The reason for my uncle's unappeasable hunger lies behind the fortieth.

The longing for love . . .

His relationship with Handan had long been over. My aunt had waited and won. But what had she won? There was a new woman in his life! An elderly, ordinary woman, devoid of charm, offering, no matter what the circumstances and without asking questions, peace to a weary man. The new woman was the final blow for my aunt, felling her; she could not, no matter how hard she tried, get up on her feet. It was the final failure of the strategy of a lifetime. She had borne the suffering infidelity inflicted with the expectation that in old age her husband would be left to her and only to her. The new affair was in no way comparable to the fire of love Handan had kindled, to that insatiable flame which in its fierce integrity had consumed itself . . . What was it then? My aunt was not remotely able to understand this recent relationship. She tried in vain to use her old tactic of patience, of pretending not to know . . . Until when? My aunt grew more bitter with every new day. The years were flowing by, life was getting shorter. Everyone in the family knew about the new woman and kept silent. Who would dare to confront the omnipotent severity of this father? Husband and wife continued to live in their elegant home, with the minimum of communication. The sons had left their father's house, unloading the continuing burden of their endless problems on his doorstep. My uncle could no longer divest himself of these inconveniences as he used to do, bribing them, reprimanding them, and offloading on to my aunt their stormy relations with the schools they attended. His sons had laid hands on his whole life, and were sucking his wealth dry. These sons were attacking from four directions at once . . . And right at his shoulder was the threatening, interminable silence of his wife, that was utterly tireless. How lonely you were, dear uncle! And you were quite unaware of it! You imagined your power to be infinite! My poor uncle, how you resembled King Lear! Burhan could not be called a very generous soul, but he would always spend freely whenever his wife or sons asked him. Perhaps it was the easiest way of atoning for his faults. He had transferred the deeds of all his properties to my aunt, back in the days of Handan, as proof positive that he would never desert his wife.

> She cared neither for wealth nor property. She knew that I was the father of a family and would never leave them. Not once did she ask me to get a divorce.

He made himself believe that he had done his duty by his family, by never abandoning them. Of course it was no use . . . Wealth and the ownership of property neither helped to soothe my aunt's suffering nor stopped her growing bitter. Finding herself suddenly in the position of a wealthy woman gave her a self-confidence which resembled her husband's, but was emptier than his, lacking any stable foundation. She simply turned into the vain semblance of a lady.

The childlike mannerisms that made her quite attractive in her young days had become repellent affectations in a woman grown elderly without maturity. She was miserable and absurd, derisory but dangerous. The toll to be levied for her being cheated could not possibly be the deeds of mere properties. How could my uncle not see that an emotional blow can only be countered by another emotional blow? The concession my aunt demanded was that he should give up all close relationships other than the new woman. In a way my aunt reduced him to a loneliness as black as hers. So in the final years of their lives they were like two wild animals kept in the same cage. My uncle's health was not too good, and he was gradually winding up his legal practice, thus losing the excuse of business trips which enabled him to be with the new woman. The power passed to my aunt's domain! The hour of revenge had struck!

In those days my uncle turned to religion. A superficial glance would have suggested that religiosity was a natural extension of his right-wing political views. It was not so simple . . . He was passionately religious, enthusiastically so. He had found God in the wilderness of his loneliness, or that was what he imagined.

Passion . . . My mother's and uncle's beings burned with a bright flame. It was not easy for me to discover this truth; it took years. The flame was hidden in the decorous, respectable shapes of their lives . . . In my uncle's life, respectability was confined to appearance only, for those who knew about Handan and the new woman. It could be thought that his professional success was no more than the flamboyant fireworks of a hungry passion that was consuming his whole life. Whereas my mother's life was pellucid; she was a flame burning in a crystal jar. The graceful, joyous reflections on the outer surface were shaped by her inner fire. My mother's passion was directed to creation, even at the risk of dimming her inner light; whereas my uncle's was directed to possession.

My uncle gave up religion in his later years when he was a weak and tottering old man. Could a true believer behave in this way?

—My back hurts badly, I can't kneel down any more.

—Dear uncle, you can pray while you're sitting.

—It doesn't mean a thing. What's the point . . .

His passion had been extinguished. God was the last lover he abandoned. A short time later he died, a few months after my mother.

How hard it is to define love! The complex of our emotions is like a sphere whose surface is covered with hairline cracks and small protuberances. Cracks which are fine but deep, going right to the core. People move towards one another and then away, like planets in space . . . Then if one sphere extends a fine filament which fits exactly into an invisible crack on another, that is love . . . A brief encounter . . . a rare coincidence . . . a moment . . . a bond destined to break off painfully, unable to sustain the combined weight of the spheres. If no other force parts those who love, death will . . .

Probably my uncle could not absorb my mother's death, his mind was too disturbed, too turbid. His wounded memory was busy with other deaths, with my grandmother, with my uncles Reha and Cumhur. Sometimes still, a youthful gleam shone in his grey eyes, like a reflection on the present of that wonderful intelligence that belonged to the past; it only lasted a short time, then the gleam died away. My uncle was sinking into the ocean of oblivion, like an old vessel abandoned to decay.

Their sons did not visit them often; my aunt pursued petty revenges like condemning my uncle to hunger. I was one of the few who knocked on their door. During that time I loved them both with a heart-rending tenderness. My aunt who refused mercy and forgiveness was preparing her own end; it was impossible to make her see this. I wanted to make my visits longer, but could not bear the smell of old woodwork, decay, and mould emitted by the deteriorating tissues and texture of that claustrophobic house. I could not endure the resentment and the anger. All their wealth had melted away, and they were on short commons. Their sons would gladly and willingly have sold the elegant flat their parents lived in, but they did not dare, as they still dreaded, by long-established habit, the old, bent shadow that had once been Burhan Yurdakul. Straight after my uncle's death, they took charge of their mother, sold the flat and shared the money. They put their mother in an alms-house, deserted her, and forgot about her.

I could not bear to visit my uncle on his deathbed, when he was unable to recognise anyone. The last time we had been together, I had confronted a creature in such a state of disintegration that my heart could not endure to witness a further stage of his deterioration. The thread that had stitched together the many fabrics of his mind had broken; his mental faculties had been reduced to the mere processing of his organic functions.

I cannot imagine a phenomenon more capable of offering proof that 'man' is an illusion consisting of carbon, hydrogen, nitrogen and oxygen, than the sight of my aged, worn-out, doomed uncle.

In all likelihood I did not visit him so as to punish myself. Witnessing the final stage might have been less painful than imagining and thinking about his end in the weeks preceding and following his death. Why did I feel the need to be punished? What had I done wrong? Remaining alive while another departed! . . . That was my guilt . . .

I only realised how much I loved my uncle when he was dying. How selfish we are . . . How much more important it seems to us that the tiny fissures in our souls should be filled, than that we should spend precious time on the differences between political opinions, the wrongs inflicted on others . . .

I have shared moments with Burhan, the memory of which is worth a lifetime. Burhan and I . . . twin souls . . . What is life, if not a long remembering . . . Raik and I always completed each other. He always anticipated my impulses which never surfaced as reactions, and balanced them against his rationality. So my husband and I always lived in harmony. Did his level-headedness ever waver? Did a gale of discontent ever blow through his spirit? He never disclosed any ups and downs. Why then the sense of guilt that has not left me since he died? What kind of path would my life have followed, if I had married someone like Burhan? Twin souls . . . With one big difference: Burhan was always quick to react, whereas I am in the habit of controlling my impulses. Burhan was the same as a child. He used to urge Reha into some act of mischief and then, when my mother got annoyed, and Reha, crestfallen, would crouch in a corner, Burhan would set up a cry of 'Please, mother, beat me, please don't touch my big brother Reha, he hasn't done a thing!' Probably he was telling the truth; but such generosity of heart and such self-sacrificial fervour would illumine his face and his way of speaking that mother simply could not believe him and so beat Reha as well.

After our father's death, I became a second mother to them. I liked them calling me 'big sister', I looked after them lovingly, washing their clothes and pressing their trousers at weekends when they were home from the Military Academy, as I didn't want mother to get too tired. Those were the days when they shared their little secrets, and giggled all the time; I was not curious about what they were up to. They would compete for my love, and that was enough for me.

Reha never grew up, he remained childlike and credulous, gazing at life with the uncomprehending eyes of innocence. Burhan . . . perhaps he was excessively grown-up . . . I could seldom share a feeling or an insight with Reha, but he could be taught things; his attention could be directed to almost any topic. It is the same with Cumhur. Of course, you should keep in mind that Cumhur and I are of different generations. Still, I have always wondered if the reason for Reha's and Cumhur's remoteness from life was the military profession. But our father was a soldier too. His kind, who had been driven from frontier to frontier, fighting and suffering, were almost like savants or saints. And then Burhan and İzzet were also trained to be officers, but they left the army early, and life took them in different directions.

Burhan has changed greatly . . . How beautiful life was, on the day we climbed Uludağ. I treasure the memory of that day in my heart, fresh and unspoilt. Some part of my soul always remembers the moment at the summit. Burhan and Reha have forgotten. No, I don't believe that they have. They don't want to remember, they don't even dare to remember. But in spite of all his denials, there's a spot in Burhan's heart as tender as mine, I know. And so I forgive him, in spite of what he did to our mother, to the corpse of our brother Reha, to the memories of Mustafa Kemal and Salonika; in spite of all the bitter disputes in our relationship, and the years of estrangement and pain . . .

The city by the sea, the avenue along the shore . . . gulls fly in circles around the Beyaz Kule, spiralling from the surface of the Aegean to the sky.

Spirals are disintegrating in Burhan Yurdakul's tissues. The strands of protein are growing thinner and fraying, memories are being cast adrift, floating away. The one that is lost last had been consigned to the deepest level, the one which consciousness relegated to the very foundations, or the one from the very beginning. The primal memory . . . the smell of the open sea, the wind . . . The maternal fluid once protected so warmly, gently, the tissue that would transform into the baby Burhan, while Fitnat Hanım walked, swaying, along the avenue by the sea, sniffing the Macedonian breeze, breathing the air laden with iodine, drawing it into her vital core, into her blood and into the foetus in her womb. Birthplace: Salonika . . .

How did Burhan Yurdakul's birth certificate reach Vicdan? It doesn't matter. The point is that Vicdan saw what had been cancelled on it. It is the late fifties, Vicdan is nearly fifty, she has put on some weight, her shoulders are broader and her breasts are bigger, but she is still handsome, and – you wonder how she still keeps her graceful, slim-seeming posture. Fitnat Hanım is very old, she has closed up her home, and lives as a visitor at her daughter's or sons'; she is not on particularly affectionate terms with her daughters-in-law, but the arrangements for her old age work out without too much friction. Then Burhan's wife announces to her in-laws that she will not be able to receive her mother-in-law any more. Why? Her change of heart coincides with the period when her husband turns all the deeds of his property over to her, with the days after the Handan affair has ended, and when the new woman has appeared on the scene.

Vicdan will not forgive Burhan's silent consent to his wife's declaration, and will hold Burhan responsible for their mother's broken heart; her relations with Burhan will cease until after Raik's death.

At the time when the wronged wife engineered her *fait accompli*, Burhan's identity card found its way into Vicdan's hands! A minor coincidence, perhaps some oversight. Probably it was Burhan who left it in Vicdan's house, although not on purpose. It could have slipped out of his pocket while he was desperately, clumsily, trying to persuade Vicdan to accept that *fait accompli*.

Before returning it to her brother, Vicdan just cast an eye over it; and was transfixed with anger and amazement!

Name:	Burhan
Father's name:	Hayreddin
Mother's name:	Fitnat
Date of birth:	1912
Place of birth:	İzmir

Vicdan's shock did not last long; what had happened struck her at once, and her anger grew.

There is no notion of 'coming from Macedonia' in Vicdan's mind. She is a citizen of the Turkish Republic, her mother tongue is Turkish. Her place of birth is Salonika, just as it was Mustafa Kemal's. She would never dream of concealing the fact. If she has to name a locality to explain her background, she prefers to say Istanbul where some of her childhood and her adolescence was spent.

Her brother Burhan has given in to the regionalism which started to show itself under the Democratic Party government, and he means to take advantage of this situation for his own political and financial ends. Macedonia and Thrace are not counted among the regions! People from these places had to cope with social ostracism when they migrated back to Anatolia; after they had lost their homelands, the migrants did not cling to their regional identity by way of antagonistic reaction, as many of them individually had moved past the stage of identification with the old localities, evolving with them and from them into a national consciousness; they spread throughout Anatolia and let the motherland absorb them. But this absorption had not been totally acceptable from the point of view of the motherland. The phrase 'from overseas' indicates the kind of exclusion experienced. Vicdan considers such expressions inevitable and of minor importance, they will disappear given time. Hadn't even Nefise, her soul mate, displayed this kind of tactlessness?

But a controversial development is being debated in Turkey at present: Turkish citizens are being categorised as Northerners, Easterners, Aegeanites, Southeasterners, and so on. Had these groupings always existed, or had the multi-party system set loose what a one-party regime had kept under control? Probably the latter. But Vicdan and Raik are convinced that supporting what has risen to the surface, trying to keep it there, and strengthening it – such tactics are pushing a nation on the verge of coalescence back into the miseries of fragmentation. Burhan and Vicdan have a serious difference of opinion over this issue. Vicdan refuses to believe that Burhan genuinely approves of regionalism. Burhan is a hypocrite! His ambition neither acknowledges loyalties nor hears the voice of wisdom. Vicdan is disgusted with her brother, the one she loves best. A part of her disbelief remains, nourishing her fury. She has analysed the situation, but her heart rebels against accepting that Burhan is at one with what she has perceived! Whereas the facts are obvious.

A man who takes all the trouble of applying to the courts, and finding witnesses to legitimate the tale that he was born in İzmir! What more is this man capable of! He cannot be the brother I love.

For the first and last time in her life, Vicdan tries to plan revenge! She will go to Burhan's office with a smile on her face, a friendly expression, take him by surprise, and watch him to her heart's content as he shrivels under the pressures of pain, remorse, and shame. Then she will pour contempt on his pettiness and leave, slamming the door!

It will be to Raik's benefit that Vicdan has dismissed Burhan from her life; as from now on she will turn wholeheartedly and with utter devotion to her husband, closing her eyes to the tottering physical aspect of their marriage.

Burhan's office. Vicdan enters smiling. She is dressed in one of her simple but elegant suits. She is an excellent actress. (Another of her hidden talents?)

After some desultory conversation . . . (Burhan has relaxed. He had thought at first that his sister's visit was another attempt to put pressure on him on her mother's behalf.) She opens her bag carefully but casually (Burhan does not suspect anything), takes out the identity card with lightning speed, opens the page where 'İzmir' is recorded, and flings the card on the desk.

LIAR! UNGRATEFUL SWINDLER! HOW CAN ANYONE EXPECT ANYTHING WORTHWHILE FROM SOMEONE WHO DENIES HIS ORIGIN!

How ignorant you are about life! As innocent and uninformed as a child. You and my brother-in-law live in a fairy-tale world made up of your lessons, your students, books, and ideals! That isn't the real world! Do you know what this country has been going through?

The sum total of compromises, of surrendering, of abandoning the ideals that reason and conscience approved of – that's being 'realistic', is it? What connection with the 'real' can anyone have, when they get entangled in all the bickerings and frustrations of daily life?
You have no idea of the people you live among.

I have taught students from all over Turkey. How can you accuse me of not knowing my people? I feel the pulse of the nation at my finger tips. I teach young people western literature, I talk to them about feelings and sensitivities shared by every living soul. I teach them how our traditional literature is not fully equipped to catch and express the evolutions and alterations in life, that we have to turn our faces towards other civilisations, and that on no account must we forget our starting point as we do so. I tell them that a tide flowing from the East to the West will ensure the uniqueness of Turkish literature, that a nation cannot survive by making war, but endures by cultivating art and literature. Can there be a better expression of truth?

Your students listen to you, but how do they react?

They are teaching all over Turkey. I know how they live.

What are their rewards then?

Who expects rewards? Our reward is our work.

You are deceiving yourself. Life is a relentless competition, a deadly struggle . . . That is what you are trying to evade. Life passes you by, your hands are empty, apart from beautiful words! You and my brother-in-law are constantly trying to design things, build things, create things, you don't take your own lives seriously, and your creations are nothing but shadows. And life is not endless. Look at me; see how fiercely I fight, I win cases, and money! In this country, business works on the basis of which region you come from. I would not have been able to secure half my cases if Salonika had remained my birthplace!

Why İzmir?

It had to be convincing. I have a fair complexion and a good accent.

It may seem valid, but what a superficial reason. It lacks roots, and so it's doomed to wither in the long run.
I know the value of my own life.

Every mortal who knows the value of life, and who has an atom of sense in his head, tries to build a 'tomorrow', simply for the reason that life is ephemeral.

If hard-working people who build the 'present', like me, didn't exist, how on earth would you people build a future, what ground would you take your stand on?

I don't take my stand on any ground remotely resembling yours! I grow from the foundations of the Republic!

Do you really believe what you're saying? That it's possible to reach your goals with illiterate peasants and a bunch of rough, coarse provincials? Atatürk's revolution has lasted until now. That's all. We are so terribly alone! That's what you so insistently avoid seeing. We are alone, especially people like us.

How dare you scorn your society in this way? Who are we, if we cut ourselves off from the rest of the population?

We, the intellectuals , the civilised few.

And pray, who are the ones you call 'people like us'?

The migrants from Western Thrace, from Macedonia!

You are a racist!

Freedom was a wind blowing from the mountains of Macedonia! It could not reach the arid Anatolian plain.

We have been spreading like fertile seeds all over Anatolia, See what shrubs we have grown into . . . This ancient soil will bless us forty times over . . .

How could anyone be so optimistic? How could you interpret this enduring faith of Vicdan's, whose whole life was spent in fearing the loss of those she loved, in disquiet and anguish, in sick imaginings?

Vicdan is not aware that she is speaking of her own experience. The young sapling, that had shot up from the ruins of her childhood, turned away from the prospect of an icy death in the northern climate she had been sent to, growing strong, putting slender roots down not only into Anatolia but into the age-old continent, and stretching her branches out to the whole world. She has managed to return to life, along with her country, and to stand erect.

Burhan felt unbelievably weary. His back ached. He did not want to lose Vicdan, but he was losing her. They stood on opposite shores of reality. Vicdan would not compromise; he would have to go over to her shore in order not to lose her. But his life was too cumbersome, too intricately involved to make such a move. Vicdan's optimism, continually refreshing itself, wearied him.

> You have forgotten, this is the land of Cybele! You have forgotten the legend I told you on the top of Uludağ. Just as you have forgotten everything else! Take Mustafa Kemal's picture down off your wall, you are not worthy to look at it! You have forgotten your mother, you have forgotten Vecdet, Handan, Dersim, and Salonika! A day will come when you will have proof that you could not forget completely! I have no wish to be at your side on such a day!

Our mother, my husband and our two brothers had died. The distance between Burhan and me seemed absurd to both of us. True, we were situated very differently in life, but that should not have prevented us from reaching out to each other. Sometimes I travelled to Istanbul and stayed with him and his wife. My sister-in-law cherished no great affection for me, but she was so terribly lonely that I think she liked my visits. In those days, they lived on the Anatolian side of Istanbul. We used to take long walks, Burhan and I, towards the hill of Dragos. His wife would not join us, she did not enjoy the open air and the meadows. I would remember when I was a young girl, and the walks I took with Nefise, back in Cambridge. Then there was the ascent of Uludağ with Burhan and Reha . . . The things we found to tell one another when we were young. We talked and talked. But now we kept silent, probably because we had no need for words. We knew everything about each other, a mass of material, the greater part of which had never been uttered in words – but we knew.

Vecdet, Handan, the women he loved, and the woman he did not love, his wife . . . And other matters, unmentioned . . . Those he called 'friends' . . . I wonder what became of the contractor? Burhan had lost his former ambitions and his violent temper.

I could not grow old with my husband. Instead, I was sharing the winter of life with my brother. We knew that we would not be together for long. His eyesight was poor, and my movements were growing slower and slower. A few more years, and we would be unable to leave our homes. And we lived in different cities. We would ring each other up. Our voices would reach out . . . But then, we had not much to talk about anyway . . . then, life would snuff out like a candle . . . and . . . I would not be at his side.

Towards the end, memory moves towards the point from which it started . . . Memory is like the setting sun, whose last rays are bright, but light a diminishing field. Burhan Bey cannot speak. Cannot utter what he remembers. He has no links with his surroundings, he cannot see, he cannot move. His mind's connections are confined within the circle of remembrance, the diameter of which is narrowing and moving swiftly to the starting point. Which electric current between which cells has decided on what shall be recalled? What chemical reaction has chosen these memories scored most deeply of all into the electrons hidden in his body's tissues? Who was the last counsel for the prosecution, the last sentencing judge? This is the last defence of the lawyer Burhan Bey! Separate off those memories where the accounts are settled, they may be forgotten now; remember those where something is owing.

Your wife and sons . . .
        I don't owe them anything . . . I have paid . . .
    Vicdan . . .
        she did make me suffer . . .
      Raik . . .
        I settled my account with him . . .

Who is left . . .

Cumhur . . . Reha. . . fighting . . . Mustafa Kemal . . . Salonika . . . my mother . . . Handan . . .

Memory works like this, sometimes leaping, sometimes skipping back. Memories mingle with imaginings . . . Cumhur . . . I met him . . . on his return . . . from where . . . from Dersim . . . by ship . . . from Korea . . . Mustafa Kemal . . . always . . . I followed in his footsteps . . . Reha . . . always . . . I was on his side . . . after . . . the fight . . . after . . . pistol . . . head . . . the side of the head . . . temple . . . morte . . . muerto . . . morto . . . a goner . . . no . . . no . . . morgue . . . he's lying . . . no . . . in the grave . . . his tall . . . bo-dy . . . in-tact . . . my mother . . . in my ho-me . . . by my side . . . Handan . . . my beloved . . . is weeping . . . my mother . . . died . . . no . . . no . . . I have/not/de-ser-ted . . . I have . . . mur-dered . . . fighting . . . command-duty . . . the dead . . . far-a-way . . . cold . . . snow . . . white . . . bl-ue . . . sca . . . ma-ma . . . ho-mc . . . my ho me . . . s..a..lo..n..i..KA! SALONIKA!!!! my ho-me . . . Sa . . . lo . . . nika . . .

A HAPPY MARRIAGE

Certainly, theirs was a happy marriage . . . An egalitarian marriage . . . He gave up smoking as his wife disliked the smell, she continued with her career, accepting a teaching job in a secondary school so as to be posted to the town where her husband worked. He resigned his post as a schools inspector, because his tours were lengthy and his wife dreaded being alone. She never even dreamed of publishing the poems and stories she had written, not wanting to outdo him. He learnt how to dance, how to enjoy theatre and opera, she learnt how to accommodate herself to her husband's provincial relatives. He put up with Fitnat Hanım's peevishness, Reha's problems, and Burhan's violent temper so that she would not be upset; she coped with his illnesses. He went shopping while she cooked. He lit the stove while she was ironing. No one ever saw them quarrel, no one ever heard them complain, until death did them part. Theirs was a happy marriage, for sure.

Mother, did you ever consider divorce? I mean, all married people do at some time or other.

No.

Were you ever attracted to another man, after you were married?

No.

How about my father? Did he ever chase after another woman?

I don't think so.

So your love lasted . . .

My mother is thoughtful, and then asks:

Why did his heart start to fail? Why did he suffer from high blood-pressure all his life?

Do you mean to suggest that he was under strain? You shouldn't ignore hereditary factors in heart and circulatory diseases.

He came from a long-lived family.

He might have suffered from stress at work, in his profession. Don't forget that we live in a country where 'Truth's a dog must to kennel'.

Yes, he didn't get on well with the bureaucrats.

You have nothing to reproach yourself for, you looked after him devotedly, you stayed awake for any number of nights without any complaint.

I loved him very much.

I know. What was your sex life like?

What a thing to ask!

I remember you two as always sharing a brotherly-sisterly kind of love.

You're too young and inexperienced to realise that what you call 'brotherly-sisterly love' is the most important bond in life, and the most difficult kind of relationship to achieve and keep between two people.

It wouldn't be enough for me – I was referring, not to something which is shaped and preserved, but to something which exists and develops spontaneously, those sensations that take you over, obliterate your will, your ability to make any independent move. A shy, youthful smile flickered across her aged face. I remembered the photographs of my parents, taken when they were a young couple, I remembered my father's handsome face, his sensual mouth, and my mother's limpid fragility, like a delicate lantern reflecting her inner fire.

We found each other very attractive.

You mean your bodies, your flesh?

It could be put like that, as well.

The attraction you felt for each other stayed alive all those years!..

During those last years neither of us was in the best of health.

I remember you two, always ailing. What were the first years like?

Wonderful.

You mean the desire or the fulfilment?

The enduring desire, and the unattainable fulfilment . . . How devastating! She had no intention of speaking. Still, I insisted. It seemed to me she was slowly opening up, and slowly relaxing.

The desire was wonderful and burning hot. The fulfilment . . . I was afraid to let myself go . . . As if some inner obstacle got in my way.

The pressure of how you were brought up.

Yes, but still, there seemed to be something else.

What?

I can't remember . . . I felt the desire and was frightened.

Were you always frightened?

Ever since I can remember.

Did something horrible happen to you?

No . . . When do you mean?..

In your infancy, or perhaps when you were a child?

After my father died . . . during the years of the occupation . . . I don't know.

At your uncle's? You disliked the place.

I can't remember, I've grown old . . . Your father was afraid as well.

What was he afraid of?

He dreaded premature ejaculation.

I was taken aback! It was the first time I had heard mother utter a sexual expression. She smiled tenderly:

And because he was afraid, it used to happen to us often.

I found it interesting that she said 'to us', instead of 'to him'.

What do you think caused it?

He was rather inexperienced. He had not known many women. He put me on a pedestal, treated me like a flower he dared not smell. Your father cherished an excessively high regard for women.

Very unusual in this country!

The resentment for the hurts I had suffered at men's hands echoed in my voice, I could not help it.

In my time, men, at least the educated ones, showed unfailing respect for women.

The success of Kemalism!

It might have been their mothers' influence. Your paternal grandmother was a woman of iron will. When I look back . . . my mother seems so too.

Fitnat Hanım?

They had to be, all those women who had to survive with their children during the war years.

'War' . . . is not as remote as it used to be in my childhood. Officers of my uncle Cumhur's generation had become generals making 'military interventions', one after another. Uncle Cumhur would joke in his rare light-hearted moments, 'Thank God I left my leg in Korea, otherwise I might have become one of them, and made yet another precipitous intervention!'

We had been living through a time of tremendous social upheaval, even reigns of terror; people had been murdered, among them some of my friends. My husband could have been killed, or I might have been! Survival was a matter of luck, just as in wartime. Then there was the era of military coups!

After so many years, my mother and I were friends at last, long after the tantrums of adolescence, and parental authority had been transcended. For the first time, I was beginning to grasp the permanent effects that 'war' had left her with.

I have a feeling that my brothers' – Reha and Burhan's – relations with our mother weren't very healthy.

A mother and her children huddled together in the midst of terror and loneliness! That kind of intimacy, the warmth of those bodies, you get used to it so easily . . . The fear of loss, the sense of possession, the love deviating into oppression . . . The hazards from which a mother can or cannot protect her children, each according to her own ability . . .

Who knows, perhaps our daughter-mother relationship was unhealthy as well. Our mother stopped touching us, caressing and kissing us, after our father died. Why? I was so sad. When father was alive, he used to make me sit on his lap, and tell me that he loved me, his only daughter Vicdan, best of all his children. He used to give me such a lot of confidence.

Good old Colonel Hayreddin Bey, how and when did you learn to act like a psychologist? When you were acting as a father to young officers and soldiers on the road to death? How did you treat your own sons, Burhan and Reha?

Everything changed after my father's death. Life was hard at my uncle's in Istanbul. Some time later, my mother remarried, and we children were sent to boarding-schools for orphans. Years later my mother told me she was afraid of dying, of being killed while living in occupied Istanbul. She deliberately stopped touching us so that we would grow used to her absence. She thought we could only be made stronger by this treatment.

Trust was being lost and destroyed, time and again . . . I was beginning to grasp the obsessive need my mother had for a stable relationship. It would not be enough for me . . . I was raised in a confined but very secure environment, in our family of three. How I loved my father, and still do! But why was there this small voice inside me, whispering that some wrong had been done to my mother? Was it the foul sediment of life silting up inside me, that muddied my perceptions?

It was the time I was making up my mind to a divorce. My mother was sad; she would have liked my marriage to continue, as she was fond of my husband. Ours was an unhappy marriage, raucous and full of rows. But it had its interesting aspect, a peculiar integrity. My marriage did not harbour secrets or hidden longings. It was peculiar in this, as people do not usually live so nakedly, and I was the perpetrator. Sincerity always distresses men! I was no longer unhappy, and was slowly reaching the satiation point of solving all the riddles of the labyrinth, of living entirely through a process, a relationship.

It was not my intention to prove to my mother that all marriages are burdened with pain. I only wanted to understand her, that was the one and only reason for my insistence. I felt I did not know her well enough, and thought she did not really know herself either. Frustrated, controlled passion . . . I had nothing to hide from her, and hoped she would have a more tranquil old age if the curtain of mystery within her were raised.

Now I am willing to admit that I really did not know my mother when she was alive. Probably no daughter (or son) can do so. My mind is drawing a different portrait of her as I go through her mementoes, her letters, poems and reminiscences, after the pain of losing her has furnished my insight with a gentle urgency, helping it to penetrate further. It cannot be proved, but some intuition stemming from my physical being, tells me that the new portrait is closer to reality . . .

When she was alive, I judged her according to the values of my generation, although she was someone of an entirely different era. Our fates were different despite our similarities.

Our rebellions and our concessions to life could not be identical. During the time which had elapsed between her generation and mine, the conceptual areas behind words like 'self', 'body', and 'present moment' had altered.

There were two men, besides my father and uncle Burhan, to whom my mother was passionately devoted, Mustafa Kemal and Nazım Hikmet. She wrote a poem after Nazım's death, addressing him as 'the man who is truly my heart's desire'. This must have been her only infidelity to my father!

She had a very simple way of linking the loves she cherished for Mustafa Kemal (the advocate of social justice but no socialist) and Nazım (a communist who was all the same devoted to the Gazi). These two loves were the gates through which her inner self entered the world of politics; historical and social issues seeped through these gates, filling her being and introducing her to complex and idiosyncratic sensations. It was utterly intriguing . . . For my generation, enthusiasm for the masses lay outside the individual world of feelings – at least such an attitude of mind was generally accepted as 'correct' . . . whereas mother drew whole lungfuls of the political wind blowing her way, assimilating it to her very existence; this process of absorption gave her emotional satisfaction, although sometimes it caused her anxiety.

I recognised precisely the same quality in elderly people whose lives had followed similar paths to mother's. The idealism of these old ladies and that of my generation were cut from very different cloth. 'Exceedingly romantic, but insufficiently aware!'; their attitude could be summed up by such a phrase, but to what extent would such a superficial pronouncement reflect the reality of any individual's existence? Politics was a subject which my mother and her contemporaries lived within their innermost selves until the very end, whereas our inner lives, during the period when we were involved in politics, were reduced almost to the point of no return.

The communication between her inner domain and the outside world set my mother's private reflections on a different orbit. The satisfactions she abstained from were not as essential to her as I took them to be. She was perfectly sincere on the conscious level when she declared, 'I have no regrets'. But what of the subconscious, the spinal cord, the muscles, veins, nerves and blood? Her body felt estranged from her, and became ill! That 'body' was not a priority with her, as she belonged to the generation which divided human existence decisively into 'body' and 'soul'.

She was aware that all her life since childhood had been a struggle demanding a huge expenditure of energy; and that awareness satisfied her. She had lived through the years of constructing the republic as if through a blissful *grand amour*! It was this all-absorbing love which was the high point of her emotional life.

I also was experiencing deep love. My daughter was still very young, attending primary school, as my mother's infirmities increased; sometimes I could scarcely breathe in the midst of my responsibilities for the pair of them; and still, in my own way, I was experiencing a *grand amour*, a happy affair. Those were the days when I quitted biochemistry and turned my attention to literature. Mother regarded this professional metamorphosis with open satisfaction, while her view of my relationship was tinged with anxiety, though not without a hint of secret pleasure. I cannot say for certain that she really approved of free love, but she did not reject it either. She learnt to accept my way of life. She realised that I had closed the book of marriage for ever.

Mine was an affair like all affairs: immediately after reaching its peak, it slid into the abyss of disharmony, smashing painfully to pieces. It would end, start afresh, and fall to pieces again. I did not mention the endings to my mother, refraining from causing her grief, and saving myself the embarrassment of admitting recurrent reunions. Mother lay on her bed, half conscious, for the greater part of the day, so I did not imagine she would notice details. At home, I would look for corners to hide in, to avoid bumping into my mother or daughter, when the longing and pain within me reached unmanageable proportions. I had an intense need to be on my own, which I was not, yet still I felt engulfed by a dreadful sense of desperate loneliness.

When the pain lessened, I clung to my domestic responsibilities, hiding under the reassuring turmoil of family concerns the signs of suffering that my eyes and throat exuded. Looking back, my condition seems tragi-comic, irrational and heroic, pushing dishes into the oven while my heart never ceased to bleed.

Mother took me by surprise! How on earth could she tell what was happening?

'The poet' hasn't been around, has he? He hasn't even phoned.

What could I say? She had diagnosed correctly. I gathered she knew 'the poet' better than I did.

He got you too easily. So now he will treat you badly and he'll soon fall out of love.

I tried desperately to defend my relationship, in spite of the existence of the 'other woman'. Then came a day when all of a sudden the large space in my heart where I had stored the pain vanished! A frenzy of violence seized me; it lasted no more than a moment, a single moment, to secure release from the anguish I had been living through. An unpremeditated, uncalculated, unexpected and unforgettable moment of violence! Probably this vindictiveness was the very last gasp of the tangle of feelings, almost crushed to death in my subconscious, and struggling for one last breath of life.

I was immensely relieved. I had no intention of telling mother about my bout of frenzy. It would be quite impossible for anyone as controlled and courteous as she was to tolerate such aggression. But in spite of my resolve, I found myself telling her:

> They were in the restaurant where we two used to dine. The things we talked about, across that table . . . How could he bring another woman to the selfsame spot? What poor taste. He could not possibly have guessed that I would pop in.

My mother laughed.

> He is a poet.

> How do you mean?

> What I mean is, it's nothing to do with poor taste; he's experimenting, wants to experience sensations that are different from those of ordinary mortals, so he's gambling with life.

The psychological analysis she had just made in her bedridden state tired her, and she let her head droop on to her pillow. What she had said surprised me; she was going through an interesting development as she aged and as her illness advanced. She was using a language, even a discourse, that was new to her during the hours when her mind was clear – pure Turkish, not the Ottoman dialect she had used from her youth!

> He imagines it's the only way to nourish creativity. It excites him to witness a confrontation between his two mistresses.

> It's a cruel game.

> So his excitement is followed by remorse. See how many feelings your 'poet' samples with one spoon!

> How can you be so sure?

Mother repeated the phrases she always used, not without pride.

> I know people. I know writers and poets as well. I have taught literature to students from all over Turkey. Literature's subject is

humanity, don't forget.

She really knew!

If you don't want to be miserable, quit the sport!

I'm driving men out of my life.

You're a happy woman.

How could I be happy when my heart was broken? I thought she had used the word 'happy' instead of another word which she could not remember, as her mind was not as clear as I had thought it was. Who knows, maybe it was precisely what she meant: 'happy'.

My mother was one of those who retreat into themselves when hurt. That was how she reacted when the *grand amour* of her life, the Republic, started to slip down the incline. According to my parents' shared opinion, the Republic had deviated from its destined path; they were truly unhappy, I knew, they felt wounded. Their common hurts bound them more closely together. They both withdrew into their shared shell of passive resistance, which could only be penetrated by means of the emotions. Their seclusion was not a sanctuary in which they had taken refuge, but their mutual resolve not to deign to play a part in a sordid world. Who knows, probably mother approved of my breaking my shell, severing my ties, and flinging them away!

She could see that all the demons she had confined in the depths of her being throughout her entire life had gathered in my mind – jealousy, outrage, vengeance, the pleasure of inflicting pain! I expelled all these demons by turning aggressive. I was free!

In the days following that incident, I felt her eyes gazing proudly at me. She was, in a way, relieved. Probably this was the first time she was truly convinced that I could cope with life on my own. She was all but revived, refreshed, and her health improved considerably for a while. I thought that 'life at that time was for her a long remembering'; that was what she had suggested. But no, it was not altogether true. She was, on her sick bed, living that 'present' that once she had continually postponed, together with that 'future' which had become impossible for her, by identifying with me. I think she had always done this, and I had always resented it. I had in my young days vehemently asserted my separateness from her.

But now, as I drew closer to middle-age and to losing her, the awareness of continuity as the most essential ingredient in life was dawning on me. One generation was born from the previous generation and blended into the following one. 'Separate identity' was nothing but a process of transition, like a wave, ebbing and flowing between two coalescing points. My mother's existence was dissolving into mine. And she was content with that. The smile which appeared from time to time on the mask of anxiety which was her face was an expression of her satisfaction, and did not only mirror the drops of delight her granddaughter splashed on her features.

Mother was having fun with water, enjoying the sensation it left on her skin, like a child discovering its body for the first time, learning with astonishment.

Her body was still beautiful for an eighty-year-old woman. I used to make jokes about it as I helped her nurse to wash her. Probably humour was my way of coping with the heavy responsibilities of our life . . . I poured a jug of water over her shoulders.

Your breasts are still like marble. What an endless source of oestrogen your body must be!

What's oestrogen?

Female hormones, material for your sexuality.

Talking about sexuality for no particular reason was an adolescent trick I had developed to tease my shy, reserved mother, to embarrass her. But she had grown used to this game and took no notice.

You are our child, Nefise's and mine.

Nefise had died before I was born. I had seen photos of her, she had been my mother's closest friend, her soul mate; I don't know why, but I had the impression that she had hurt my mother as well.

> She used to tease me like this. She was a joker, and a great expert in literature.

> I thought I was the daughter of you and Raik.

> Of course you are. But you are Nefise's child too.

Mother patted her arms and her thighs, enjoying her bath. Let this moment last for ever . . . The interplay of body and time slowly grew clearer to my mother's intuition as she grew childlike again. Body and time . . . It all came back . . . Nefise . . .

The flame grew feeble, and the lantern cracked, the flame touching the broken fragments of glass before it snuffed out, recalling the first and last person to enjoy its warmth . . . Nefise . . .

> My soul mate, I did not have to be discreet with her. My sister . . .

Soul mates are fictions, mother.

> Nefise was a skilled translator. She enriched our language with many works of literature. A pity she died so young. She used Turkish beautifully.

I had no doubt that my mother handled our language as skilfully as Nefise. In her last days, when the doctors were amazed as to why she did not suffer from dementia, she spoke Turkish better than I did. Language was something more than a conscious skill with her, it was instinctive. Why did she never have her prose and poetry published?

> Nefise's soul would be hurt.

Was my mother a saint or a coward who was scared of living? I do not know.

Nefise's ghost haunted our house, when I was a child. I sensed it. She was a shadow between my mother and father. I did not like this woman with her gamine hair-style, her broad shoulders and heavy bones.

And now I wished that I had known her. My mother had forgiven her, as she had forgiven everybody in her life.

While her body was slowly passing away from life, Vicdan's mind hovered above the ailing organism, like a meta-organ liberated from the body, continuing its slow, calm, tremulous functioning, as if intending to prove the separateness of body and soul.

She had never been untrue either to a person or to an idea. Was this luminosity within her mind the inner bond holding it together, preventing it from disintegrating into fragments?

TIME IN BURSA

An old mosque courtyard in Bursa
The small fountain splashing water
A wall from the time of Orhan
An ancient plane tree just as aged

Time's a crystal chandelier in Bursa
Made of wings' flutter and splashing water

Ahmet Hamdi Tanpınar

On the fifteenth day of July, 1935, Raik sat under the shade of a four-hundred-year-old plane tree, in an open-air café facing the back yard of the Bursa jail. On the wooden table, a cup of medium sweet coffee, and a glass of sweet fruit-flavoured soda water.

Day tastes like a ripe peach on the palate. Time is suspended in the air, thought Raik, like an element, like oxygen or nitrogen. Like honeyed sherbet in a misted glass, time falls in large, heavy drops . . . Raik lifted his head . . . from the leaves. To anyone looking down from the peak, the humidity must seem to shimmer like a white mist over the plain of Bursa. Vicdan is climbing Uludağ with her brothers, how crazy! Raik took a deep breath and thought, I am inhaling time. How quiet everything is . . . Like the moment a camera freezes; not so much as a leaf trembling, as if time has stopped . . . such a moment resembles looking at space through the wrong end of a telescope, in an effort to grasp infinity. In relation to eternity, the present moment is like a dot on a line extending to infinity.

A dot is immobile. That is why I have the impression that time has stopped, Raik conjectured. The present moment is only a dot . . . but why does the image of eternity figure in my imagination like an infinitely large projection of the present moment – like an infinitely large drop – and not like the streak of an arrow? . . . Because I'm tired. He pushed his felt hat to the back of his head, unbuttoned the collar of his shirt and loosened his tie. There's a kind of wistful sadness in me. A poignant sense of joy would be a better phrase.

With a sudden movement, he thrust his hand into his pocket, bringing out a small notebook. At such times, an overwhelmingly strong urge to write poetry erupted, like a compulsive pressure forcing up from inside him; he felt shaken, as if experiencing an earthquake. For a while he drew geometric figures, then put the notebook and his pencil back into his pocket. The seething desire had calmed, had retreated into arteries and veins – a little hurt, mildly angry, disappointed – intending to put pressure later on the artery walls, of a different, malignant nature.

From time to time Raik wrote masterly satires, but he was quite incapable of pouring his innermost emotions – that turbulence seething in his veins – on to a blank page. Words, once they were woven into ink's black lace, frightened him, or rather discomfited him. Like some strange creature begotten by him and rebelliously confronting him! No matter how violently the storm raged within him, it spun – like a maelstrom – around its own centre and within its own sphere. His emotions which, while part of this upheaval, he felt to belong strictly to himself, as he could always keep them under control by exerting enough pressure to counter their explosion, if ever they were to discover a channel to flow through, reaching the blank page, would cease to be his – certainly he would have been unable to express them adequately – no doubt words dropped dead when their links with related sentiments and facts were severed – no doubt words were simply that, just words – and when they had found their proper shape, they seemed alien to him.

He read his satires to Vicdan, they would laugh together. His other verses? No . . . Instead, he preferred to read to Vicdan poems by Ahmet Haşim, Ahmet Hamdi, or Nazım Hikmet. Raik and Vicdan both loved poetry passionately. Wouldn't it be insulting to these great masters if a novice like himself attempted to scribble verse, when Ahmet Haşim or Ahmet Hamdi, for instance, expressed so exquisitely the sweet sadness of the East, and Nazım Hikmet the erupting energy of revolution?

The great poet, Nazım Hikmet, had been here throughout the previous summer, behind that wall, in Bursa jail. Raik's cousin was still there, imprisoned for his Bolshevism, just as Nazım had been.

Raik was staying in town to visit his cousin. Vicdan knew the situation, he concealed nothing from his fiancée. The others, Fitnat Hanım and her sons? No. They knew neither Raik's reason for not climbing the mountain, nor that his cousin had been convicted of Bolshevism. The young couple had not mentioned the matter to Burhan or Reha, showing some consideration for the latters' uniforms, and some for Fitnat Hanım's nerves. Raik had met Vicdan through his cousin, who was a friend of First Lieutenant İzzet, who in turn was Burhan and Reha's friend. İzzet shared Raik's cousin's way of thinking, but was careful – being in the army – to limit their relationship to the exchange of ideas. Burhan shared the passion that nourished the ideology, but Reha was not interested in politics. Now everyone thought Raik's cousin was a teacher in some distant eastern province, İzzet included.

Each visit to his cousin upset Raik, and also strengthened his resolve. The pleasure at being reunited and the sadness of knowing that the young man's imprisonment would last for years, exerted contradictory pressures on Raik. He loved his cousin very much. In a word, the situation was absolutely agonising for Raik.

But the young prisoner was strong and cheerful. You could not help feeling optimistic after witnessing his undaunted resilience.

Raik and his cousin, all through the years when they were students at a teacher-training college in Istanbul, would discuss the problems of their motherland into the small hours, after long evenings when their only sustenance was tea and simit. The power of the international proletariat movement burnt in Raik like an ardent flame, reshaping his thoughts and feelings. But Raik, just as he hesitated on the brink of poetry, stood motionless on the verge of the vista opening before him; it was neither interdict nor fear that held him back, but a powerful intuition that the humanitarian beauty of communism was no more than a dream. It had nothing to do with foresight, but probably had its roots in the past, in his childhood, in some childhood memory that Raik had forgotten long ago, or had wanted to forget.

Raik knew that those who joined the 'Party' although it was banned in Turkey and in spite of realising the weaknesses of the movement, as for instance its inappropriateness for a largely peasant society, took this step because they could not resist the temptation of the political dream. So did Raik lack the ability – and certainly it was an ability – to respond to the attraction of a passionate dream? Or did his self-control exactly counterbalance the attraction? If so, wouldn't the inner tension thus created break a man? No . . . Raik seemed so strong.

With the simple determination of a man of the soil who would sniff the air and predict the direction from which the storm would come, Raik opposed his cousin, although the need and longing he felt for the brotherhood of man had sculpted his very soul.

His cousin thought hostility to the Muscovite was the main reason for Raik's attitude. During the Great War, Czarist armies had occupied Trabzon, and Raik – who was then only ten – had to flee his father's house in a small boat, together with his parents and younger brothers. The cousin came from a branch of the family that had settled on the west coast of the Black Sea, and so had not experienced the devastation of that occupation. He thought he understood Raik's feelings, but there was something Raik for his part could not comprehend: the tremendous difference between the Union of Soviet Socialist Republics and imperialist Czarist Russia. Over this issue, the two of them argued. Raik could not make his cousin believe that he did not hate the Russians, that he was not afraid of them; what he actually dreaded – although he never admitted it even to himself – was the creature called 'man'!

Such depths of feeling were not usually expressed in so many words by either of them; their conversations centred for the most part on day-to-day political developments. No, Raik could not possibly trust 'Comrade Stalin', and he was sure that the Nazis who were in power in Germany would spell disaster. The incidents that Vicdan had described would give birth to terrible and ominous events. Berlin . . . No, Vicdan's view of it was certainly not the pessimistic interpretation of a young girl orphaned by war; on the contrary, it was a human being's understanding which, having experienced atrocities, could discern, like a sensitive antenna, the first signs of impending disaster and file them away in a quite different category from the bulk of life's happenings. No, Raik did not trust the German working class, which had either capitulated when exposed to Nazism or had become Nazi, which was even worse. And the worst was that 'Comrade Stalin' was trying to find ways of getting along with these Nazis.

Stalin is struggling to ensure the survival of the first workers' state.

That's exactly what I mean! The dream of international communism is over. History is forcing the first workers' state to fight for its life. The defence has to be labelled 'nationalism', whether you like it or not.

In fact, the labelling would be even more disastrous! Raik knows, but prefers not to remember, that in the struggle between survival or destruction, the innocent and the guilty, the victim and the executioner, can at any moment exchange roles.

They fled from Trabzon in a small rowing boat. His mother rowed for many days and nights. Her two elder sons had been slaughtered with the army of Enver Pasha, which was annihilated at Sarıkamış in the Caucasus, fighting against Czarist Russia in the Great War. The third son would take part in the War of Independence. The mother – endlessly self-sacrificing – endured constant agonies, trying to save her two youngest from starvation. Raik watched his father founder in the minefield between survival and destruction, while his mother strove to survive on the same treacherous terrain. The War of Independence, peace, and the Republic . . . Raik only realised how dearly he loved his hometown when he was restored to Trabzon, their family home on a hill overlooking the sea, the small tobacco field surrounding it, the fig trees, the geraniums. The carefree years of his childhood were interwoven with this very place. Raik would never ever forgive those who abandoned his town and its people to destruction, the forces of illiteracy, religious bigotry, and the accursed 'imperialism of capitalism'.

During the years when he was studying in Istanbul on a state scholarship, his antagonism to these three enemies was purged of destructive rage and evolved into positive action. From then on, he became a teacher, bringing education to the children of Anatolia, and performing his duties to perfection. Now he could allow himself the luxury of forgetting the Great War, and the anguish associated with Trabzon. He had no wish to suffer, which is the legacy of hate. He turned his face to the new life of which Vicdan was a part, brightening his existence like a ray of light.

Raik forgot, or thought he did: his mother had been an angel up to the time when they returned to Trabzon, enduring her sufferings like a saint, without complaint, without reproaches; the fountain of love in her heart had never dried up.

But another family had settled in their house in Trabzon, one that had been unable to flee when the invasion came, and had remained under the invaders, perhaps serving them, perhaps experiencing oppression at the hands of those occupying forces.

The situation brought Raik's mother's patience to an end. She turned into a female panther, tossing and swirling her black charshaf like a tornado and, by the sheer force of her rage, drove these people out. Later, Raik met one of them, an old man – he was begging on the street. Did his mother not know that she was condemning those who had occupied her property to starvation?

Raik does not want to remember his mother, with her stately carriage, parading through the house like a victorious commander, after all had been said and done. She cleaned the house with her strong arms until it was bright and shining, then drank her refreshing coffee with great relish, taking great gulps of the hot liquid. Raik hated his mother that day, hated her strength. Could that be why he fell in love with a delicate-looking woman like Vicdan?

Raik thought a lot during the period when he lost his heart to internationalism: could they not have shared their home with those poor people? No, not after all those years burdened with poverty and wretchedness; there was little enough room for his family in any case, and they were living on short commons. Raik was appalled to discover that he himself rejected such a sharing to begin with! The sense of proprietorship, the right of precedence . . . to forget all that and endure a twofold poverty. No, he could not . . . Probably no one could. What about communism, then? What right did he have to bear a grudge against his mother? Did he not rather owe her thanks? His indebtedness fuelled his rage against himself as well as his hatred for his mother.

His self-reproach grew as he realised that he had been countering his mother's tenderness over many long years with the fury of a moment. But what a moment! A moment pregnant with damaging, long-term effects.

Nobody could make Raik believe that a people trapped between survival and destruction would act more generously and less selfishly than an individual in the same position. The instinct for survival in individuals and groups, colliding, savaging each other, and hiding behind words and phrases supposed to convey momentous and profound meaning, while in fact betraying that meaning and deceiving those who had not yet lost their innocence, would transform life on earth into a fine temple to malignity, built of terror, lies, illusion, deception, treachery, and crime.

Raik did not tell his cousin, who had no knowledge of the incident, the story of how his mother reclaimed her property. He only mentioned the memory of this moment to Vicdan.

Yes, the two cousins discussed the events of the day; like all those living at that time in the cities, towns, and villages of Turkey, who had felt the violent impact of the collapse of the Ottoman, they were devoted to the Gazi and to his men who had fought in the War of Independence, to those who had fallen and to those who survived to become veterans, with a passionate love. But Raik's cousin was increasingly inclined to take a critical view of the Gazi's economic policies.

Raik was aware that the situation in Turkey was developing along different lines from those envisaged in the euphoric visions of the Republic's early years, but it was only the people who had these dreams; Gazi Pasha had never promised a paradise. No need to look far for the evidence . . . even his mother-in-law, Fitnat Hanım, had been exposed to injustice; it did not bother her sons and daughter who were floating on clouds of optimism, but Raik was trying, with quiet determination, to see to it that his mother-in-law received just compensation for her property in Salonika which she had lost by the terms of the Exchange agreement between Greece and Turkey in 1924. With this in mind, there was not a single door to officialdom that he did not knock on. If you did not have a friend in a government office, you could not possibly unearth your papers, what with red tape and reluctant officials. 'Be fair,' Raik would say to his cousin who kept on criticising the Republic, 'haven't we inherited this unwieldy structure from our empire? Only we, the younger generation, can alter it.'

The frustrations Raik experienced were certainly nothing compared with what his cousin's radical criticism was directed against: the Gazi is trying to create a national bourgeoisie. Raik defended the idea that in a country where industry was non-existent, a working class could not possibly be created, and that the ideology of the proletariat must constitute a further step in the life of Turkish society. The cousin talked about the workers in the dockyards of Istanbul, whereas Raik referred to the vast horde of impoverished peasants in Anatolia. The cousin asserted that the masses did not have the patience to wait for centuries, whereas Raik spoke of the impression he gained while doing his military service in Erzurum, and while teaching in Sivas, of the infinite patience of the Anatolian peasant. At this point, the enthusiasm of Raik's cousin would boil over; while he could not remain seated and would jump to his feet and start rampaging round the room, roaring like a caged lion, Raik would grow even more sedate, and tell him how a people, just like a plant, ripened gradually, and that if certain stages of the ripening process were omitted as a result of outside interference, the process would not be shortened as expected, but a freak of nature would occur. His cousin would grow furious.

Yours is typical Islamic patience, the apathy of fatalism.

Could he be right? Isn't faith the easiest part of religious instruction to lose? What about modesty, humility, unselfishness, accepting your lot? Are they easily obliterated? Or should they be? Raik wants to get rid of every particle of the religion which his mother, in his infancy, added to his make-up. Is it possible? Ever since the day he saw the old man who had been driven out by his mother, begging in the street, Raik has felt his mother's religious observance is a sham. He knows that she derives the strength to endure the pain at the loss of her sons from the sincerity and intensity of her faith. But that faith is tarnished! Is that why Raik lost his? Unaware that his quiet way of thinking, that sometimes carries him up into the foothills of wisdom, is a new form which he himself has shaped for the devout resignation of his mother.

His cousin would attack him:

You are supposed to be a follower of Mustafa Kemal! He's a great revolutionary! Not an idle peasant waiting for the shoots to ripen.

Raik remembers the peasant boys he taught at the Sivas High School, students on state scholarships; he remembers how their passive intellects could be mobilised by love of their country and by hope for the future.

He had seen how high these minds could jump to achieve success. He resembled his fellow countrymen on the land, waiting for a late spring. And spring is here at last! Spring is the Anatolian revolution.

Mustafa Kemal intervened in this late birth, like a surgeon performing a caesarian operation. He saved and gave life. He did not force an infertile womb into producing.

It is the coming of spring that transforms Raik's disbelief in humanity into optimism, which is probably why he loves Mustafa Kemal so much, Mustafa Kemal who, by the miracle he performed, has saved Raik from his very self. Raik's faith in his fellow countrymen is no dream, but has its foundations in his teaching of village boys. The near-miraculous interaction between Gazi Pasha and the ordinary young people springing from the masses has functioned like a lever, like a vaulting-pole that lifts the athlete, in its effect on these youths who have outstripped themselves. Why should Raik brush aside an experiment that has been proved to him, in order to embark on a fresh unknown, Bolshevism?

His cousin would listen carefully to him, and then explain to Raik that he was swimming in a sea of dreams, repeating one after another the rules that societies were expected to abide by:

The awakening and arousal of the peasants in the Anatolian Revolution is destined to end. Wait until the bourgeoisie gathers strength; at that point, why should the upper classes tolerate the social improvement of the rural masses who would otherwise provide cheap labour? The bourgeoisie will sooner or later find a way to suppress this enlightenment. If the Anatolian Revolution expects the bourgeoisie to realise industrialisation, then the Revolution must cut the selfsame branch it has climbed and clings to!

Now all these discussions are in the past. Raik and his cousin will perhaps never again share this brotherly affection which never hurt either of them even though it involved some serious disagreement, as their relationship was based on the mutual knowledge that they would never betray one another.

Betrayal! This is the real cause of the pain Raik suffers. Betrayal runs in both directions, like foul currents, far below the surface. The path of the Turkish Bolshevists following comrade Stalin has deviated from that of the Anatolian Revolution. But their being sentenced to heavy terms of imprisonment, for an exorbitant number of years, smells of betrayal too! Betrayal of the humanitarian ideal! At that turbulent spot where two undercurrents meet like gales roaring in opposite directions, Raik feels an appalling weariness. At that precise moment he closes his eyes and listens to the voice of the water sounding from the nearby courtyard of the mosque, the water of the marble fountain which would continue to flow in the same rhythm even after thousands of years.

This moment will pass away, as will this century . . . Raik is well aware that what is being experienced is devastatingly important, but he can also sense that neither ideological movements nor revolutions, which are unable to alter the texture of the contact between water and rock, count for much in the lives of the plane tree, rock, and water, the true owners of our earth . . .

Evening in Bursa . . . The garden of the hundred-year-old house. The table, with its starched white linen cloth, set under the apricot tree. Aubergine salad, white cheese, fried green peppers. The melon cooling in the water-well.

This is the house of Fitnat Hanım's sister. The table has been laid especially for the conquerors of Uludağ! The oil lantern shines like a pale full moon among the pine-tree branches.

A little while later, young people will fill the garden. Lieutenants Reha Bey and Burhan Bey, their sister Vicdan and her fiancé, Raik, the mathematics teacher. Little Cumhur will certainly follow them.

Fitnat Hanım is in the kitchen which overlooks the garden, preparing delicacies with her sister. Her sister has been luckier than Fitnat Hanım, since she received this much finer house as compensation under the Exchange agreement between Greece and Turkey. As she has grown older, this sister has turned to religion; she will not sit at a table where rakı is served, but tolerates the young people who enjoy drinking. How Fitnat Hanım would enjoy a glass of rakı, that 'lion's milk', during her two days in Bursa, with all her children round her – how lovely – and her husband back in Istanbul – which is even lovelier! But it wouldn't be right to leave her sister on her own, and to step into the garden to join the young people. So Fitnat Hanım resigns herself to working by the kitchen's fiercely burning gaslight throughout these beautiful evening hours, as refreshing as cool lemonade.

Reha's thin, dark face flickers like a shadow in the light of the oil lamp. Burhan's fiery hair flames, shimmering. My two sons, how different from each other! Vicdan is happy, full of satisfaction. Raik is thoughtful. Cumhur adores his big sister; he is also very fond of his brother-in-law-to-be. Cumhur has settled in Raik's lap, his head on Raik's shoulder, staring at his sister.

(Cumhur would lay his head on Raik's shoulder once again, eighteen years later, on the İzmir-Ankara train. Raik would meet him at İzmir harbour, where the American ship, bringing the Turkish Korean Brigade home, would berth. Raik would meet Cumhur, whose leg had been amputated and whose military career had come to an end. God knows in what forgotten barracks Reha would be by that time, as officer in charge of supplies and equipment. And Burhan . . . Aah yes, he would of course have very important business to attend to, as usual.)

Burhan is telling in his eager voice how they climbed the mountain; Vicdan is supporting him, while Reha stares round silently, as if rather detached. Raik is listening.

Vicdan leans towards Burhan and whispers something. What? What has she said? Raik could not hear. Cumhur is fidgeting on his lap, wanting to attract all of Raik's attention.

Vicdan wanted to share with her brother Burhan a realisation which had suddenly dawned on her. Since the evening began, or rather all day long, the melodies they hummed on the summit had been going round in her head, 'The Maya Mountain' and that symphony! And she had solved the riddle! There must have been some chemical compound among the delicious scents of the garden that stimulated the brain! Vicdan could not and would not restrain her thoughts which were rushing off like a horse at full gallop. She was discovering brand-new forms hidden within the accepted shape of the life you grew accustomed to. Was she arriving at some truth or being driven to fantasize? She did not know, but loved the sensation. All of a sudden she thought she understood the reason for the Gazi's admiration of Western classical music. She had been to many concerts in England, but never before had she been able to interpret the harmony called music, as now she could, sitting in the garden of an antique wooden house in Bursa, with her brothers and her fiancé. Her mind and senses, that were busy interpreting the music, had been rendered fantastically acute by the effects of a day which had been filled with various images of various kinds of love, and by the liberating thrill of climbing the mountain. A multiplicity of feelings expressed simultaneously: that was Western music. Did not an orchestral conductor control the movements of sounds according to a system bordering on the mathematical, and did he not resemble a commander of armies? Was not the strong, durable symphonic structure, stroked softly and elegantly into being by the interaction of the musical notes, the very Republic that the Gazi dreamed of? The metaphor she had just invented further intensified Vicdan's excitement. She could open her heart only to Burhan. She could not share her power of association, that leapt from orchard to music, then bounded from there to the Gazi and his Republic, with Raik. Raik would advance with slow, sure steps from one fact to the next, painstakingly arriving at a just conclusion. He was a typical mathematician. But as for Burhan, he sprang forward with the speed of the wind.

Raik watches Vicdan ruefully. Today, the three of them have shared the experience of a lifetime that excluded Raik. A precious and momentous experience for them, that would leave deep impressions. Raik has to accept the fact. Reha is not as fully aware of what they have experienced as Vicdan and Burhan, whose eyes are shining. Reha . . . he is like a young plant, he can forget his very existence and drift into a different awareness responding to sap, soil, and rock. Raik thinks that he can understand Reha with that part of his being that senses and dreams about the life of the soil. The real owners of our earth, both organic and inorganic matter, attract some individuals towards their material unity like a powerful magnet. Reha is one such individual. You can only withstand that fatal attraction by the power of reason. Will Reha manage it? Who knows?

Burhan . . . He is different. He is Raik's real rival, and will remain so. Raik's flesh is about to surrender completely to the dissolution of sadness, when habit reasserts itself, he deluges his nerves with rational optimism, and there he is, lively and vigorous again! Well, so what? Only a brother! That is all the rivalry he has to put up with.

Vicdan's face looks pale and thin in the lamplight, her delight of a moment ago has evaporated. Is she tired? Her brothers' posting to the east is getting closer. Is that worrying her? Raik has an irresistible urge to reach out and touch her hand. Only one single touch. No, it would not be proper. He draws back. His fiancée is looking down at the ground; is she reminiscing? About England? Or Nefise, Raik's other rival? Maybe Vicdan does not even know herself what she is thinking of, she is so timid . . .

> *How sweetly summer passed*
> *The nights in our small garden*
> *You white as any lily*
> *In timid contemplation*

Their shared life would pass like that. Raik relaxed and leaned back in the wistful security of that knowledge.

Is it the future that scares Vicdan? The future . . . is dark . . . The world is doomed! Raik knows that his thoughts, his inner turmoil, his speculations about the future go on sporadically for days after a visit to his cousin.

If war breaks out . . . even if it doesn't . . . if salvation lies in industrialisation, and . . . if the future looks none too bright as the bourgeoisie gets stronger . . . then what magic would transform the peasant masses into a class-conscious proletariat? Impossible . . . Then what would the Republic of Turkey do? What does Gazi Pasha think? From whatever angle you view the prospects, it is clear that a difficult and contentious era is beginning. Then . . . there's the problem in the eastern provinces. Reha and Burhan will be going there, to Elaziz. The four of them will probably never be together again, never again share such an evening of intimacy. (Come on, Raik, it's because you have just left your cousin that you feel so gloomy. No one loses everyone they love!) This isn't weariness, this is perception sharpened by gloom. Is there a single instance of prophesy that's proved correct, that is made by those who are sated with happiness?

God defend Reha and Burhan from being shot in armed combat . . . Vicdan would not be able to bear such agony . . . Yes, Raik thinks that a fresh uprising will definitely take place in the east. While doing his military service, he had met many easterners. They were honest, brave boys. They could easily turn merciless and aggressive. Who was ever proof against turning merciless? Who? And they were the children of relentless winters and isolated plateaux. The breakdown in the east sprang from differences in lifestyles rather than in a dispute about authority. Would a tribal chieftain ever willingly exchange the boundless freedom of the mountains for the settled, restricted life of a citizen of the Republic? The nomadic tribes lived in a different age. Another uprising seemed inevitable to Raik.

The Republic was caught out in the cold! Raik was breathing with difficulty. What did Gazi Pasha think? Oooh, Raik, surrender to pessimism, climb down into the bottomless well of grief! Don't worry, it does have a bottom! Hit the bottom, let your whole self be shattered, smashed to pieces! Destroy that steadfast reasonableness of yours that keeps your inner structure from foundering! Then, only then, will your pessimism seem to you exaggerated! Only then, when your being has been reduced to organic and inorganic matter, when your consciousness hovers above and gazes with the eyes of a stranger at what is left of you! Only then will you see a new radiance, in the darkness that shreds like a stretched and peeling skin, a radiance that will inspire you with the endless durability of matter; hold to that, and gather yourself together! But you insist on stopping halfway, like a stubborn child! . . . Ooohh, I see, your generation has inherited this false optimism from your mothers.

Hold on, children, soon your father will come bringing bread. Don't be frightened, children, the enemy will retreat. Kemal Pasha, like a golden-haired wolf, will drive them away.

I've come to realise that individuals brought up in a country which foreign invasion has devastated can never quite achieve personal freedom.

Then Burhan, one of those selfsame individuals, radiating hope, brings his fist down on the table, crushing pessimism like an insect!

'You will see, brother Raik, how Turkey will progress, young people like us will create life out of the bare stones!'

How he believes in himself! (He addresses Raik, for whom he would always, throughout his life, cherish an unalterable respect. He would always try to prove himself to Raik, try to win his approval.)

'New suns will rise, brother! Wait and see!'

Burhan can't stop himself breaking into verse.

I come from the East
I come crying the East's revolution
I have run with the winds blowing northwards
Along the roads of Asia
And have reached

You
Come, open your arms
Embrace me

Raik is excited, his heart is beating fast. How well Burhan recites Nazım's poetry, his voice beautifully modulated.

Oh dear! Fear seizes Fitnat Hanım's heart, she turns to her sister in despair, 'He is reading the Muscovite poet's verses'. Her sister shrugs her shoulders. Please Burhan, at least lower your voice, the neighbours will hear. One of them might inform on us!

Reha stares at his brother with uncomprehending eyes. Vicdan looks at Burhan, her face flushed, her eyes two great pools of a deepened, intensified blue. An ocean! The timidity has vanished from her eyes! Could the ocean ever be timid? Vicdan is transported on the mystical fervour evoked by the harmony of words and Burhan's intoning of them. Burhan is enraptured by his own voice. Only Raik listens to the message behind the words. Yes, here it is possible to merge the various loves that divide his suffering loyalty, the loves he cherishes for Mustafa Kemal, for Nazım Hikmet, for his cousin, and even for historical materialism, here at this meeting point of genuine, fervent concern for the east and commitment to it! Raik takes a deep breath and leans back. His muscles relax for the first time today.

Reha is no longer listening to them, he has moved further away from the three of them, or perhaps they – Burhan, Vicdan, and Raik – have abandoned Reha. Although as the evening began they were all enthralled by the sweet sadness of the *hüzzam*'s minor key, now the three of them have punctured the membrane of its heavy droplets of time and have rushed off! But Reha's ear is still attuned to the gramophone, forgotten under the pine tree. The record revolves slowly, the dimly heard melody is one of Bimen Şen's.

Come, sing my song in your voice of love.

Reha feels like weeping, as he hums the song and dreams of Yıldız. He casts a quick glance at the table, frightened and shy like a naughty child caught in the middle of some mischief. No, no one is taking any notice of him; they are riding horses with flaming manes, galloping further and further away from him towards horizons Reha can't even imagine.

Reha relaxes into melancholy, murmuring the song . . . the sense of being apart makes his heart ache.

But what's happened? Reha has heard a great shout proclaiming 'the starving'! Raik rarely recites verse at a party. But now it is his turn. He recites Nazım Hikmet's 'Eyes of the starving', about starvation in Moscow, just after the Revolution:

> *Those who are starving stand in line, those who are starving!*
> *Neither man nor woman, boy nor girl,*
> > *feeble and fragile*
> > > *stunted trees*
> > > > *with stunted branches!*
> *Neither man nor woman, boy nor girl*
> > > *those who are starving stand in line!*

(Why did you turn back again, Raik, to pain? Speed like an arrow to the future! Yet the future curves like an arc, does it not, to perfect the great water drop of infinity . . .)

Hunger! Yes, it is a sensation Reha too has experienced. Hunger is an experience common to all at the table except Cumhur.

'Dear God, now they are all reciting "The Starving"!' cries Fitnat Hanım . . . and she remembers:

They are on the boat which will cross the Sea of Marmara from Mudanya to Istanbul. The year is 1922. She is on her way with her children Vicdan, Burhan, and Reha to seek refuge at her brother's. For the last forty-eight hours nothing but sesame bread has found its way into the children's stomachs. She herself is keeping going on water alone. They are on deck. All of a sudden, a fresh, warm, somewhat sickly smell reaches their noses: rich, buttery kasar cheese and freshly baked bread. Burhan's eyes, huge with hunger, are glued to the passenger's lips.

The cheese, shining like yellow amber, is still before Fitnat Hanım's eyes. The man, wearing peasant shalvar and potur, with a turban wound round his head, takes a piece of cheese and offers it to the child. Fitnat Hanım seizes her son's quick and eager hand in a clawlike grasp.

'Thank you,' she says curtly, 'he has had his meal, the spoilt child.'

Fitnat Hanım, daughter of the Sultan's aide-de-camp, widow of the late Colonel Hayreddin Bey, veteran of the Balkan War, she herself one of the army of widows created by the First World War, is starving but proud. She knows that the moment she loses the strength to refuse such an offer, she will have reached the end of her powers of endurance, so she holds her head high and proclaims, 'No, thank you.'

An evening in the summer of 1935. Tears spill from Fitnat Hanım's eyes, like a string of pearls. Fitnat Hanım is weeping for the jailed poet.

> *From farther away*
> *Dark piercing points*
> *Stretch out, like a row of dots, and stab*
> *   into your arteries.*
> *Like clog nails with big heads*
> *Are the crazed eyes*
> *   of those who are starving.*

Burhan's angry voice, Vicdan's valiant tones and Raik's determined ones have dissipated the gloom at the table. Cumhur is enjoying the harmony around him, on his big brother Raik's knee, shouting delightedly 'The Starving', half asleep. Fitnat Hanım thanks God for her future son-in-law who usually irritates her. All her children are here with her, just a step away, in the garden.

Reha, my son, where are you? Reha, I know you're there, but why, oh why can't I see you?

Night in Bursa. Starlight sprinkling like a shower. Raik is sleeping on a sofa on the ground floor, Vicdan upstairs with her mother. Fitnat Hanım will not be able to sleep tonight, she will watch over her daughter! . . .

Raik's flesh stiffens with desire as he imagines Vicdan's graceful, elegant body between the white sheets. Blood rushes to his loins. Yearning! Why does the image of Nefise suddenly appear, her dark, dark hair and eyes, dark skin, her body covered with dark down, her large mouth? The strong bare calves of women who polish the wooden floor with their bare feet? How Nefise resembles Raik's mother! Raik does not like Vicdan's soul mate one bit, not one bit!

Nefise has shared an experience with Vicdan, England, which Raik knows nothing of. Is Raik jealous of Nefise? Probably – while Nefise actually found Raik attractive. She gazed at him with hungry eyes when they were first introduced. Raik recoiled and rebuffed her. But here she is now, her breath is here. Raik drives the image out, furious. Is he aware that he is warding off the ease, the relaxedness of marrying a woman like his mother?

Raik imagines he hears a sob in the sensual silence of the night. Fitnat Hanım is weeping . . . for her lost youth, for the dangers awaiting her sons and daughter, for the misfortune of the prisoners in Bursa Jail . . .

THE OTHER SIDE OF THE MOUNTAIN

My youth vanished in a series of exiles, migrations, deaths, and poverty. The very last of my money has gone. I am so tired. But I did manage to have my children educated, fighting against all the odds. Where is my reward, where? They have never forgiven my second marriage. The Republic was supposed to be the remedy for all ills. Where is my remedy, where?

Can this house, number 8, Sakızağacı Road, be adequate compensation for all my father's and husband's property in Macedonia? After those compensation deals, business premises, large buildings, were granted to some, whereas my claim was met by this dilapidated house. I live here. Alright, what am I supposed to live on? I am only a weak woman. Your stepfather pays no heed. Neither do any of you. Where is our Gazi Pasha? Isn't he the father of the nation? Why does he allow such injustices?

Her mother's poor health and fractiousness oppressed Vicdan's spirit, as it reached out towards the new horizons of the Turkish Republic. She was tired of listening to stories about the property in Macedonia owned by Fitnat Hanım's father, a former aide-de-camp of one of the Sultans, stories about how the gold coins, sewn inside the quilts folded into packs to conceal them during the migration, were found by the Greek soldiers, stories about the family jewels which had reached Anatolian soil safely, hidden in underwear, but had been sold one by one for survival's sake during the war years. Vicdan neither cared for nor dreamed of wealth, as ever since she had been aware, she had been lapped in poverty. She could not understand what was the matter with her mother. She missed the mother of her childhood, who had hugged Vicdan to her, comforting the little girl during the nights when the poor child wrestled with the phantom of that wretched deserter hanging on his rope, she missed the nationalist mother who had introduced the love for Mustafa Kemal Pasha into her child's heart. When and how did that sanguine, resolute young woman turn into the Fitnat Hanım of never-ending complaints, and an unsmiling face? Vicdan, educated at boarding-school, was away from home and did not witness the transition. Was her stepfather's drinking wearing Fitnat Hanım out? Fitnat Hanım fought for breath now; her face and neck flushed up. Fitnat Hanım sweated. She shut herself in darkened rooms and cried her heart out.

She shouted and screamed, scolding little Cumhur, the son she had conceived by her second husband. She interfered in everything Vicdan, Burhan and Reha did. She did not approve of Raik. Her endless fantasies, ever since she lost faith in the justice of the Republic, centred on the expectation that Vicdan would marry a wealthy man. And now Vicdan had chosen an orphan just like herself, from a teacher-training school! Raik, the Laz, a teacher of mathematics! Could there ever be any chance of this fellow making money? What's more, he had no intention of doing so! An admirer of the 'Muscovite' poet, Nazım! I wish Vicdan had never fallen for him! Well, this is what happens to girls when they grow up away from home and a mother's authority!

Dark memories of her youth drove Fitnat Hanım, on the verge of old age, into anxieties about her own and her children's future. Anxieties which seemed contemptible, pitiful to Vicdan, Reha and Burhan, fortified as they were by hope . . .

The fact that Vicdan had been received by the Gazi, and her subsequent relations with the Dolmabahçe Palace, opened up entirely new prospects of hope for Fitnat Hanım's feverish imagination.

Listen, listen to my idea. Could you speak to that gentleman, the aide-de-camp? He could probably arrange another interview with the Gazi, and perhaps you could tell the Gazi about our situation, how your stepfather's business is not doing at all well. If the Gazi was to move even his little finger, the slightest gesture from him would be enough to put right the wrongs done to me. I don't want anything I'm not entitled to! I only ask just compensation for my father's property.

Fitnat Hanım tries to speak in a soothingly soft and affectionate voice. But now it is Vicdan's face that flushes up! Her eyes, wide with shock, are fixed on her mother! She feels shame and rage.

Fitnat Hanım loses control. Her voice grows hoarse with resentment, as she calls one by one the roll of those who have grown rich during the republican years, hurling her words savagely against her daughter's eardrums, words which fall deafeningly from Vicdan's ears into a void of unmeaning.

The sole meaning her mother's display of rage conveys to Vicdan, the only reaction it evokes is the disgusted question: 'How could anyone, even for a moment, think that the Gazi should be disturbed for the sake of any individual's personal problems?'

Vicdan and Fitnat Hanım stand screaming from opposite shores, and swim swiftly away from each other. The space dividing them swallows their voices before they reach one another. Words can only hurt like hurled stones.

You have a high and mighty opinion of your self, haven't you? You look down on your mother, whom you should be thanking for the education you received. God knows how many people manage to reach the Gazi every day, appealing to him on God knows what personal grounds. You have the opportunity right to hand, and you knock it away, out of pride. You have made yourself secure, won a lifetime's guarantee, and don't care one iota for the rest of us. Alright, you don't mind about your mother, but at least you could bother about your little brother, Cumhur.

(You are wrong, Fitnat Hanım. You know very well that Vicdan will always care for you, her brothers and her stepfather. You give yourself leeway to talk in this particular vein because you are absolutely certain of Vicdan's concern for you, and aim to hit the tender, vulnerable spot in her heart. Don't, Fitnat Hanım! It doesn't become you! And besides, you will never get anywhere by this route.

Your daughter is an idealist who is surrendering personal advantage for family responsibilities, and family advantage for the country's good. You have brought her up like this. You don't have the right to complain! And Vicdan knows nothing about the stages of womanhood. Neither do you. Neither of you is aware that the factor contributing to your anxieties may be the menopause.)

Is it the menopause that brings these shameful ideas into your head, Fitnat Hanım?

When the Gazi's summons reached you, you were terror-struck, Fitnat Hanım, imagining that the Gazi might have his eye on your daughter, your heart palpitated, blood rushed to your head, you felt dishonoured. But what about the rose-garden secretly blooming in your self-esteem? What a glorious honour was being bestowed upon your daughter and naturally on yourself as well! Does your head ache, Fitnat Hanım? The snake curling round the intricate structures of your brain is hissing unspeakable thoughts with its venomous tongue to the blood circulating through your capillaries. Shame on you, Fitnat Hanım! Does this opportunism suit you?

Vicdan's limbs are paralysed, she can't move hands or feet. She is in shock because of the Gazi's summons. Fitnat Hanım is rushing about. Bring that muslin dress, the pride of Fitnat Hanım's heart, and the single-string pearl necklace. Vicdan must be dressed elegantly. Vicdan is amused by her mother's fussing. She could perfectly well go to see the Gazi in a plain skirt and jacket, but she does not oppose her mother's efforts. As she rides in the black official car from number 8, Sakızağacı Road towards the Dolmabahçe Palace, she waves through the rear window, in her pink muslin dress. Her heart in her mouth, her mother sees her off to an unknown future.

(Fitnat Hanım, be honest, do you secretly want the Gazi to keep your daughter? Then the engagement to Raik would be broken. Then . . . Would it be possible to refuse the Gazi? There isn't a soul in the whole of Turkey who can utter the word 'no' in the Gazi's presence! Then . . . all Fitnat Hanım's financial worries would be over!)

The black car came back. Vicdan stepped out, smiling. Fitnat Hanım, prey to the desperate tensions between contradictory emotions, had not for so much as a second left her post behind the net curtain, ever since the car took her daughter to the Palace. She had waited, her eyes fixed on the road. Thank God, her daughter is back, safe and sound, honour unscathed. The serpent in Fitnat Hanım's mind has curled up in a corner! The dreams of wealth are over!

Vicdan sensed her mother's anxieties over the Gazi, she was even amused, not knowing the guilty hope that lay in ambush behind the anxiety.

Fitnat Hanım cannot begin to solve the problem. The value the Gazi places on her daughter owes its being to what, if not to Vicdan's body? How can anyone believe that, in a huge city like Istanbul, another teacher of English cannot be found for the people in the Dolmabahçe Palace? Isn't there any other worthwhile person in the whole of the Turkish Republic to give a talk on the English Radio? On the other hand, how honoured Fitnat Hanım feels! She feels proud in the presence of her excited neighbours, who follow Vicdan's Dolmabahçe adventure with disbelief. In all the houses of Sakızağacı Road, behind every net curtain, stands a female sentinel, for every arrival and departure of the black car, to and from number 8. If a relative of some neighbour hadn't been on duty at the Dolmabahçe Palace, nobody would have believed in this business of private English lessons. Fitnat Hanım's daughter Vicdan goes to the palace, gives her lesson, and comes back! That is all! . . . No secret sequel to the story! But that's impossible! Well, there are witnesses! Very strange indeed . . . Well, nobody can fathom the Gazi's doings, any more than anyone can fathom those of God the father. Do you think his drinking habits make our Gazi behave in such odd ways? Hush . . . Be quiet . . . Don't even mention such things . . . Hush . . .

The gossip reached Vicdan's ears, but she did not mind; she told Raik, and they both laughed . . . But . . . Her mother's behaviour . . . Vicdan cannot begin to follow the rapid evolutions her mother is going through.

Fitnat Hanım gave up thinking about the reasons for the

Gazi's honouring of her daughter – she could not solve the riddle – now her mind is working on another matter, her fevered imagination fantasises richly, and she fancies her dreams are true. Her daughter is a very important person, almost wields power over affairs of state.

Raik, I sometimes think mother is going crazy.

Why won't such an important person listen to her mother's pleas? Why won't she talk to our Gazi . . .

Mother, the Gazi is absorbed in the affairs of state. He can't be worried with what are simply personal problems.

Listen to her! What do you take yourself for? Do you know the old saying about the chestnut that scorned its shell? I am the shell you are treading on! Affairs of state, my foot! Everyone knows what he concerns himself with, with drinking rakı! Just like your stepfather!

Rage, tears, private anguish . . . Fear, caution . . . Walls have ears . . . Somebody might hear . . . The neighbours might report you . . . How can you do it, Gazi Kemal? . . . How can you drink? . . . Disappointment and tears . . . Like a low-down drunk . . . Like that fellow I can't love any more, like my husband . . . The smell of mixed rakı and vomit always hovers before Fitnat Hanım's nostrils.

Vicdan is worn out. She does not know what to say. She watches the changing expressions on her mother's face. For a fleeting instant, through the overwhelming weight of her weariness and the mists of her longings, she can catch a glimpse of her mother's true self. A face taut with pain. Vicdan is startled.

'Mother' . . . Placatingly, her voice tries to reach Fitnat Hanım. But the space that divides them swallows Vicdan's words. Fitnat Hanım does not hear, keeps on muttering through her misery.

The poverty I suffer, the injustice I have been subjected to, do they mean nothing? Who shall I appeal to about my situation? Tell me, daughter, who on earth can solve my problems?

Vicdan cannot offer any answer.

When her mother stifles her, Vicdan either clings to her hopes or to memories of England. At this very moment, Victoria Station appears before Vicdan's mind's eye, with its grey dome, and its dark, dignified, solid presence.

How relieved they felt, when this great structure confronted them after that ghastly visit to Berlin, embracing them like a crusty elder, soft at heart. A building that might stand for a thousand years . . .

—Institutions, said Vicdan, they could solve such problems.

—Institutions, echoed Fitnat Hanım, from her place on the opposite shore. Where are they?

And indeed, where are they?

—They will be set up, replied Vicdan.

—Whoever will set them up, and where are those who should have done so?

Vicdan went on talking, as if speaking to a feverish child.

—You know where they are, mother. They fought and died in the trenches of the Dardanelles, in the Gaza desert, in the Caucassian mountains, in Galicia. But we shall rise up, the young people of today, and set up these institutions.

—Then, said Fitnat Hanım, what will become of me, in the meantime?

Vicdan ran into the garden, smiling, her heart warmed by the image of that solid Victoria Station, pushing away her mother's anguish which for a moment had touched her heart, without realising, even for an instant, that her mind had inherited, directly from Fitnat Hanım, the ability to jump from her mother's suffering to the vision of Victoria Station. During that lightning flash of identification with her mother's feelings, Vicdan could sense another fact linking her and her mother, the difference between them. Vicdan's mind could hold more that one thought and emotion at any one time, she could look at reality both from within and without, whereas her mother could not. Probably this quality of Vicdan's was the solution to the riddle 'Why did the Gazi choose me?' Vicdan could just as well take a bird's eye view as look through a magnifying glass.

—His Excellency the Gazi requested information on and the credentials of the students he chose for an initial interview. He resolved the problem of whom to choose for the talk on the BBC after his interview with you. He seemed to have found what he had been looking for. 'My child,' he said to me, 'I have tested her and she will do.'

—Then, Aide-de-Camp Bey, what were my merits?

—He did not explain. But he followed your progress, and all the positive results of your visit to London; then he said to me, 'See, my child, I have not been mistaken.' The success of his choice made him as pleased as a child himself. He asked for your papers once more. 'Hmmm, she has not yet been assigned to a post,' he said. 'If you give the order, sir, I shall see to it that the procedure is speeded up,' I said, but 'No,' he replied, 'let her be treated in exactly the same way as her comrades are. But please arrange some private tuition for her; the poor child must be in need.'

The Gazi haunts my dreams. Every time I go to the Dolmabahçe Palace, the same thoughts possess me. I cannot wish to meet him again. Even dreaming of such a wish frightens me as I would not be able to face the excitement of the event a second time. My mind strains to comprehend the greatness of his genius. The mainstream, its details, and their inter-relations are equally clear to him. I am only a detail, as is my talk on the BBC, and as are my lessons at the palace.

But if the fine strands connecting the details to each other were worn thin, would not the entire structure be weakened? I have understood the Gazi's struggle to create flesh-and-blood models of the modern Turkish woman. I am committed to this particular aim, and realise that this goal is just as vitally important as the army, the taxes, educational and internal cultural projects. I feel he trusts me, and I am gratified, and grateful to him. I love him.

His eyes appear time and again before me and attract me like a powerful magnet, and in my mind a journey begins towards what lies in the depths of those eyes, learning to differentiate one from another the mass of emotions and expressions gathered there – discovering new meanings each time – I dive down to the depths, to the precipitation of pain. His suffering cannot be uncomplicated, nor is it personal. His suffering is a complex of hurts from the past, the present, and in all probability the future. The Gazi can by no means forget any jot or tittle; his genius rules out oblivion. But are not we human beings in need of forgetfulness from time to time, so that our minds can enjoy some repose? I am worried that his inability to forget will consume him! I wait, sleepless and apprehensive, like a desperate mother whose child is being worn away by an incurable fever.

Mustafa Kemal loved his study which caught the morning light. He was in the habit of contemplating fresh enterprises in this room. The future . . . was the drug needed by the life of the individual, as it drew to a close. Turkey's future should be planned; she had to be protected from the great conflagration which would certainly erupt within a few years from the bosom of Europe, and would seer and burn down the world of men. How? Turkey's very existence had not yet been secured.

THE PAIN FELT TIME AND AGAIN TO THE RIGHT OF THE BELLY INTERRUPTED THE FLOW OF IDEAS. MUSTAFA KEMAL WAS IRRITATED. HE WAS NOT ACCUSTOMED TO HIS BODY'S INSUBORDINATIONS.

Very soon the problem existing in the east would be solved once and for all, the uprising put down. A country damaged from within was like an organism harbouring an incurable illness, and would not be able to survive a probable world war.

THE ACHE IN THE BELLY WHICH HAD BEEN CONTINUOUS FOR SOME TIME NOW, ERUPTED TIME AND AGAIN INTO VIOLENT PAIN. A LITTLE LATER THE SYMPTOM OF ENDLESS EXHAUSTION MADE ITSELF FELT, TOGETHER WITH DIZZINESS AND HOLLOW ECHOINGS IN THE EARS. HE HAD NEVER ATTACHED MUCH IMPORTANCE EITHER TO HIS BODY OR TO HIS HEALTH. HE HAD SIMPLY RECOVERED FROM A WHOLE SERIES OF SERIOUS ILLNESSES WITHOUT TAKING HEED OR PRECAUTIONS. THE WORKINGS OF HIS MIND HAD NEVER BEEN AFFECTED BY PHYSICAL DISORDERS.

MUSTAFA KEMAL WAS AWARE OF A FACT THAT NO ONE CLOSE TO HIM HAD NOTICED AS YET. HIS BODY, ONLY FIFTY-FIVE YEARS OLD, BATTERED BY TWO DISASTROUS CENTURIES, WAS DESERTING HIM.

Disaster was at the door! It was there, because for Europe, the bloody carve-up after the First World War was not yet over. Europe's bloodlust would endure to the bitter end. As the world was hurtling towards its catastrophe, HE WAS ON HIS WAY TO ABSOLUTE PASSIVITY. THE ABILITY TO INTERVENE WAS BEING DENIED HIM, UTTERLY AND FOR EVER. HE FELT A SORROW HE HAD NEVER KNOWN BEFORE. FOR HIM, DYING MEANT NOTHING LESS THAN A FALLING AWAY FROM ACTION. FOR YEARS HE HAD LIVED CHEEK BY JOWL WITH DEATH, FLYING AT FULL STRETCH ALONGSIDE HIS SKULL, EXPLODING TO HIS RIGHT OR LEFT. IN BATTLE, DEATH WAS ONLY A PART OF THE ACTION, WAS THE OTHER FACE OF ACTION, AND SO WAS NOT UNFAMILIAR. BUT NOW . . . WOULD HE HAVE TO DESERT HIS COUNTRY, THE SOLE GREAT

PURPOSE OF HIS BEING, ON THE EVE OF DISASTER, ONLY BECAUSE OF HIS WEAK BODY'S BETRAYAL? WOULD HE HAVE TO GIVE IN AT THE SUMMIT TO WHICH HE HAD RAISED HIS COUNTRY, WITHOUT HAVING ENOUGH TIME TO SECURE THE CURRENT VULNERABLE BALANCES? DWELLING ON THIS HOPELESS ASPECT OF WORLD AFFAIRS INTENSIFIED THE PAIN. YET IRONICALLY, MUSTAFA KEMAL'S MIND WAS BURNING BRIGHT WITH THE BLAZING FLAME OF HIS PASSION FOR GRASPING THE TRUTH, AS HIS BODY WAS BEING EXTINGUISHED. He had been pessimistic for some time, ever since the Depression of 1929 to be exact, when he lost all hope that world peace could be achieved in the twentieth century. The Depression had been the final, decisive stroke, crushing the last chance of those nations which had emerged, battered, from the Great War, to realise that their new leaders were nothing but puny souls in thrall to the compulsive appetites of their own personal ambitions.

Historical events, like the links of a chain, were quickly interconnected in MUSTAFA KEMAL'S INTELLECT, AND THE FUTURE APPEARED, INCISIVE AND BRIGHT AS STEEL, TO THE VITAL FORCES FLOWING THROUGH HIS BRAIN'S BLOOD VESSELS, EXERTING AN URGENT PRESSURE POWERFUL ENOUGH TO CRACK THE CAPILLARY WALLS; there was a brand-new link in the chain, those champions of the future, The United States of America and the Union of Soviet Socialist Republics, countries which had not yet been worn down, and were nurturing fresh ambitions. The twin opposites that mother Europe had given birth to. One day one of them would destroy the other.

ALL HIS ABILITIES WERE CENTRED IN HIS MIND, AS IF HIS SKULL HAD EXPANDED, HIS FEATURES MAGNIFIED. DIZZINESS WAS OVERRIDDEN BY A HEADACHE. THE THROBBING IN HIS TEMPLES HAD ALWAYS BEEN A REGULAR FEATURE OF HIS EXISTENCE.

HIS BODY, A STRANGER NOW, LAY IN INSIDIOUS AMBUSH, JUST BELOW HIS NECK, A THREAT THAT WAS BIDING ITS TIME; BUT HIS FERVENT DEDICATION FORCED THIS THREAT TO THE FARTHEST EDGE OF HIS MIND'S RANGE OF PRIORITIES. THE COMPLETE CONCENTRATION OF HIS INTELLECT PENETRATED LIKE AN X-RAY THE TEXTURED COMPLEX OF HISTORY AND POLITICS, REACHING THE SHARPLY DEFINED SIMPLICITY OF THE BASIC STRUCTURE. TURKEY'S VITAL PROBLEMS CRYSTALLISED UNDER THIS PERCEPTIVE RADIATION.

From the centre of the crystal shone the ray of civilization. On the threshold of the coming disaster, the difficulty lay in correctly estimating the direction the ray would take; that faint gleam of light which had gone on existing under the debris of those catastrophes the human race had suffered for thousands of years, continued to shine, its beam now declining to the West. If the sun of civilization were to rise again in the East, as was his heart's desire, then it would have to be impregnated by the seeds of fire thrown out by the sun setting in the West.

Kemal Pasha interested himself personally in the matter of young people sent to Europe to study. While he sipped his morning coffee, he went through the photographs of the students who had come from the schools for orphans, and had been sent to Europe after passing the state scholarship examinations, and he took his time scrutinising their faces through a magnifying glass. He thought that these orphans whom the collapsing empire had left homeless and who were growing up to form a class of intellectuals with a strong faith in the republic, were a suitable group to broadcast to the world the Republic's pacifist stance.

He put to one side the photo of a graduate from the Çapa Teacher-Training School, who had been sent to England to study literature and had recently returned home, having completed her education – that of Vicdan Hayreddin. He thought that the girl's face showed an imaginative intellect balanced by gentle determination.

Only young people and children could stimulate something akin to joy in Gazi Pasha. Only then HE BECAME AWARE OF HIS BODY WITH A PANG OF SOMETHING LIKE SORROW. WAS THIS SADNESS A YEARNING FOR A LOVING FEMALE BODY? A yearning for a child? No, it was impossible to convey in any close relationship how human existence, which had been disastrously divided into a trilogy of body-mind-spirit by humankind's definition, had in his case blended into wholeness, although intellect and insight outweighed the physical. Maybe he was recalling his youth. No, he never indulged in nostalgia. Yet time and again his birthplace, the beautiful town by the sea, Salonika, emerged in his imaginings associated with lost loves.

No, he regretted none of his decisions. He had followed his destiny to the end, had succeeded and paid the price of success, had lost the joy of living.

A commander who had implemented battles – unless he saw human beings as ciphers – was bound to lose his *joie de vivre*. For Mustafa Kemal, victims of all the conflicts that had taken place and would take place were tragic figures engraved on his heart.

He had not forgotten how a soldier felt at the front. In no other situation did the chances of living or dying confront the individual so utterly devoid of social trappings. The gap between the soldier and his chances is infinitesimal. There is no hole to hide in, and the gap rapidly narrows. The moment when fear is overcome is glorious. The ability to face, dismiss, and scorn death is both superb and terrible. The only thing the soldier has at his command is his weapon. With his rifle his fear disappears, his anger aroused, and if he cannot rein himself in at the point where fear vanishes, he falls prey to the fantasy that he has boundless freedom in a world without horizons, and is drawn into a trance of cruelty. Mustafa Kemal has always known how not to cross the boundary where balance is maintained. He cannot bear any being or circumstance controlling him, not even his own power. The driving force of his dauntlessness has not been his weapon but his purpose, the justification for which he has never doubted.

How many people can be like this? A fighting man is only aware of a small part of reality, of what he is living through at any precise moment. But the President, from his summit, has a bird's eye view. He is the one who positions the policies. He knows all too well the yawning abyss in character between himself and those who carry out and implement political decisions affecting individuals, in face-to-face contact with them. No other name can be given to their relative position than 'an abyss apart'. It is utterly different from defects of administration, and is related to an individual's temperament, to his capacity for mercy and cruelty. To bridge the abyss between his personality and that of others is beyond even Mustafa Kemal's power. This is where his destiny frustrates him. Abysses drain away the successes, and insidiously nurture the seeds of coming conflicts, like those clefts where poisonous grasses grow.Who on earth can induce Gazi Pasha to forget about the precipices on the flanks leading from the summit to the foothills? Who indeed? The young people?

He made up his mind to see Vicdan Hayreddin.

No, no, he would not wish for a son or daughter OF HIS OWN FLESH AND BLOOD. Moreover, was not the desire for the partial continuation of one's BODY and mind in somebody else a kind of egotism? That BODY which would soon disappear . . . They would bury his body in the soil of Anatolia. Very probably they would perform some huge ceremony.

His people would grieve sincerely for him, that he knew. His people who loved him unquestioningly, unconditionally, with feelings of gratitude . . . They would hang his picture everywhere when he was gone, put up statues. At first the images would be handsome and elegant, in later years they would grow plainer, even ugly, carelessly carved. They were of no importance, those stone images. But some would think them so, and demolish them, deface them. Then crowds would come to his grave to ask his pardon. If he were to mention these presentiments to those near him, they would not know what to say and would mutter, 'Oh, my Pasha, please don't talk like this.' In all honesty he would have enjoyed having a friend – male or female – beside him, at least from time to time, a friend who had the gift of seeing the future. Still, in an odd way he did not doubt that he would be understood in the future, that they would understand him more profoundly than any living soul did at the moment, those children yet unborn. Children of those like Vicdan Hayreddin would understand and love him. These would be his true sons and daughters.

As he stretched out to ring the bell to summon his aide-de-camp, HE PUT HIS HAND ON HIS LIVER. COULD HE MAKE FRIENDS WITH HIS BODY? THE PAIN HAD CEASED.

ON ANOTHER SHORE

JOURNAL FOR MY DAUGHTER

A limpid blue day on the steppe. I am at Cebeci cemetery. I feel beneath my feet the autumn soil still harbouring its warmth; I feel the skin of the earth. If the leaves I am careful not to tread on crackle, I know it is the sound of a thin fissure being torn open in my heart. I know that the leaves are 'them'.

They all lie here, my mother Vicdan, my father Raik, my uncles Burhan, Reha and Cumhur, my grandmother Fitnat Hanım. And Nefise . . . They are all here. I think of the old cemetery in Trabzon that looks over the Black Sea from the heights, where my father's mother and his brothers have been sucked into the texture of the earth. And those uncles who, at the beginning of the century, were whirled away and dispersed by the storm of war in the Caucassian mountains . . . I remember Neruda's verses.

I know only the skin of the universe
And I know it has no name

For better than the pleasure I derive among flowers
Is what I feel when living among their roots

What name can be given to the substance of the earth that finds new life in decaying human corpses to breed its plants?

I walk beneath willows, poplars, and cypress trees. I am a writer . . . Once in a Mediterranean town, where my mother's professional career had its glorious beginning before her monotonous years of teaching on the steppe, I looked in the mirror and saw her! She had died a few years before. The oval shape of my face in the mirror trembled with the translucent vibrations of an egg about to give birth to a new cell, and the image of my mother slowly appeared, coming from beyond the grave and reflecting her hidden desires. I am a writer, a woman whose body has been estranged from men . . .

After my mother died, I went travelling around the world. I

flew with those birds of steel which frightened me. If I had crossed the Mediterranean on a pitching ship, would I have been less afraid? Nobody sails in ships nowadays . . .

I remember the Italian vessel, the *Théophile Gautier*, which sailed through storms to reach the harbour of Marseilles in the autumn of 1929. No, I am only imagining her, with her two passengers, Vicdan from Salonika, and Nefise from Karaman. A girl from the seacoast and a child of the steppe.

I am travelling to the West, as they did.

I am at the intersection of 0.2 degrees longitude, 5.2 degrees latitude, in Cambridge, where my mother and Nefise deposited their youth before returning home. In the dream-town of my childhood. The timelessly green meadows, the river on which slender punts and elegant swans are sailing, the tiny bridges, the noble towers, the old narrow streets murmuring softly of the darkness of the Middle Ages as if recalling a forgotten verse, the wisdom gained by this precious experience of time – they are all as they used to be. Mother, Nefise, where are you? In the 1930s, pre-war? No, I don't want those days back, those green and cool years that secretly nurtured in their bosom the century's ruthless destiny, like some malignant seed.

At five o'clock a cup of Ceylon tea, with a slice of cake, on a terrace adorned with roses. Tea should be served in Chinese porcelain. An Indian butler should wait. The conversation should dwell on tasteful and elegant subjects. Hitler? . . . Oh, what makes you think of him? Who is he anyway? I should think the Germans learnt their lesson in the Great War. It is absolutely ridiculous to suppose they would attempt another imprudence. Besides, it does sound unlikely, I mean, to expect malice from the nation that nurtured Beethoven, does it not? The Jews? We have no such problem, here in Britain. Churchill does not trust Hitler? Oh, come on, forget that fat fellow, just because he has failed in politics, he thinks he has the right to doubt everybody . . . Besides, the incredible amount of cigars he smokes . . . The oil in the Middle East? What about it? Oh please don't, why should we bother about politicians' affairs? The situation for British miners is deplorable? Well, I suggest that we close all the mines, they are spoiling our lovely meadows, would you please pass the milk – and darling? You aren't a leftist, are you? Oh, these young people, they follow whatever is in fashion . . . Oh please stop talking about those dreadful Russians, I believe I asked for the milk. I can't drink tea without it, you know. Besides, let us not bore our Turkish guests with such tasteless conversation . . . Oh, what a delightful summer's day, cool and green, like lemonade . . . Miss Vicdan, Miss Nefise, where do you spend your summer vacations at home? . . .

Summer vacations! . . . Mother, Nefise, how did you reply to your hosts, on the terrace adorned with white roses? . . .

During those first years we kept quiet and were rather hurt. Then we spoke. We told them about Virginia Woolf, how her perceptive pen had discovered the current of terror streaming beneath the quietly flowing days. Then we told them about war and invasion. They were silent and they listened to our words.

Mother, Nefise, I am in those same meadows still recognisable in your snapshots after sixty-five years. Vicdan's pearl necklace, Nefise's sporty jumper and unruly hair appear before my eyes.

The air is no longer like lemonade, the temperature is 32° Centigrade. The pressure of an atmosphere laden with carbon dioxide is suffocating us, trapping the town in a hothouse exuding green vapours. Towards the end of the century, each summer is warmer than the previous one, in Northern Europe . . . Beggars stand at street corners, unemployed youths crowd into the pubs, violence and crime lying in ambush within their tense male muscles. Crowds fill the streets, still baffled by their confrontation with the secret face of their dispersing empire. The crimes of the past erode the people's self-confidence. The ghosts of my mother and Nefise cannot recognise this new Cambridge.

I left the town by its river together with their ghosts.

I passed through London and crossed Waterloo Bridge . . . I looked down at the river washed with acid rain, a metallic sheen was flowing over its waters which I remembered as dark but clearer in the late sixties. Once upon a time I had wanted to merge with these waters, I remembered with a smile, now that I no longer had such a desire, now that I was calm, no longer perturbed. The suppurating, poisonous currents of the river drove me away.

I left the British Isles and entered the core of the ailing, bloody, ancient continent, finding hypocrisy and lies.

One day my country called me back. When my mother was alive, I wanted to escape her and longed to travel. The dead call us back . . . The lure of the land filled with those we love is strong. Now I was making my way under the shabby, yet proudly worn, garments which prevented any contact with my country's pelt. To the shore from the steppe, and back again.

Is this place Antalya? This huge excrescence by the sea, moulded out of white cement. Where has the little harbour gone, round the corner from the modest little mosque? Old, wise hands used to carve the most durable craft in the world out of wood in that tranquil harbour, while young travellers sipped hot tea from small glasses shaped like slim-waisted women. What had become of the wooden houses, whose kitchens were filled with the smell of red cabbage, where tobacco leaves would be left to dry in semi-darkness? I mean those houses where old women, wearing their white prayer-scarves, would, on the creaking parquet floors of their halls, beg heaven's mercy for their faithless sons who had cast anchor in a materialist philosophy. Is this Istanbul, the imperial throne of Byzantium and of the Ottoman? Her blue enamelling has become suspicion's colour, the grey shade of lead, the colour of air pollution and dirty banknotes . . . The Aegean towns spread from the shore towards the interior. Whitewashed houses with colourful shutters. The sea towns where the cobbled streets used to smell of olive oil and of jujube, where songs sung in Greek hung in the air – and those sullen, conservative towns further away from the sea.

Towards the East, from the Ionian columns of Ephesus to the earthenware jugs of ancient Phrygia, to the nomads' tents, to the carpets of the Yörük, towards the endless expanse of the steppe, towards – farther east – the mountains where terror dwells . . .

Is this the central Anatolian town, dating back to the days of the Seljuks, with her gracefully slender minarets, and her caravanserai carved with reliefs? The same town where the cold bred in the eastern mountains would settle down? The self-same town where my father, when he was a very young mathematician, fresh from the school for orphans, would earnestly reflect on the Anatolian Revolution, while listening to the stringed saz of the great troubadour Veysel? He did not yet know my mother, but he was already in love with her, the 'new woman' of his national dream. The vision of my father's favourite town, mother of troubadours, nurturing them for centuries with the precious milk they sucked from her austere breasts, basked in my father's love within my imagination. Is this the same town? The cindered remains of a conflagration.

Look at her, tearing her troubadour sons from her shrivelled breasts empty of milk, hurling them to the ground, and torching them with her own hands, reducing them to ashes along with her own sense of justice. No, I shall not utter her name, lest it scorch my tongue. I reject this treacherous, cruel, and stupid town! I want nothing of the steppe, I repudiate it!

How could any town, how could any country degenerate into a bloodsoaked fire festival erasing both conscience and poetry? While the pockets of the landowners bulged with filthy banknotes, while coins clinked against the whisky glasses of weavers and cartwrights, while the gallows performed its hangings, while the relentless waves of the starving surged over the steppe, while a midget, the puppet of capitalism, after settling on the loftiest perch, in a single stroke destroyed justice after splitting it off from success; a town, a country, turned into a bloodsoaked festival of fire!

Am I like a Jew fleeing Nazi Germany? It is not my fear that pursues me, but the anguish of a daughter whom the mother sets fire to. Besides, I have no refuge to which I can escape (but yes, you do! You have the natural universe! Your physical being would dissolve, penetrating and mingling with the molecular chains of matter; you would be saved, just as when – you remember – you were drawn by the pull of dark water as you stood on that riverbank in a North European city, like Virginia Woolf, like Vicdan who, in 1929, longed to melt in the grey mist of England, like your uncle Reha who blew out his brains.) Where shall I run to? To the outer layers of the earth, to the membrane of the universe that covers its organ, earth . . . to the soil . . . But then I turned my attention to the soil and realised that Neruda's verse was absolutely true – 'The flesh of the earth is made up of people'. No, it is not a metaphor. The soil filling my hand, the physical texture of the very matter I feel on my palm, is made up of generations of people, living and dying . . . Just as the history of the universe has been carved into the trunk of a tree, the history created by men has been cut into the texture of rocks and earth, into their molecules, their electrons! No, I reject this planet! Would there be a place for me in space? No, by no means! (You cannot run away, because you are made up of the very things you wish to escape!)

I turn my attention to my innermost self, and can find there nothing but the rhythms of nature and the history of the earth. It dawns on me that compassion and cruelty have always existed, will always exist in the texture of earth and in the history of mankind, just as they have always been and continue to be in my being. All heroes and heroines – those history salutes, and those it has forsaken and forgotten in some remote corner – have sucked mercy's milk and been poisoned by treachery's venom; they have vomited up the bitter, poisoned gall, and have spun mercy with the patience of a thousand silkworms . . . And no other way out exists! The flesh of earth, which finds fresh life in decaying human corpses to breed the plants which are my sisters and brothers, bears the name of 'homeland'!

I have to keep in touch with the flesh of this homeland as intimately as I do with my own. I have to burrow through the filthy quilt of sizzling, hissing electromagnetic noise, covering seas, mountains, plains, and steppes, and touch my country's flesh. I have to thrust my way through layers of electromagnetic waves loaded with images of ugliness and foul phrases, flowing from the quarters of the masters of finance to the hostels of those few who aspire to wealth but aspire in vain, flowing into and flooding the magic boxes of deception in the hovels of the poor, streaming out as lying shadows from screens claiming to mirror the truth, shadows that cast a spell over their audience, paralysing mind and conscience. How does one get rid of this modern invader? How does one infiltrate the still-functioning tissues of mind and soul? The living organism right there in the depths, which merged Ionian vases with Phoenician amphorae, and porcelain decanters; the powers which refused to surrender to personal, material gain, and so refused complicity with those who invaded in the first two decades of this century; the powers that post-modernity thinks weird and eccentric because they put the survival of their homeland above individual gain?

Such powers are in fact the collective unconscious of eastern peoples, in whose innermost being the basic code of the universe, 'the self is identical with the other', has not yet been obliterated.

Can I reach my country's flesh through the tortuous passage of my own history, by deciphering the history of close relationships, of love and partings inscribed in my own flesh? A blue limpid day on the steppe. I am at the Cebeci cemetery, I have old letters with me, the witnesses to bygone days.

10 September 1935
Istanbul

My dearest Vicdan,

I haven't known whether I am on my head or my heels for the last three days since I have been away from you. I am so wretched and unhappy. My head and the whole of my body ache.

I can scarcely move. Am I suffering from influenza? But I don't have a temperature. It isn't just exhaustion of the body; my soul is sick with longing for you. I simply can't make up my mind to do anything. My tongue's sense of taste has vanished. Whatever I eat tastes like straw. You left for —————, and I felt as abandoned as an orphan child in the heart of Istanbul. Miserable and aimless, that's what I am. I crawl out of bed with difficulty each morning; going to school is a torment. I want only one thing: the one consolation of holing up in some remote, dark corner away from everyone else, dreaming of you. But your image only gives me pain. My sole consolation increases my distress.

Ah Vicdan, how merry and resolute you were when you left me. The sight of you climbing on to the train, your head held high, never leaves my mind's eye. How you waved to me, smiling, from your compartment. Whereas I had considerable difficulty in restraining my tears. You hurried cheerfully to your new task. What can I say, I hope you will prove useful to our country, our nation. I wish you every success. I expect our separation which devastates me doesn't affect you. Yes, that has to be so. Your strength of purpose, your willpower, the resolution within you scare me, Vicdan. How can such courage radiate from such a slender body? You love your work better than me. You probably don't love me at all, but only think you do. Maybe you don't consider me good enough for you. In fact, I'm not. I'm only a rough, provincial guy.

Vicdan, you can't imagine how hypersensitive I've become. Istanbul is meaningless without you. Yesterday I paid a visit to your mother's, looking for friendship from Reha and Burhan, thinking my mood might improve in their company. I felt a coldness in your mother's attitude to me. And your brothers left me alone with Fitnat Hanım, and popped round to your neighbour's. Could you call this courtesy? You always criticize people's manners. It was only young Cumhur who didn't leave my side, calling me 'brother Raik'. I expect Burhan will eventually ask for your neighbour's daughter's hand. If this isn't his intention, then I have to say he's playing a devious and risky game. What will become of Vecdet then? How will Burhan look İzzet in the face? I tried to learn what his intentions were about getting betrothed before the end of his tour of duty out east, but when the conversation touches on Vecdet, he won't meet my eye. The explanation he gives is quite rational. A tour of duty out East . . . You never know what may happen. But how can his attachment to this young girl of your neighbour's be interpreted? I find it hard to believe that it is simply a brother-sister affection.

About Reha . . . He is head over heels in love with Yıldız, but Yıldız has considerable social ambition. I feel your mother, like me, is aware of Yıldız's aspirations, but Reha hasn't the slightest clue.

These problems occupy my mind, as if we haven't enough difficulties of our own, you and I. Tomorrow, I'm going to apply again to the local Department of Education, if I can find sufficient strength in my knees to walk there, asking for an assignment to where you are. They keep producing endless objections. 'If you wanted to move to the capital, we could arrange it immediately, there are many vacancies in high schools there for mathematics masters,' they say. I tell them that my fiancée has been commissioned with an important task. I don't think they understand. 'Isn't she, when all is said and done, teaching English?' they ask.

I wonder if it would be a good idea to go to Ankara, and try to sort things out with the Ministry of Education! I think my chief trouble is this question of my assignment. Tension raises my blood pressure. But . . . please don't worry. I know how much your mission means to you. I shall do everything in my power to be united with you, and with the town of ———. I know you don't like Ankara, and wouldn't enjoy settling down in a town away from the sea.

I kiss your beautiful eyes, your silken hair, your honey lips with longing, my only one.

Raik.

15 October 1935
Istanbul

My dearest darling,

As soon as I laid hands on your letter, my depression vanished. Oh my love, the way you can affect me! First, I cast a casual glance at the post box . . . 'No, I won't be getting the letter I've waited for so long, not yet,' I thought hopelessly. I was anxious, and imagined you would leave me, break off our engagement. The moment I saw your letter, my heart started to thud madly with happiness! Then a sudden rush of anxiety returned. Was it good news? My hands were trembling as I opened the envelope. I saw your beautiful handwriting, your lines flowing like rows of pearls, and immediately calmed down. My only one, you cannot imagine the happiness induced by your words, 'My Raik, I wish I were at your side cradling your aching head and resting it on my bosom.' You write, 'I thought you were very quiet when you saw me off at the station, and was hurt, thinking you did not care about our parting; so I tried hard to seem carefree.' Oh my love, don't you know that silence overwhelms me when my heart is heavy with sorrow and anxiety? My tongue loses all feeling as if it has suffered a blow, I can't find words to utter. Only a warm smile or a few comforting words from you are enough to make my heart take wing and soar . . .

Raik

18 October 1935
Love, no news about my assignment. It is perfectly understandable that you want to teach in the institution you are setting up. But after facing so many obstacles, I am driven to wonder from time to time whether we should accept posts in Ankara. The crucial point is that you are the one who is literally building that institution, the honour for such an undertaking will always belong to you. I am by no means insisting, but only

suggest that we ought to consider our position from this point of view as well. As we can't get married before the beginning of summer, there's no need for you to leave before completing the academic year. From then on, you and I would teach the children of our country together. What do you think?

My dearest, don't worry about me, I am taking good care, my health has improved. I am yours, Vicdan, I belong to you. I attach importance to my body and its health for the sole reason that they belong to you. If I stop being yours, my darling Vicdan, I shall lose every reason for living.

Vicdan, if I hadn't already tasted the pain of parting from you, I would have accepted your invitation and come to ———, for the celebrations of the Republic's anniversary. There's nothing in this mortal life that I want more than to touch you, hear your voice, gaze at you until my eyes are filled with your image. But please don't ask me to go once more through the desolation of parting after being reunited with you. In ———, we would not have our families with us, and so none of the preventatives forcing us to control our feelings, and so we would rush into an even closer union. Parting after such intimacy would be even harder to bear. Besides, a little bird tells me there is a wedding this coming summer! We have to save, and haven't been able to economise yet, have we? Let us live through the winter dreaming about the day of our reunion. Wait for me in your dreams, Vicdan . . .

> *I kiss your rosy lips longingly,*
> *Your fiancé Raik*

I touch my skin. Am I a female body which opens up when sensing sincerity, but is alienated and closes down when it senses niggardly selfishness, or am I not, any longer? Does my flesh pulse to its own special rhythm, established by a special agreement with nature? Perhaps freedom starts here, at that very first instant when all contradictions are assimilated, and the bitter wind of confrontation and dilemma no longer chills the physical self. When your attention turns to your innermost being, brushing away the complexities of your own emotions.

I touch my father's letter tenderly and place it upon the earth. I lay his handwriting, covering the silken surface of the paper like a lace of black ink, softly upon the earth. I leave his love together with his manipulative selfishness – probably not even admitted to himself – which were interwoven with the netted texture of his emotions and laid before my mother, upon the earth. Without disturbing my tranquillity.

3 January 1945
Konya

My dear Vicdan,

For some time I have been sitting idly, my head in my hands. Boys are playing football in the school yard. For many hours I have been busy compiling my reports on the inspection. For the time being this tiresome task is over and at last I have the leisure to write to you.

Vicdan, the room I share here with three colleagues, which has been reserved for our use by the headmaster, is claustrophobic; what's more, the ceiling leaks badly. The weather is exceedingly cold. We are trying to keep warm beside the dilapidated brazier, the smell of which gives us all headaches. We are all longing for our homes and families. Spending New Year's Eve away from our loved ones has depressed us. However, we hide our burdens of weariness in our hearts and do not utter words of complaint to each other, doing our best to carry out the duty the state has commissioned us to perform. But all the same, I can't help wondering, when on my own, whether all our lives will be wasted in partings! First my second dose of military service because of the War, then this mission, inspecting secondary schools . . .

It has been a month, my love, since we parted, and there is still a spell of more than a month before this tour of duty is over, Remember saying, 'Winter days are short, and pass quickly,' when you saw me off? I wonder if they have really flown by for you? My experience is rather different. Do you know this saying of the poets: 'The longest nights are known neither by astrologers nor by muezzin time-keepers / Ask him who suffers the pangs of love how long some nights can be.' ?

I am waiting for the moment when I shall be with you, anticipating the moment when I shall embrace your strong, healthy body, hugging you to my chest. I keep myself going with dreams of our day of reunion which will bring all life and all passion to us. But the waiting is a torment greater than I can bear, destroying my being, reducing me to ashes. I kiss your sea-green eyes again and again; I embrace you, my dear wife, again and again.

Raik

P.S. I wonder how many days it will take for the box of apples I sent from Ereğli to reach you in Ankara. I hope they won't freeze. Beware of the cold, my love, keep warm, and don't catch the flu.

The passion of Raik's love, still continuing after ten years of married life, exhausted me. I felt stifled. If a day comes when the material obstacles of life have been overcome, will men and women give up loving each other, seeking refuge in each other? Or will they learn only then how to really care for one another?

My father wrote my mother the minutest details of the complicated journey, fraught with difficulties, which he made during that winter of 1945, as an inspector of secondary and high schools, for the National Education Board, going from Ankara to Konya, and from there to Antalya and Mersin. A long, difficult journey by coach, train, and jeep. Was transportation so hard to come by, was travelling so hard in my country, half a century ago? A big land . . . Steppe and mountains . . . A thin coastal strip of plains, barely visible. A big country, compassionate and cruel, a timid, stuttering heart beating on the steppe . . .

15 January 1945
Antalya

Darling,

Our itinerary was changed again. We could not follow the route I told you about in my phone call from Konya. When it proved impossible to reach Bolvadin from Akşehir, we changed the order of the provinces on our inspection list, and went as planned to Afyon where we arrived at midnight. We spent the night in the high school, got up at 5 a.m. the next morning, and at 6 am, caught the train which leaves Afyon once a week for Burdur. When we reached there, we didn't have to wait long – thank God – and we simply boarded a coach for Antalya. At one of our stops, we came across an old peasant man with his grandson by a fountain. The grandfather had taken off his jacket and put it on the child, to keep the little one warm, and he himself stood just in his shirtsleeves. With infinite tenderness, he was feeding the frail child all the food he had. It was a sight well worth seeing. Does any other nation love its children as the Turkish people do? Fathers of this self-same nation sometimes beat their sons, forcing them to slave-like labour in the fields, loading heavy baskets as tall as themselves on their slender shoulders, without mercy. In all probability the community of poverty and ignorance is identical the world over. When I see such sad sights, I feel ashamed of my own weariness, and realise how much more there is for me to attempt as a teacher.

As soon as we reached Antalya, I rushed to the post office, to send you a telegram. Unluckily, no way of phoning Ankara. And I have only just found time for a letter, as we left very soon after our arrival for the Aksu Village Institute, 15 km. from Antalya. The achievements of the teachers and of the students as well are terrific, Vicdan! Impossible to capture in plain words! All my resistance vanished on the spot. I felt my inspector colleagues rejoicing with renewed hope and enthusiasm. When such institutes really increase in number, our country will be happy.

Only then, Vicdan, will the Gazi's bones lie in lasting peace.

When we'd finished our job, we returned to Antalya. Tomorrow we will be on our way to the township of Elmalı, for which journey we shall have to borrow a jeep, either from the gendarmerie or from the forestry overseers. We are planning to inspect the schools in the townships first and then the ones in the main centre of the province.

Antalya basks in clear, bright sunshine. With warm weather and a pure air which has none of the interminable dust of central Anatolia. A land living in an endless spring. But you lose all contact with the rest of the world here. A spot of utter deafness! When we were back in Konya province, we could learn a little bit more about the goings-on in the capital, the developments out there in the rest of the world. Here we are completely devoid of such facilities. But there's not much you can do about this dismal state of affairs. Our days here will be over soon; we have to be patient and stick to doing our duty. We shall be in Antalya province for about a fortnight, then we will go on to Isparta and from there to ——— . Then back to Burdur, then to ——— ...

My father's odyssey on land made my head spin. His letter continued, after these passages about his itinerary, with detailed information about the oranges and bergamots he planned to buy in Mersin, stressing the fact that my mother was particularly partial to bergamot jam.

When we came down to domestic details, after the hazards of love and the Taurus mountains, I was relieved.

My mother's reply to this letter of journeys and oranges was particularly important to me.

25 January 1945

My darling,

Thank you very much for your long and interesting letter from Antalya. Believe it or not, Raik, but I had such a passionate desire to climb the cloudy peaks of the Taurus mountains by your side in that jeep. I was really touched that, despite all your tiredness and demanding work, you could remember that I liked bergamot jam.

Dear Raik, I hope the telegram I sent this morning will reach you. As soon as the news broke that there had been an explosion at the gas factory, I rushed to the post office despite making myself late for school (believe me, even in our flat in Sıhhiye, so close to the factory, the noise was not loud), as I realised that you would read the report in the 'Ulus' newspaper in the next few days and would go crazy with worry, as you would have no means of making a phone call.

Don't worry about us. Both of us, nanny Faika and I, are quite well. You know she has always taken special care of me, and nowadays she is particularly attentive. I shall explain why soon. For the time being, just wonder why.

Your positive impressions of the Aksu Village Institute made me happy. I too am pleased with my students; I am quite confident that we do teach them well. Do you know, Raik, my classroom is the only place where I forget about my longing for you?

In my spare time, dear Raik, I read a lot; probably in the coming months I shan't have enough time to read. I am going through Virginia Woolf's 'The Waves' once more, after a gap of a few years, and wondering what the spell is in this novel which enchants me. It's been suggested that all the characters are in fact different aspects of Virginia Woolf herself. Do you agree, Raik, that we individuals are really more than one person? You, me, all people . . . How many Vicdans exist inside me, and how many Raiks inside you? You probably love some of the Vicdans in me passionately, but probably dislike some of the others . . . Maybe you aren't even aware that there are others. Now I can imagine you protesting that you are the one and only homogeneous Raik, and vehemently professing that this man is passionately in love with me! But where is the proof?

Anyhow, soon a mixture of some of my Vicdans and your Raiks will be born. Darling, do you realise what I have said? I am pregnant!

Dearest, I'm not sure whether this letter will reach you before you leave Burdur. In case it does not, and you learn the happy news after my mother and brothers, please don't immediately jump to the conclusion that they are more important to me. I am doing my best, and writing to you immediately after learning the positive result of the test.

Darling, live through the rest of your inspection tour basking in the joy of this blissful news. Please don't conjure up fresh sorrows, such as 'Why can't I be close to my wife?'

Raik, I hope we have a daughter. I am sure you would wish the same. I would like us to bring her up as a modern Turkish woman. Educated, courteous, kind, but strong. Raik, I am not strong, you wish to think I am strong, that's all. But please, let us bring up our daughter to be really strong.

Do you know, recently I keep thinking of Nefise; I think I've grown used to Ankara for her sake. The dead tie us to a place, a city, a country, with stronger bonds than the living. It is a deep hurt to miss someone who is dead.

If God is good, and all goes well with my pregnancy, I shall give birth round about the anniversary of Nefise's death. She was my only woman friend. Her place remains empty. Please don't be hurt, my love. Of course my perfect companionship with you fills my life. But sometimes a woman simply needs to talk to a woman friend. There is no one who meets my need.

Vicdet could have been just such a companion. I met her recently, can you believe it, just outside the Özen bakery. We embraced very warmly. She was happily married, and happened to be in Ankara accompanying her husband, who was on a business trip. She asked about Burhan, as casually as if asking about someone of little importance to her. I felt a sudden, acute pang of pain . . . Raik, I could not ask about İzzet! I don't know why. Maybe I dreaded the news I might receive; maybe I was being careful on her account in these difficult times.

Don't get the impression that I am feeling apprehensive. I am genuinely happy, and look to the future full of hope. Of course there must come a time when our country will be an unreservedly good place to live. The war is nearly over, isn't it? Even an incurable pessimist like me believes that the world will attain peace soon. Still, sometimes I shudder recalling your words. Do you remember, when the war began and I was shaken with grief, you used to say, 'Don't worry, our country will survive the hurricane, but we shall have to pay for our good luck.' Have these six years of our lives, times of impoverishment and hardship, come to an end, Raik? Or do we still have more to suffer and to pay? What do you think? What will our child have to face?

I am sending you Cumhur's latest photo in his War Academy uniform. Isn't he handsome? He is like a son to us, isn't he?

> *I embrace you lovingly and longingly,*
> *Your wife*
> *Vicdan*

I have perched on the edge of Vicdan's and Raik's grave, listening to the sounds of the soil and the voices of the leaves. My mother and father lie here, merged at last in one another's being.

I have lain on the ground which absorbed the material essence of their physical selves. At the touch of my body, soil and leaves merge with the images of the dead – my dead – which I restore to life in my imagination and emotions.

(Such an experience is quite impossible. Lying on a grave, in communion with the beloved dead!)

(Impossible! How could you possibly avoid all those beggars who water the graves, those reciters of prayers, the entire company of graveyard workers? Especially on a limpid blue day! Impossible! The sky is thick with the foul vapours of the final part of the twentieth century, with particles of carbon and sulphur, with exhaust fumes, with the gaseous waste of industry. Even the rain is tainted.)

Feelings are biochemical in essence.

Let us first consider the external and internal stimulants

triggering chemical reactions as a result of which, 'feelings' are born. According to this method of proof, such an experience is 'real'. Do we agree? Now, the second method of proof. If the same chemical reactions are stimulated by some inner resource, and if the chemical activity ends in the arousal of the same 'feelings' as in the first instance, should we suppose that the second result is 'unreal'?

At this point, can we postulate a theory? If 'feelings' are products of biochemistry, might not the reverse statement also be true? That biochemical reactions are actually 'feelings'?

At this point all the obstacles, the boundaries and the walls within my mind are removed. Like the essence of a cell pouring out into neighbouring tissues when the cell walls have dissolved, my mind flows into the universe. A brilliant light illuminates my thoughts. How simple everything is! Is this a rare moment of enlightenment, or the onset of lunacy?

The revealed mystery of the structure called matter, or an organism, melts into its strands, the structure deconstructs, and its DNA is subsumed into an alloy of universal sensations. If this is so, then it is possible, on a given spot and at a given moment, to distinguish, even (so to speak) recreate the feelings belonging to another specific place and time; and the reconstruction will probably be quite close to the original material form, is in all likelihood identical with it, from the points of view of biochemistry and literature.

At this point I contemplate myself and those Kemalists nourishing the slender roots of plants. I am the daughter of Vicdan and Raik. I can distinguish the strands I have inherited from my parents, and from others. They are within me, the Kemalists. At the same time, I am different from them. Because I do not believe in molten individuals subsumed in ideals and in relationships; but believe in what ideals and relationships contribute to the individual.

And I perceive that Vicdan, Raik, Burhan and Cumhur pursued their destinies to the end. No, they did not run away, but fulfilled their fates. What is destiny but the limits of the epoch you find yourself born into? I am their child.

Only Nefise, only she rebelled against her destiny. She who wrote letters on a typewriter, who drove a car, who fell in love with a British officer, who desired her best friend's fiancé, who divorced, who could put her name on the books she published! She who opposed her destiny and whose material being fell to pieces when she was only thirty-two. Yes, mother was right, I am Nefise's child. I can comprehend her place in my mother's life. Nefise was the thread that held together the various segments of Vicdan's life, providing continuity and wholeness from the destructive days of the invasion to the establishment of the Republic, from the schools for orphans to England and the new Turkey, from girlhood to marriage, from security to the Second World War. There was no one else who had witnessed my mother living through these stages. Nefise was the mirror-image of Vicdan, her other self, the one Vicdan wanted to be; the firm bond between my mother and reality, the link between Vicdan and Vicdan's innermost self which was broken in 1942. I was born three years later, and from then on witnessed all subsequent happenings in my mother's life. Yes, I am truly Nefise's daughter.

Born of Vicdan and Nefise, suckled at the breast of Cybele, begotten by Raik and Turkey, I dip my hands into time, the past laps against my skin. Bygone days, rising from the tombs of the Kemalists who gave me life, start to circulate through my body, touching the memories stored in the protein spirals within the honeycombs of my organisms, making them thrum, those memory-laden threads that lay coiled in my cells without the decoding recognition of my awareness, probably even before my awareness was born; time past, circulating through my body, renders these previously unknown recollections my own.

The century draws nearer to the horizon, we stroll towards a lurid sunset resembling the hazy brightness of a dawn. All things change shape as twilight deepens, flowing back to the original state which existed at the dawn of the century; like a rewound film, we approach the beginning as we draw closer to the end.

Is this a nightmare about a vicious circle, or history itself?

Was the entire optimistic enterprise of this century, gaining access to the age of information, to atomic energy, to technological revolution, to social justice and democracy, a huge mantle woven to conceal the painful, ugly realities? Now the fabric of that mantle is being stripped off, and there remain, confronting us, those ancient forms of life and death as hard and as merciless as ever, perhaps only minutely altered. I am distressed when I put the question: Has nothing changed?

We are approaching the end, the end, the end . . . Clouds thick with burnt flesh obscure the falling dusk.

Soot hurts my eyes. Plants are scorched, the thin, eroded soil is fissured, the rocks remain hard but red hot, the birds have migrated, humankind has lost sight of its dreams. The dead incinerated, gassed; the dead riddled with bullets, mutilated on the road, organisms decimated by explosions . . . Blood drips from the fiery clouds. I close my throbbing eyes.

When I open them again, I can glimpse the sunset light which resembles that of dawn. At the century's end, the savage alloy of civilization is a deadly slurry in which millions of atoms, billions of electrons bubble in the rhythms of dissolution, but which is still pregnant with vitality. The light will fall upon this hellish brew . . . And a miracle! The atoms absorbing light energy are mobilized, they crash into each other by an irresistible attraction, new molecules are born; the energy concentrates and see, how the fine threads of protein appear; living matter! Billions of years ago, when our earth was just a very young planet, was not life born in this way?

The past, made up of shadows, is animated by the mysterious light, and the story of my country starts to run on the shadow-screen of the imagination. The past appears in flesh and blood, just as energy concentrates into matter, and steps off the shadow-screen, right into the present, into life. There it is, the past, confronting me and within me!

I see dreadful, bloody scenes. I see the 'fire and treachery' of Nazım Hikmet's poem . . . 'Fire and treachery', whose despicable shadow looms over the present like a crimson cloud of flame . . .

The earth splits with a thundrous crack. It is the twentieth century! Splitting before me like an abyss insatiable for violence and victims! How far away the vale of security seems!

He is standing on the threshold of the century, not yesterday but now, with his 'eyes lightning flashes' and his head unbowed, ready to play his part at the moment when the coincidence and compulsion born of nature and history intersect. He resembles a natural phenomenon. He walks to the 'edge of the abyss' not yesterday, but now. His keen gaze embraces infinity. He senses time, 'flexing his slender haunches', waiting for the auspicious moment, not in the past, but now, he will leap and 'speeding through darkness / Like a shooting star' he will gain a place for my country in the vale of security.

I know that he is here, in the plain, unassuming land of the steppe and not in that huge monument of stone. I know that his being, which became the conscience and hope of my people, has been transformed into sustaining drops, quietly nourishing the steppe and those living on it.

The century has been drawing to its end, has drawn a huge arc and is heading for its beginning. I am lying on my parents' grave, waiting for the circle to be completed.

I wait in vain, yet grief is out of place. Time never closes the circle; time flows in spirals. Now, let me repeat my former question. Has nothing changed? I am that change! If the fragmentation of my being on this, the fiftieth anniversary of Nefise's death, does not result in my physical dissolution, but on the contrary leads to a new integration, my claim is justified!

I am lying on my parents' tomb, contemplating and exploring myself. I begin to realise that my body is not empty, incomplete and sterile as it used to be when divorced from a man's touch. I am alive and I am free!

What a vast contradiction exists between myself and my suffering, bleeding, miserable and merciless country! But I am made up of that contradiction. I, who am the offspring of the wounded children of a people felled in the short, spiralling interval between the beginning and the end of the twentieth century, of those children who became the creators of their people's miraculous resurrection, I am the change.

I left the Cebeci cemetery. My daughter was waiting for me. She was only a small child when I was lost in the forest of images. She was a mixture of honey and pepper, a little cross, often naughty, her face gentle with angelic dimples, imps twinkling shrewdly in her eyes.

When did she grow up to be a slender valley plant, standing so gracefully? I know that her supple tissue could be all too easily shattered; I know how fragile she is, standing out there and waiting for me. My child . . . She is identical with her mother and yet so different. I know the calcium forming the slender structure of her stem-like body, the iron circulating through her veins, are rooted in the bone-dust and fragments of marrow dispersed throughout a landscape which has been torn apart from Macedonia to Crete, from the Aegean to the Caucassus. I know how enduring her young tissue is, and how ardently it can mend.

Mother, it is getting dark, where have you been?

I am beside you, my daughter, I am within you.

I give my hand, drenched in light, to her.

LETTER TO THE READER

Dear Reader,

If, after my mother's death, I had failed to find whole piles of letters in her room which she and my father had exchanged throughout the thirties and forties, this book would never have been written. Later, other letters turned up, my mother's correspondence with her own mother and brothers and also with friends, both Turkish and foreign. Naturally, what interested me most was my parents' correspondence. And what did I find between the lines? The spirit of the past. The toughness of the hide concealing that spirit, which is to say the harsh outlines of everyday events, had no place in the language of these courteous and rather shy people brought up under the strict family discipline of Ottoman society.

The letters unlocked a door for my own insights, intensified by the pain of loss. Crossing this threshold, I seemed to enter into my innermost self, into a domain of my own being of which I had not been aware. My parents' generation stood there, the anguish of their lost motherland, the anguish of migrations. In that domain were the orphans of the First World War, children of a nation condemned to death by the world powers, and also the generation of rebirth, young citizens of a young and eager Republic, the endurance and effort that carried them from their schools for orphans and set them among the creators of the 'resurrection', their faith in the ideals of their youth, their disappointments, their hurt silences . . . all these were there.

The century is drawing to a close. Those still remain of the generation born in its early decades are leaving us one by one. A generation is slipping away like a receding wave. New deaths bring back memories of older ones. And the Kemalist generation is being born once more in my imagination.

My mother Hadiye was a student in a teacher-training school for girls in 1929, when she won a scholarship awarded by the state. The examination was inaugurated by order of President

Mustafa Kemal Atatürk himself, and the aim was to raise an educated generation as quickly as possible, as the country was in dire need of trained personnel and of institutions, after the heavy losses she had suffered during the War and the invasion. The revolutionary aim of the Republic was to create a social and cultural synthesis of East and West, and so bright students were sent to leading European universities to be educated not only in the sciences and technology, but also in literature, music and art. My mother was in a group sent to Oxford University. One young girl in the group could not cope with living in Britain and committed suicide. The rest graduated very successfully and returned home to found the English Language and Literature departments of Ankara University and the Gazi Teacher-Training College in Ankara. All of that group are dead now. My mother graduated from St. Anne's College in 1934, returned home, married my father Faik, who was a mathematics teacher, in 1936, and later founded the English department of the above-mentioned teacher-training college. She taught English, English literature and translation classes for many years and also translated into Turkish works by Webster, Marlowe, and later Oscar Wilde and Somerset Maugham. The heroine of this book, Vicdan, is based on my mother, the character Raik on my father, and Vicdan's mother, Fitnat Hanım, on my grandmother. Those unfamiliar with the process of writing fiction may have doubts about this approach, but let me say that it is quite impossible – let alone unsatisfactory for the writer – to construct reality just as it is or was in a novel or story, quite impossible because of the inner dynamics of the text. So here are Hadiye and Vicdan, Faik and Raik, Fitnat Hanım and my grandmother Elmas Hanım standing before me. They do resemble each other, but in a strange way are strikingly different.

In my previous works, I have always called characters Raik who were inspired by my father, and always those inspired by my grandmother, Fitnat. It is a common device in fiction to give different names to different – usually contrasting – aspects of the same character, so suggesting divisions within the personality. I do admire some works of this kind, but do not feel drawn to them. I think my different Fitnats and Raiks in different texts can stand on their own feet, as well as meeting and blending harmoniously in more fully-rounded characters. This is what fascinates me: not the dispersal of a personality into discordant parts, but the formation within the same personality of a harmonious whole made up of different characteristics which are sometimes quite independent of, or even opposed to, one another.

Among the other characters in the book, Vicdan's friend Nefise, with whom she shares the England experience, is completely imaginary. Vicdan's three brothers, Burhan, Reha and Cumhur, are syntheses of many uncles, on both my mother's and father's side, whom I have lost recently, one after another. It is by my choice that they are all army officers, a choice which aims to uncover clues as to the metamorphoses the character of the army officer has undergone throughout the history of the Republic.

About what happens in the book – for me, incidents in themselves, either in fiction or in real life, are not terribly important. My memory for factual detail has always been rather weak. But the essence of things that happen, the reasons for them and the results, the impact they have on individual psyches, the impressions on inner selves, have always been the issues of paramount importance to my mind.

All incidents in the book, except two, are imaginary (I am not referring to the family histories of Vicdan and Raik during the Balkan War, the First World War, or the years of the Occupation). The things that actually happened are, strangely enough, those that seem remote from probability: Vicdan's meeting with Kemal Atatürk, and her ascent of Uludağ (Mount Olympus, near Bursa, northwestern Anatolia) with her brothers, wearing her elegant Irish linen suit and high heels! In 1936 my mother, the daughter of an ordinary middle-class family, was summoned by the president, who took a personal interest in the students sent abroad on state funding, and talked with him for about an hour. The president asked her about her impressions of England and also made mention of his views on world politics.

My mother was, naturally enough, utterly fascinated by him – Atatürk being the great hero he was and also a very impressive person – and described the interview to me, using Atatürk's exact words. Vicdan's impressions of the interview coincide precisely with those of my mother. My mother left the president's office feeling anxious and with the gloomy conviction that the president was seriously ill, just as Vicdan does (Atatürk would die a few years later from cirrhosis. At the time of the interview, he might possibly have shown early symptoms of liver failure, such as tiredness, pallor, heavy breathing, and so on); and she was also sent back to England on a mission, as Atatürk's special envoy, to give a talk on the BBC about the women's rights movement in Turkey, just as Vicdan is.

The other incident took place in the summer of 1935: the climb up the mountain. In the faded snapshot of sixty years ago, the enthusiasm of the young people, their self-confidence, their – rather childish – challenge to the whole world, are still clearly visible, shining like a beam of light, and not without pathos.

Vicdan's education in England plays an important part in the book, and takes place not in its actual location – which is Oxford – but in Oxford's sister Cambridge, for no rational reason at all. I had been to Oxford when I was a child and cannot remember the city clearly, whereas I spent some time in Cambridge as an adult. While I was writing my novel, I found that I simply could not realise the setting as Oxford. Cambridge, like a magnet, kept on drawing my imagination, so I just shifted the location (it may well be that female students were not even accepted in Cambridge during the late twenties).

The stories about the 'Dersim Rebellion' are completely fictitious; but I had heard as a child many grim anecdotes told about those who had been in the military units commissioned for the suppression of the armed Kurdish uprising. The function of Dersim in this book is to offer a tragic example of fellow-countrymen, forced to oppose each other in armed conflict, and secretly carrying the wounds of that experience throughout their lives, like an internal haemorrhage.

Conversely, the stories of the Korean War are based on documentary evidence, such as letters which soldiers at the front wrote home, newspapers, and the thesis of a young Korean woman, Eun-kyong On, on the Korean War in the Turkish press and in Turkish literature.

In this book, dear Reader, you will come across some letters. Before starting this book I had read hundreds of them without having the faintest idea of writing a novel like this. My mother's correspondence, not only with my father, but with her brothers and with friends in Turkey and abroad, helped me to capture the spirit of the first half of the century. I spent a great deal of time thinking about how to shape the book. Form in itself does not mean much to me, its value lies in its capacity to integrate with its content, in its ability to convey the content to the perceptions and imagination of the reader. I think the material I was dealing with directed me towards the form I have chosen. This structure, made up of stories which are related to each other, seemed appropriate for narrating the worlds of Vicdan and her three brothers, worlds which, although they drifted apart and grew remote, still – at least from Vicdan's point of view – remained linked by threads of love, loose, drawn thin, but nevertheless enduring.

The inner dynamics of prose always pose a stumbling-block for the utilisation of documents. I had to assimilate the letters I had read, forget them on a superficial level, and then create brand-new letters from the essentials I remembered. Except for technical data about various battles and some chronological details of the Korean War, no passages have been quoted from the Korean letters.

I have quoted freely, not from the documents to hand, but from poems and songs. I believe national culture – or indeed world culture – to be a unified whole, not a patchwork where all the bits and pieces belong solely to the one who has fashioned it. The presence of our great poet Nazım Hikmet resonates throughout this book. It is quite impossible to overestimate his influence on the shaping of my generation's perceptions, sensitivities, and aesthetic sense.

My reader will know me as a feminist writer, and this book he or she is holding at the moment may come as a surprise. The feminist sensibility of this book is masked, and reveals itself only to the observant. I discovered something about myself while writing it, which I should like to share with my reader. Both my mother and father were among the orphans of the First World War and Armistice (i.e. our occupation) years. By force of circumstance, their families were transformed into matriarchal households, and this may be the starting-point for my feminist awareness.

On the subject of feminism and world culture . . . There is a metaphor in the chapter 'Time in Bursa', an allegory linking infinity and the 'arc'. After I had finished *The Other Side of the Mountain*, I began reading Nietzsche's *Thus Spoke Zarathustra*, and when I came across the metaphor pointing to the resemblance between 'infinity' and the 'arc', I felt a surge of excitement. A Turkish feminist writer living in a different cultural climate and a different epoch from those of the great philosopher – arguably a misogynist – shares the same plane of instinct and insight where time and infinity are concerned . . . I think it fascinating that we are all children of the same mother nature. We live, as a poignant reality, the differences between men and women, but what is both beautiful and a cause for hope, in spite of all differences and divisions, is the sure tie of brotherhood and sisterhood that exists between all of us human beings.

Many people have contributed to this work. I thank the members of my family, and those relatives who have opened their hearts to me, their memories of war and peace. I thank those friends who have put documents at my disposal, for their contribution to my own enlightenment, and for their inspiration; I thank those who have read drafts for their encouraging criticism.

The poems in the chapter 'Vicdan and Nefise: The Kemalist Girls of Cambridge' are by the English poet William Wordsworth and were translated into Turkish by the author. Poems in the chapter 'Journal for My Daughter', are by Pablo Neruda and were translated into Turkish by Nuran and Hilmi Yavuz and Enver Gökçe. I thank all the poets writing in my own language and the above translators, together with Naciye Öncül and Tomris Uyar who have translated Virginia Woolf's works into Turkish.

Let me once more call to mind with respect, admiration and love the three great people whose influence on my heart and mind resonate through this book: Mustafa Kemal Atatürk, whose being supplied the sap which has sustained my country's life; that major poet, Nazım Hikmet; and the major writer Virginia Woolf, whose work has drawn me ever closer to the writer hidden within me.

And let me finish by thanking my daughter Reyhan who, although only a teenager, has supported me with mature love and understanding throughout the writing of this book.

From Erendiz ATASÜ
With love